MERMAIDS
NEVER DROWN

MERMAIDS
NEVER DROWN
TALES TO DIVE FOR

EDITED BY
ZORAIDA CÓRDOVA
AND NATALIE C. PARKER

Feiwel and Friends • New York

A Feiwel and Friends Book
An imprint of Macmillan Publishing Group, LLC
120 Broadway, New York, NY 10271 • fiercereads.com

Our books may be purchased in bulk for promotional, educational, or business use. Please contact your local bookseller or the Macmillan Corporate and Premium Sales Department at (800) 221-7945 ext. 5442 or by email at MacmillanSpecialMarkets@macmillan.com.

Library of Congress Cataloging-in-Publication Data is available.

First edition, 2023
Book design by Maria Williams
Feiwel and Friends logo designed by Filomena Tuosto
Printed in the United States of America

ISBN 978-1-250-82381-6
1 3 5 7 9 10 8 6 4 2

To our readers—from vampires of the
night to mermaids in the sea. We thank you
for joining us on this magical enterprise.

CONTENTS

INTRODUCTION

A Note from Your Editrixes:

Let's just start with the obvious: Who *hasn't* spent hours sitting on the bottom of a pool pretending they were a mermaid with a gorgeous tail and the ability to breathe underwater? Or, in Zoraida's case (because, spoiler alert, Zoraida can't swim), staring at the glorious expanse of blue and dreaming of what lay beneath? Just us? We don't think so.

Natalie was so enamored of all things aquatic that she started begging her parents for scuba lessons at eleven years old (though they held out, citing something about "being too far from the ocean" as if that would stop her); and Zoraida received a VHS of Disney's *The Little Mermaid* when she was three and watched it on repeat so many times she taught herself English, and came away with a lifelong love of mermaids.

When we started thinking that maybe, just maybe, we could turn our first cryptid collection into a series, we knew that mermaids would be our second installment. Mermaids, like many folktales and legends, have taken on a life of their own. These beings change from culture to culture—sometimes there are fins and sometimes tentacles, sometimes they sing you to the bottom of a cold sea, and sometimes they fall in love with lonely sailors who most definitely weren't hallucinating. No matter what, stories about merpeople are an invitation to dream about the mysteries of our own world.

With each story, our authors invite you to imagine mermaids in a wide variety of ways. There are mermaids who dream of being on land and mermaids who dwell in the deepest waters. There are stories of transformation and magic and of yearning to belong. As you read, we hope you will explore these endless, magical possibilities, because, let's face it, the ocean is big enough for all of us.

Cheers,

Zoraida & Natalie

STORM SONG

Rebecca Coffindaffer

To feed the magic, you must first yourself know hunger.

It is your turn to call down the storms tonight.

The waves are wild already, white fingered and clawing at the rocks that line the coast. Above you, the star-scattered sky is clear and waiting.

No moon, though. That part is important. The magic is at its most powerful when she is hidden, and you've watched carefully every night, tracking her as she slipped farther and farther into shadow.

She is at her darkest now—right now. And the current brings the ship you chose closer every moment.

You've timed everything perfectly. You had to.

You need every advantage you can get because your song . . .

Your song. It isn't ready. It may not be strong enough.

You'd wanted more time to find your melody, to hone that power that sits deep in your stomach. But the season already grows late. The elders—those sirens who've been around the longest, who know the seas best but no longer travel so far to join the singing—told you it cannot wait any longer. If you don't call down the storms tonight, the cycle will break. Everything will suffer.

Abalone slips up beside you, curling gracefully around the rocks. Even in these waters—darker and colder than the warm, tropical currents where the elders hold the heart of your people's power—she stands out, vibrant as a flower. An ombré of rich blue and gold, touched with streaks of pink, from the bright yellow tips of her billowing hair all the way down to the deep navy ends of her fin. Everything about Abalone is provocative, shimmering.

You, on the other hand, blend in up here along the jagged coasts of the northern seas. Your scales and skin and hair are mottled dark gray and brown and rust orange. The ends of your fin are bristly and sharp, and long, thin, venomous barbs line your spine.

Abalone twists her arms, her hands, her delicately webbed fingers in a smooth series of movements, signing to you, "Everyone is ready. We wait on you."

"Don't worry," you sign back to her. "They're coming. Can't you feel their wake?"

Even if you could easily speak down here, deep underneath the waves, signing is the only safe way for your people to communicate. The voice of a siren is too dangerous for casual use, capable of turning tides, shifting currents, altering the ocean waters in a million tiny ways that could upset the delicate balances of life.

Every siren grows up knowing the weight of this power, how vital their voices and songs are in governing the seas.

But to call down the storms? That is another kind of magic. A magic of sacrifice and bargaining.

The waves are hungry, the elders always say. *Feed them and the skies will listen.*

"There! I see them now," Abalone signs, pointing ahead at the sharp keel and curving underbelly of a ship as it cuts through the waves toward you. A glow gathers around the edges of her scales. Anticipation stretches her mouth into a grin, baring viciously sharp teeth.

She looks almost as excited as she was when it was her turn to call the storms last season. Her first time leading the song, just as it is yours tonight. She had chosen a shoreline instead of a ship, closer to your home waters. A sprawling town stretched along a coast of white sand. Every unique note of her song had risen flawlessly from her throat, and humans had thronged to the water toward her, wading in up to their necks.

The other sirens had slipped easily into her cadence and harmony, the ocean had taken its bloody sacrifice with vicious waves and greedy foam, and the storms that had been born out of that night had been the most powerful in generations. Churning up vital nutrients from the seafloor and pouring rains across the dry lands of the surface.

Vibrant, violent blooms of new life, above and below the water.

Abalone curls her fin around yours, brushing her hand down your barbed back without fear, and you lean into her touch for a moment. Then you kick upward, spiraling along a twisted stack of volcanic rock and breaking through the surface. Just barely. Enough that you can see the full ship rocking up and down over the waves. Brought here on a current you created and cultured yourself, singing soft tones to the waters so that they would wrap around its keel and pull it here:

Where the sirens are gathered.

Where it will be dragged down to its grave.

It's quite the prize. Triple masted with stacks of white sails that are rounded with the breeze. Not a fisherman's ship or that of rough sailors scraping for trade or coin. You chose this one because it's richly outfitted, newly painted, crowded with humans who always have gold and gems glinting on their fingers and earlobes or along their belts and decorative sword sheaths.

One of them—a woman with bright yellow hair piled atop her head—has a necklace that encases her whole throat in sapphires and gold. She can't even comfortably drop her chin when she's wearing it, but you don't think she minds that part. She seems used to viewing the world down the length of her nose.

Every time you see that necklace, you think of how much better it would look on Abalone. You imagine the gems dripping between your fingers as you fasten it around her neck.

Tonight is not supposed to be about riches or the spoils of the kill. It is supposed to be about continuing the cycle, blessing the lands and seas with storms for another season.

Still, you think. *Maybe if I am good enough, if my song is strong enough, there might be room for both.*

You look up at the dark-faced moon, at the alignments of the stars. You see the roll and flash of sirens' fins—bright orange, vivid pink, metallic black—as they twist through the waves and rocks and wait. On you.

Now is the time.

But there is a tightness in your chest so fierce it squeezes your voice into silence.

You have sung before—to the currents and the tides, to the pods of whales that pull you along in their enormous wakes as they croon back. But those are different songs.

The storm song is about lust, about *wanting*. It is about drawing all the humans on that ship to your call, filling them with such desire for you that they throw themselves into the arms of the sirens and let their blood spill across the seas in red ribbons.

You must sing to them about allure and longing until it builds a fire in their groins that burns away all logic and reason, until all they can think of is getting to you, pressing themselves against you, even as you rip them apart. It is about the *hunger*.

But you don't know how to sing this song.

You've never really known how to sing it—because you've never felt it.

You will, Abalone told you at the last new moon, as the two of you swam along the coral at home. *When it is your turn to lead, I'm sure you will. It is a powerful feeling.*

You have joined the songs of other sirens before. You remember what it was like to sing with Abalone's song, to see the hunger alight in the humans' eyes and how the sirens had thrummed with the power of it.

But it hadn't felt powerful for you. It had felt . . . uncomfortable. Wrong. Their blood had tasted sour—it always tasted sour.

Maybe Abalone is right, though, you think. *Maybe it's only because I haven't led the song myself. Maybe it will be different tonight.*

Your people have been singing the songs of storm season for generations without fail—surely, you can't be the first who has felt like this. Who has come to this ritual without feeling fully connected to the hungry magic you're calling upon. They managed it anyway, so why can't you?

The water twists around your body, and Abalone rises up next to you. Starlight shimmers in her hair and along her high, curving cheekbones. Her hands move above the surface.

"It will be all right. The skies will listen."

The tightness in your chest loosens. Just a little. She believes in you. And maybe that will be enough. Just for tonight.

You dive deep, pulling the waters around you, letting them push you up until you rise well above the surface. Water pours from your hair, curving down your body, and the air up here is cold against the bare skin of your chest.

This—the display of yourself, your body—is part of it. You know that. You know so many sirens who find strength and plea-sure in this part of it, and you try to be like them.

But it doesn't feel any less uncomfortable to expose yourself like this. To have to present yourself in such a specific way. Not even as you open your mouth and start to sing.

The first notes come out wavering and weak, but they are still enough to draw the eyes of one human on the ship. And then another notices. And another.

You try to build the melody, stringing the next note and the next. Like trying to find your way in the deepest, darkest waters. You have no instincts for this song, no sense of how to shape it, so you try to sing it like you've heard the other sirens before you do. You mix deep, low notes with sweeping highs, like Abalone did. You push and pull at the volume like Thessa's song, three seasons ago.

None of it sounds right in your throat.

But it seems to be working, which is what matters.

The humans have all clustered against the railing on the ship, pressing against it, their eyes fixed on you. Far above, dark clouds start to spool from the horizon, obscuring the stars.

The sharp waves die suddenly, going eerily still as the other sirens break through the surface, glowing with bioluminescence as their voices join yours. It shines in their eyes and the strands of their hair, around the scales of their fins and in delicate patterns across the skin of their chests.

Abalone was right. There is something powerful here. In hearing them match their songs to yours. In tasting the bargaining magic, like ozone on your tongue, as it starts to unfurl.

But the song . . .

It won't flow from you as it should. You can't find its natural rhythm, and the melody scrapes against your throat.

The next note comes out in a stuttering rasp, but you catch yourself quickly. Throw yourself back into the song before the other sirens hear.

On the ship, you spot the woman with the sapphire necklace. She blinks, and the lust starts to fade from her eyes.

No.

You yank the melody up from your chest, singing it louder. You can't lose them. No siren has failed in calling the storms before. You can't be the first one. Without them, there will not be a renewal of life in the oceans. Drought will strike the lands, and wildfires will paint the air with ash and smoke.

The woman in sapphires blinks again—and then she looks away. She turns toward a man on her right—a soldier in uniform—and leans into his ear to whisper something.

He looks away, too. No longer transfixed by you. Or by Abalone. Or any of the other sirens.

A shudder ripples through the ocean currents. Above you, the dark clouds begin to stretch and thin.

No. No no no.

You choke on the next note and can't find your way back into the song. Beside you, Abalone's voice wavers—and then drops to nothing. One by one, each siren goes silent. They turn their eyes to you, expressions tight with worry, with fear.

Abalone slides in front of you, brushing her webbed fingers down the sides of your face. Her hands move, trying to speak to you, but you can't look at her—your eyes are fixed on the ship and the quickly clearing sky.

Panic grips you by the throat. So tight that you have to drag every breath into your lungs.

The stars wink down at you, bright and sharp against the dark night.

Then the people on the ship begin to move. They scatter and shouts ring out from bow to stern as the most richly dressed of them pull back from the railing. Soldiers surge to the side of the ship, all in uniforms of black coats and gold buttons, some with gold epaulettes on their shoulders. They line up with muskets held in front of them, silver bayonets glinting as they point the muzzles down at the water.

At you. At your sirens.

Another shout from the ship, and then there's an explosion of noise.

Crack. Crack. Crack. Crack.

Smoke curls from the muskets as bullets hit the water, sending up sprays. Over by the rocks, Thessa cries out with pain and slips beneath the surface.

Horror swells in your chest, choking you. You open your

mouth, but nothing comes out. Not a wail or a shout. Definitely not a song.

The ship towers above you, all noise and movement. The people on board are cheering. Excited. You see the woman in the sapphire necklace applauding, laughter dancing across her face.

Crack. Crack. Crack.

They are shooting at will now, over and over. Another siren gets hit, red blood splashing against the ship's hull. You hear the cry of another far off, back by the stern.

Abalone screams.

Your heart stops as you turn and see her, clutching at her shoulder. You dive for her before the soldiers can fire again, dragging her below the surface.

The waves close over your head as you sink down and cradle Abalone against you, her cheek resting against your bare shoulder, her hair and yours mingling together in the current. Thin ribbons of blood twist upward from the wound in her shoulder, and she shudders with pain.

You bury your face in the billowing forest of her hair and sing to the waters, so quiet, so soft. It's the song one of the elders sang to you when you lost control of a riptide and crashed against the coral, gouging scrapes all along your side. It's a blood song, a healing song, and Abalone starts to relax as it eases her pain and knits at her wound.

The soldiers are still shooting. You can see the sharp, straight trails the round lead balls make as they cut through the water. In the shadows of the waves, sirens are scattering, diving deep.

"I'm so sorry," you tell Abalone. "I failed all of us. I couldn't feed the magic. I couldn't make it listen."

She presses a hand against you, right at the base of your throat.

"You tried to sing my song. You tried to sing Thessa's. You didn't try to sing yours."

Her heartbeat is strong under your fingers, pounding in her chest, reassuring you that she, at least, will be all right. The relief that fills you at feeling the rhythm of her pulse is cool and calming.

And clarifying.

You have been thinking, all this time, that there was a way to do this wrong, but that is impossible. Songs, after all, are like sirens. Unique and the same all at once. Abalone's had been full of allure, brightly colored and impossible to ignore. Thessa's had been sweet and warm, a melody that lapped gently at your skin and drew you in with slow fingers.

Every song you've heard and joined since your very first storm season had been perfect because that siren had simply sung who they were to the stars. Without hesitation or regret.

You look up, watching the faint ribbon of Abalone's blood drift above you, the dark shapes of your sirens, fleeing, in pain, scared. The bottom of the ship looms on the surface, blotting out the sky above.

There is hunger inside you after all. You know the taste of it now.

You help Abalone to that twisted stack of volcanic rock, leading her to a tucked-away spot where she has shelter from the bullets still raining down. And from what you are about to do.

"Stay here," you tell her, and then you kick up to the surface.

The ship is right where you left it, its sails now bound against the masts as the people on board mill about. The finely dressed passengers—in their tightly fitted coats, their hose and heeled shoes, their gowns with layers and layers of skirts—laugh and cheer and call out to each other as the soldiers pace from railing to railing, searching the waters as they reload their long guns, shoving black powder and lead balls deep into the barrels. Every now and then they take a shot, the harsh crack and acrid scent of smoke raising the barbs along your back.

In the corner of your eye, you spot Thessa, huddled and shivering in the shadow of a rock where the humans can't see her, the water around her colored red with her blood. She sees you and shakes her head, motioning for you to leave, to disappear.

But you just smile at her, the points of your teeth dripping venom. You're not afraid anymore.

This time, when you part your lips, the first notes come out strong. Deep, low notes that vibrate in the bones and send ripples down into the seafloor.

Come back, you think, hoping the other sirens hear you, sense you. *The ocean is calling. Come back. I know what I'm doing now.*

You build the new melody piece by piece, calling up a song from all the secret corners inside you. The notes spill from your mouth, growing in resonance and force. They ring off the rocky cliffs and rattle the deck of the ship. They whip at the water until it froths and boils.

And from out of it, you rise higher, borne up on a towering column of sea-foam. Light radiates from your scales and your skin and your eyes and your hair, and aboard the ship, all the humans pile against each other on the railing to witness you.

They stare, transfixed, their faces stretched not with lust or desire, but with amazement and fear. It is the look of someone witnessing the earth splitting at their feet. The look of someone standing on the beach as the hurricane bears down on them. The look you get when you're in the path of something magnificent and terrible.

You are that magnificent and terrible thing. You are beautiful and monstrous. Sharp as the barbs that bristle across your body. Dark as the clouds starting to knit together in the sky.

The woman in the sapphire necklace shoulders her way to the front, disdain written across her face. She's the last person to lay eyes on you, and as soon as you see her, you twist the song like a snare, rounding out each note with the rich clarity of the sea shimmering under a bright sun, the ferocity of the orca on the hunt. You watch as it floods her ears, molding her disdain into awe.

The water breaks to your left, and a siren sister appears, joining her voice seamlessly with yours. From her spot behind the rock, Thessa starts to sing as well, and the blend of even just two harmonies with this song—your true song—fills your chest with fire. The melody spills from you faster now, fiercer. You taste the bargaining magic on your tongue.

More sirens return, layering on deep bass notes and rich altos and high tones that ring bright against the air. Dark clouds boil outward across the sky. Lightning flickers in their bellies and then—that quick—lances down in a jagged arc and strikes the tallest mast of the ship. The wood bursts into flames, quickly catching on the canvas sails, the network of ropes.

Your voices, as one, climb higher, rising to a fever pitch. There is no sweetness in it, no niceness. It is filled with chords that drive shivers up your spine, and you know it will not inspire any of the people on board to leap over the side, into your deadly embrace.

But that's all right. It doesn't need to. Because you are not singing to drive the humans mad with want.

You are singing to the storms.

You are singing to the ocean, telling it to take what it is due.

The waves claw against the hull, tossing the ship in their grasp. Wind rips across the cliff face, driving the fire down the masts. Screams fill the deck.

Still, you sing.

You sing until a loud crunching sound cuts through the air and the whole ship shudders as it smashes against a rock, splitting the hull right in two. Wood splinters and cracks, and the ocean rushes in to fill the gaps, scooping out crates and chests, barrels and bodies. Fire still burns on the masts as the hungry waves pull the belly of the ship apart, greedily sucking everything down.

Thunder rumbles in your ears, and the clouds burst open, sheets of rain pouring down on your head.

Only then do you let your song die. You float at the surface, content to let the rain and wind batter you as you watch the other sirens dive into the wreckage of the ship, their fins flashing bright amid foam that gradually gets redder and redder.

Lightning flashes, and your eyes catch the sparkle of sapphires. The woman with the necklace clings to a flat of splintered wood. Surprising that she wasn't dragged down by her own gown and the weight of all her jewels. You watch as another human swims toward her, their hand outstretched for help, but she smacks at them, pushing herself away from their reach.

Your lips pull back from your teeth, and you run your tongue across their jagged points. Tasting venom.

Abalone still sits where you left her, perched on the ledge of dark volcanic rock, tufts of red algae and green seagrass waving around her. Even wounded, she looks like a benevolent queen.

You reach around her neck, draping the necklace of gold and sapphires on it. You were right—it suits her perfectly. Even with the bloodstains smeared across parts of the metal. Or, maybe, especially because of them.

Abalone runs her fingers along it, smiling at you. Her teeth are like knives.

"I told you the skies would listen."

WE'LL ALWAYS HAVE JUNE

Julian Winters

I'm ten years old the first time the ocean whispers her name to me: *Death*.

One moment, I'm on the edge of the boat, singing along to the music coming from someone's phone. My moms are laughing with their friends on the other end of the deck. Then we hit a wave. I lose balance and the ocean takes me.

She doesn't embrace me like a concerned parent. No, she swallows me like a starved shark.

The descent is quick. I'd secretly slipped out of my life jacket ten minutes ago because we were headed back to shore, and it felt so constricting while I sang. Now, the ocean's strong fingers tug on me. I fight to hold my breath. I thrash and kick, but I'm not a great swimmer, so I sink.

Down, down, down.

Everything slows like the space between the end of a dream and waking up. I almost don't believe someone is swimming toward me.

A boy, who looks my age, but different.

His eyes are amber like Mom's favorite pair of teardrop earrings. Short locs dance in the current. Rich brown skin all the way to his navel. After that, it's a burst of fire and gold. He has a tail. The scales shimmer like a slice of the sun.

But shock and fear seize my limbs. It's just the two of us in the pounding silence of the sea.

His small hands catch my limp arms. He studies me with sad, bright eyes. Carefully, he pinches my nose and leans in. His mouth covers mine. It's not a kiss. He exhales small pockets of breath into me. The coil around my lungs loosens.

I'm . . . alive.

He propels us up. I don't struggle. I let this boy with a tail rip me from Death's determined hands.

In the distance, I hear the ocean again. This time it shrieks my name:

Kai!

Or maybe that's my moms. They find me spluttering on the shore. Soaked clothing pinning me to the soft, grainy sand. Salty water burning my eyes, scratching my throat.

Echoes of "Are you okay?" surround me.

Am I?

My only response is, "A boy . . . saved my life." I know what he is, but I don't want to say it out loud. Not yet.

No one listens. And the boy with a tail and careful touch is gone.

Six Junes Later

"What's the worst that could happen?"

Nothing good has ever come of those words, especially when said from the wolfish mouth of Vicente Pérez.

We're at our favorite spot—the railing leading down to the beach. The sky's an explosion of crimson and tangerine. Sunset looks nice on his tawny complexion.

Vic knots his hair into a messy bun. "Just ask him out already."

Me and Vic are complete opposites. He's loud and reckless. I'm chill, cautious. Even down to our bodies—where he's short and defined, I'm long and lean, a level above scrawny.

We've lived on Talisa Island, a coastal town deep in the belly of Georgia, all our lives. Nine months out of the year, nothing really changes around here. But summers are different. Every June, tourists pour into our town for the beach and ocean.

One of those visitors is Marc O'Brien, the boy who's stolen my attention for the last two summers.

Even from here, I can see him kicking a soccer ball along the shore with kids from my school. Floppy ginger hair like a crown of flames. I can picture the spill of freckles across his face contrasting with his very green eyes.

"Your pining is embarrassing." Vic hops off the railing, checking his phone. "And my break's over."

He works part-time at the surf shop. I pick up shifts at my moms' restaurant. Being a busser isn't glamorous but I'm already saving up for college. I'm looking at universities closer to the city. Far from the ocean.

"So," Vic begins, a smile teasing his lips, "band rehearsal tomorrow?"

I roll my eyes. We've had this conversation a hundred times. Vic plays bass guitar in an amateurish cover band. He's tried persuading me to sing lead for years. Everyone said I had a beautiful voice when I was younger, but I haven't sung in front of people since almost drowning, only to myself or when goofing off with Vic in my bedroom.

I worry the moment I sing in public again, something awful will be waiting to swallow me whole.

"We need you, Kai," Vic continues. "We landed a gig at my dad's karaoke bar."

"I'll think about it," I lie.

It's the same answer every time.

Halfway back to the main road, Vic pauses. He looks out toward the beach, where Marc is still dribbling a soccer ball between his feet, then to me. "Kai," Vic shouts, eyebrows waggling, "you're a six-foot god! Stop being scared. Any boy would be bananas not to want you."

I wave him off, nose wrinkled. If my best friend only knew about the boy I really dream about.

⬤

When the sun kisses the horizon, the beach empties out like a flood. Locals and tourists pass me on the wooden walkway. Everyone but Marc. He's hiked to his usual hideaway—atop one of the shallow cliffs overlooking the water. For nearly an hour, I watch him from a distance, unsure my clumsy feet will carry me all the way up the rocks without tripping and landing right back in the ocean's dark, possessive grip.

Eventually, Marc fades into the night.

Now, I'm standing on the beach, arms folded across my chest, legs trembling. The water's briny, salty scent fills my nose. I glare at Death as she unleashes her nightly hymn.

I rarely come this far into the sand. This close to the ocean. Over the years, my moms and therapist have gently nudged me toward giving swimming another chance. Trusting the water again. But every time it brushes past my ankles, climbs up my shins, I freeze.

What if I get it all wrong like I did as a kid? What if there is no magical merboy waiting? Who will save me? My moms didn't then, not that I'm upset with them. They tried.

As much as I want to learn how to swim better, so it never happens again, I'm scared the only thing that'll catch me when I fail is Death.

Anger coils in my throat. I yell to the water, "Why won't you let me forget?" My voice echoes into the night like a broken note in a quiet room.

Death doesn't reply in words. Instead, the wind lets out a low howl, and the ocean answers in a slow-building wave. My eyes catch on something moving along the crest. A flicker of fiery, glittering light. The quick whip of a tail emerging, then disappearing.

Stunned, I instinctively shuffle backward, but I don't notice the hole some kid dug up hours ago. My foot catches. All my weight shifts and then, my balance is gone.

As I'm falling, I almost laugh. This is what I get for being bold. Classic Kai.

I thud onto the beach, eyes closed. A groan escapes my lips as the back of my skull throbs.

Can you get a concussion from sand? I think. Then: *Who's gonna delete my browser history if I fall into a coma?*

My eyes pop open when a throat clears above me.

It's *him*, standing over me. The full moon weaves silver garland through his dark locs. He has a delicate, beautiful smile like blown glass in the light. Shiny drops of water slip down his deep brown skin. There are two legs where I remember a tail being. And he's—

Naked.

"Oh shit," I gasp.

He stares at me for a moment, an eyebrow arched, before glancing down. Reality sets in. "Sorry. I forgot." His grin widens before he jogs down the shore, ducking behind a large rock.

Lethargically, I sit up. *He's not a dream.* My brain's barely calibrated those words before the boy's returned, settling next to me in a loose, short-sleeved Henley and board shorts. "Are you okay?"

I nod slowly. When the waves dance up the shore, I finally scoot back. I don't let the water near my feet.

"Just a bump on the head," I say, rubbing my skull. The short hairs of my taper fade tickle my fingertips. I blink, then gaze at him.

In the moonlight, his eyes are less bright. He's toned like a swimmer. Nothing different from the boys I see at school, except . . .

"Sorry." *God, was I really just* staring *at him?* "I was expecting . . ."

His mouth tilts curiously, waiting for me to finish.

"Uh, nothing. I'm—"

22

"Kai," he says, his voice like salt and honey. Rough but sweet. The curves around his mouth deepen. "I know."

My heart tumbles like rolled dice in my chest.

"I'm Cyrus," he says. "We've met before."

"You saved me. A long time ago," I rasp out. "Do you always go around rescuing drowning boys?"

"No," he says. "Just you."

My eyes widen. He ducks his head, face scrunched as if he's just grasping what he said.

I glance at his feet, toes wiggling in the sand. "No offense, but I have to know," I say. His eyes narrow suspiciously, but I can't stop. "You had a tail that day, right? You're a . . . merboy?"

A pause hangs between us like the moon in the indigo sky. Tension shifts through his jaw. He's thinking. Finally, he whispers, "Yes. I am."

His eyes scan my face, waiting for a reaction. I don't flinch. I shift closer so he knows I'm not scared of what he's just told me. He saved my life. How could I ever be afraid of him?

"But you have legs now," I blurt, breaking our stare.

"Only during the full moon." He dusts grainy sand from his palms. "Every twenty-nine days, for two to three nights, my people can walk the shores."

"And the rest of the time?"

"A tail. Gills." He grins. "Of the sea."

I'm transfixed by his face, those high cheekbones, until another wave washes up, brushing the tips of my sneakers. I reflexively pull my legs to my chest.

"You're scared of her?" he asks.

Frustrated tears prickle my eyes. "I can't swim really well," I admit. "Practically the only kid in this beachside town who can't. It's embarrassing."

"We all have at least one thing about ourselves that's embarrassing." He tucks locs behind an ear, sitting a breath closer to whisper, "I can't sing."

Seconds pass before I laugh, which is high and thin like a wheezing cat.

Cyrus frowns, confused.

"Sorry," I rush out. "It's just that—lots of people can't sing? Not good, anyway. My best friend can't. Don't tell him I told you."

His expression doesn't alter. "It's not a joke. Where I'm from, our song is important. It's part of our magic."

My hands fidget anxiously. I want this boy to smile again, to know I'm not an asshole. "*Oh.* I'm sorry. *Seriously.* Tell me about your . . . magic. Please?"

The sea's haunting chant softens as if she's listening. She wants to know what secrets Cyrus is holding. So do I. Gently, I nudge my knee against his, encouraging him.

"In my kingdom, our voice is an instrument of power." Beads of water slip down Cyrus's cheek like dew on a peach. His eyes never leave the water. Dancing ripples disrupt the moon's doppelgänger on its surface. "When we sing, it shows the god of the ocean we're worthy of her gifts. That we can command the waters. Bring peace to a storm. Call on the creatures that live among us. It's a rite of passage for royals. But if you can't find the right pitch, then . . ."

"Then, what?"

He frowns. "Then the people of my kingdom won't respect you. I'll never ascend to the throne like I'm supposed to. No royal has ever failed to find their song. Until . . . well, me."

I lean away. "Wait, so you're a . . ."

Cyrus winces like he's said too much. "A prince."

"Whoa." *Being kissed* by a prince of the sea wasn't on my bingo card. Though technically, it wasn't a kiss. CPR? Mouth-to-mouth?

"That seems like a lot of pressure," I say. "The singing thing."

He nods solemnly. "Have you ever felt that way? Like a failure?"

My eyes immediately focus on the shallow waves. I hug my knees. Words sit tangled like a knot in my throat. I nod once.

"What if I teach you to swim?" he offers. When my head jerks in his direction, Cyrus quickly adds, "For your safety. I don't mind saving cute boys like you, but . . . just in case. I can teach you to trust her."

"I—" Nothing else comes out. *He thinks I'm cute?*

"And you can teach me to sing!" he insists, grinning.

A sputtering laugh escapes my lips. He can't be serious. I'm not a trained vocalist. Even though Mama says I could "outsing Tevin Campbell," whoever that is, and Mom used to sign me up for every school musical that promised a potential solo performance, I'm not qualified to *teach* anyone.

I tell Cyrus that.

"Kai," he says, "I heard you sing. When we were younger. And tonight—"

"That *wasn't* singing."

"Point is, *I heard you.* It's how I found you both times." A loc falls over his forehead. "I've never stopped thinking about how beautiful you sounded that day."

I bite my lip. My lungs fight for oxygen.

"I need to learn or—" Cyrus swallows hard, and I see it. In the pinch of his mouth. The hollowness of his cheeks. A melancholy shine to his eyes. It's the same face I make in the mirror whenever I think about that day:

Fear.

I rest my hand on the back of his. His skin's warm like a cookie fresh from the oven. His gaze meets mine. "You'd be out there"—my wobbly chin jerks in the direction of the dark water—"with me the whole time?"

He nods enthusiastically.

"And I can quit when I want? No questions asked."

Another nod.

Already, my stomach is sinking into my feet, but I say, "Tomorrow night? Meet here?" with more confidence than I feel.

The edges of Cyrus's mouth twist up and he says, "Tomorrow night."

Cyrus's voice is a collision of dissonance. The rumble of earthquakes. All snare and cymbals, no bass. It scares a flock of birds into flight. Unleashes a wail from the ocean.

We're standing face-to-face, alone on the beach. He's in the same clothes from last night. I'm wearing a tank top and, reluctantly, a new pair of swim trunks. Sneaking out of the house with them on didn't go as planned.

"You're learning to . . . swim?" Mama asked, panic etched around her eyes.

"Yes?"

"From a boy we've never met?"

I grimaced. "He's, uh. Here for the summer. He knows his stuff! I'll be safe."

She pursed her lips. "Years of offering to *pay* for swimming lessons and suddenly one boy comes around and you're—"

Luckily, Mom interrupted. "Carolina, we can trust him." Turning to me with narrowed eyes, she warned, "Phone and location on. Home before eleven. No practicing in the water after dark."

"And get the floaties!" Mama yelled when I ducked away to run all the way here.

To Cyrus.

For now, the floaties are lying discarded on the beach. The usually pale-gold sand is brushed smoke gray by the moon. The night's eerily quiet except for us.

We've done this for an hour—I hum a melody, then he echoes. Our notes never sound the same. Mine are a mellow tenor. His are a boom of noise. I don't laugh or scold him, and he smiles appreciatively at my patience, as if he's used to people giving up on him.

After another failed note, I ask, "Isn't there anyone who teaches you how to sing?"

"No," he says, chin lowered. "We believe this kind of power isn't taught. It's supposed to come naturally. And only wielded by royals."

"So, technically, what we're doing is . . . forbidden?"

"Yes?" He grins slyly. "Again?"

I finally laugh, then give him a new chord. He destroys it but with crinkles around his eyes. We trade unmatching melodies for another ten minutes before he asks if I'm ready to get into the water.

I chew my lip. "I guess?"

He peels off his shirt. When his hands reach for the waistband of his shorts, my throat releases an awkward noise that sounds like his singing voice.

Cyrus flexes an eyebrow. "I can't get in the water with shorts on."

Of course. I quickly avert my eyes. Just because there's no shame in being naked in his culture doesn't mean I have any right to *look*.

Soon, there's a small splash. I wait another beat before turning.

When anyone else is in the ocean, it looks too big, swallowing them whole. But not with Cyrus. It's too small, barely containing all the light and beauty radiating off him.

Ten feet out, shiny beads of water gather on his skin like stars broken from the sky. He's visible from the chest up. Beneath the surface I spot the gilded fire. Behind his shoulder, a peek of tangerine fluke emerges. I glance apprehensively at my floaties.

"Kai," he says, "I won't let you drown."

The promise in his voice carries me to the sea.

Shivers race up my muscles. The cold mixing with stubborn fear. I'm only waist-deep when receding waves knock me off balance. Cyrus races forward. His strong arms catch me before I go under.

"It's okay," he assures.

My fingers pinch his biceps. I count backward from ten. He keeps my chin above water, waiting for the tremors to subside before slowly floating us deeper into Death's embrace.

"The mechanics are different for merfolk. Tail versus legs," he explains as we drift. Past the sea's inky surface, his tail moves in effortless motions. Fire and grace. "But the main things are the same."

"Like?"

His grin inches into something mischievous. "First, you have to trust her."

Somehow, he persuades me to lie back. Fall into his arms. Into the water. I want to crawl out of my skin. Instead, I stare up at the jeweled moon, letting my body adjust.

A weightlessness comes first. Then a quiet in my chest that matches the noiseless night. The ocean hasn't pulled me under.

"Safe," he whispers.

I try not to flinch. He warned me about sudden movements. With one of his hands cradling my neck and the other tucked behind my knees, I stay afloat.

"Okay?" he asks.

I exhale. "I think so."

We've floated farther out. I don't try to crane my neck and see how far we are from shore. I let my brain remain connected to his hands, the occasional splash of his tail, the lightness of his breathing.

"Why are you only allowed on land during the full moon?" I ask, seeking another distraction.

A fondness stretches across his words. "It's an old story. My mother tells it best."

"I want to hear your version."

"Once we were free to roam the waters and land. To be seen by humans. But the sun gods hated how humanity gave attention to us rather than worshipping them. Gods are equally benevolent and jealous. They promised protection from humans who'd want to capture us, learn our magic, if we stayed hidden beneath the waves. Never to be perceived above the surface."

He rotates us in a wide circle like a carousel.

"We were safe, but unhappy," he continues. "We missed the freedom to be wherever we wanted. So the moon gods granted us a gift—once a cycle, we're allowed to walk the shores under their watchful eyes."

I study his face. He's talking about gods and magic as if they're real. As if these things exist. It's impossible. Then again, I'm floating in the sea with an actual merboy, so maybe . . .

"What else?" I say.

His smile ticks up. "What do you want to know?"

Everything, I almost reply. "Do you have any siblings?"

He laughs and I hear it in his voice—the rippling melody. A soft current of notes dancing from his throat. It's not quite a song, but the promise exists.

"Four younger sisters."

"I'm an only child."

I tell him about how my moms fell in love. The family restaurant where Mom cooks, and Mama bakes sugary pastries—my favorite being sticky cinnamon rolls drizzled in cream cheese icing. Then about my friendship with Vic. How we came out at the same time. How I wish I had his confidence. The reason I yelled at the ocean last night. How I'd do it again if it meant he'd hear me and come.

Overwhelmed with embarrassment, my feet kick up water. That's when I notice Cyrus's hands aren't supporting me anymore. He's hovering nearby, beaming. His touch is gone.

Panic lurches through me but I breathe through it.

I'm floating on my own. The water hasn't betrayed me. No, she's steady beneath me. She brushes softly against my skin. When I inhale, it's the scent of salt and green.

I want to scream victoriously. My eyes tread over Cyrus. "I'm . . . okay."

He wades closer. Cool fingertips skim my forearm until he finds my hand, squeezing. "More than okay."

As we drift back to shore, I comment offhandedly, "I wish you were always here."

"There's a myth about merfolk becoming human," he explains.

"If they find true love on land, and if that love is returned, then the ocean strips them of their magic. She refuses to let them come back once they've given their love to another."

He reminds me that gods are jealous, sometimes spiteful, but they're also compassionate.

"Do you think it's true?" I ask.

"I've never seen it happen." A hush briefly swirls between us. "But that doesn't mean it's not real."

When I'm drying off, the moon's footprint circling his face, I ask, "Will you come back? During the next full moon?"

Hesitation tightens his features. He's almost neck-deep in the water. It's gleaming like black sapphires.

"Is it fair to make you wait that long?" he asks.

"I've waited six years to see you again," I say. "I can wait twenty-nine days."

"What if—" He stops short. Never finishes.

I want to run back in. Tug him into my arms. I've spent almost half my life being terrified of the sea. But, in one night, Cyrus has shown me I don't have to be afraid. If I can trust the water not to take me under, then I can dive into almost anything and know that I won't drown.

I clear my throat. I use the one weapon I always had: my voice.

"Cyrus, what if I told you I've been dreaming about you ever since that day?"

He blinks hard, startled.

I smile, my resolve persisting. "I was ten years old and obsessed with a boy with a tail." The ocean swishes and sloshes. Her song never reaches the volume my voice does. "I'm not done learning to swim. And you—you're gonna learn to sing. You're a prince and I know you can use your voice to show everyone how much respect you deserve."

Cyrus pushes locs away from his face. My stomach tightens thinking about those hands holding me up like an offering to the moon. Gentle palms like a place to call home.

I stand taller. "I'll wait for you."

He exhales. The ocean's surface quivers.

"Will you come back?"

It's a long, painful silence. Nausea bubbles in my stomach. "Yes," Cyrus finally says. Glimmering drops of water slide down his chin as he smiles. Big and unafraid.

In my mind, I roar, *I'll wait. I'll be here.*

July

I'm nearly bursting the first night of the full moon. So much has changed in twenty-nine days.

I've traded weekend shifts at my moms' restaurant to give voice lessons in our garage.

On Saturday mornings, I meet up with Vic's band. We rehearse for two weeks and then, one warm and humid night, I hop onstage with them at his dad's karaoke bar. I perform in front of a cheering crowd. I soak up their energy. I show them what I can do without once thinking about drowning.

Twice a week, I drag my moms to the beach. I practice floating in the ocean with them nearby. Mama tries to hide it, but I catch her crying on Mom's shoulder the second she sees me in the water with no floaties. Safe and comfortable and free.

When Marc comes by the restaurant, I don't hide in a corner and watch him like I used to. No, I give him a nod. Bus tables around him. Wave goodbye when he leaves. He was a distraction, and I'm not wasting any more time on those.

Every night, I watch the moon shift from waxing to quarter to a crescent sharp enough to cut stars from the sky. Through every phase, I dream of a boy with thunder in his song and a fiery gold tail.

Now, I'm racing from my house, my towel fluttering like a cape in the wind. My heavy feet thump against the wooden planks leading to the beach.

I'm chasing the moon.

When I finally stop, breathless, there are footprints in the sand. They turn left, then right, like someone's been pacing. But the shore is empty.

It's just me, the moon, and the ocean.

Panic itches up my spine. Prickles along my neck. Settles like a hook in my head, the tug too strong to fight against.

Am I too late? Did something happen to Cyrus? Did someone scare him away?

"Cyrus?" I say.

The ocean answers back with rocking waves and nothing else.

Without warning, sharp, unforgiving tears flood my eyes. My hands shake. What if he decided I wasn't worth the wait? My knees weaken. I'm back to the boy I was before—trembling, barely able to stand in front of the water, scared and frustrated.

Why did Death give me hope only to snatch it away?

After a beat—my brain trying to will my body into turning away, walking back home—I hear it.

"Kai!"

The voice comes from behind a large rock almost ten feet away. Cyrus steps into the silvered light. His shirt's balled in one hand. The same shorts from last time. His locs are pinned up with shells and seaweed. He's as beautiful as I remember. Uncertain but unforgettable.

I stutter, "I-I'm here."

A smile pokes at his lips. "Me too. I was just—I thought you might've changed your mind? Or that what I said about the ocean's magic and true love being able to turn merfolk human scared you away? And then I wasn't sure if that's what *I* wanted? Do I want to leave my home and family behind? Do I even want to be the next king? Twenty-nine days is a lot of time to think and—"

He's rambling, and there's nothing left holding me back. Sand flies from my heels as I run to him. I squeeze him tightly. His laugh vibrates against my cheek.

"You came," I say into his locs.

His forehead presses to mine. "I couldn't stay away."

"You don't have to make any decisions now," I tell him. "It's all still new. *We're* new. But this is enough."

Him and the moon and even the sea.

"Actually, I lied," I whisper. "I want one more thing—to kiss you. If that's okay?"

"I've never kissed anyone."

"Do you want to try?"

His answer comes in a head tilt. A slow closing of the gap between our mouths. Our first kiss tastes like salt and need and a refrain waiting years to be played.

Cyrus draws back first. "I have to show you something." He turns to the water. Inhales deeply before opening his mouth.

He *sings*.

It's not perfect. His pitch wobbles. But ripples turn to waves, building to small crests before dissolving. In the distance, a whale leaps out of the water, gleefully crashing back into it. The ocean's black canvas cracks when a series of dorsal fins appear.

"Never trust dolphins," he whispers into my ear. "They're tricky monsters."

I laugh loudly, then beg him to show me how to breathe underwater. "I brought goggles!" I say, tugging them out of my pocket.

I want to see everything he does.

Cyrus takes my hand. Guides me into the sea. Each of my steps are steady and sure. When we're deep enough, his mouth slides over mine, fire and gold on his tongue. I sigh happily into the kiss before we're submerged.

He never leaves me. His breaths fill my lungs until I learn to blow bubbles through my nose. Our bodies sway together. Synchronized. Tethered.

Underwater, the ocean whispers something new to me:

Life.

THE STORY OF A KNIFE

⚓

Gretchen Schreiber

We have always lived in the house on top of the hill, on a cliff overlooking the sea. Unlike the rest of the town, where houses clump together like seaweed around the shops of Main Street.

Just another tick in the strange column for Strand women.

Scars laddering up our legs.

Lingering on our widow's walk, staring out at the sea.

No fathers.

I've heard the whispers about what goes on in our house. *They have bones buried in the cellar or the ocean below their cliff. Bones of their fathers.* I know very little about my father aside from the fact that he was a boy from town, and he was gone before I was born. His family had been here since the town's founding, but one night he packed his house and left . . . whether of his own volition or something more nefarious depends on the rumor you believe.

As long as we remember our place, we are begrudgingly accepted in Brimshore. Not because my mother brings cupcakes to school for my birthday or volunteers for anything the town offers, but because of her work. Our island town subsists on tourism, and my mother's photographs have a way of drawing crowds. Her photos of the ocean awaken an ache in so many that we never have to worry about food or repairs on the old house. Never mind that she fears the water.

The shop, like the house, has always been ours—an anchor keeping us tied to the community. Each generation turns it into something new, but it is always ours. The familiar bell chimes as I push the door open, ignoring Mother's photos on the walls.

I don't need to come here but I do, hoping that Mother will be happy to see me. That her expectations of me picking up her mantle and becoming the next Strand woman with the shop and the house on the cliff will shift. That she will just see me. And perhaps see how, every chance I get, I look to the ferry that shuttles tourists and supplies from the mainland.

I pause by the door at the basket of wishing stones my mother collected from the beach, pocketing a few. I could pick my own from the beach below our house, but there's something about taking them from my mother that is more satisfying. Wishes are for people with futures.

"Aurelia?" My mother's head pokes out from the back room. Her long black braid hangs over her shoulder, making her fair skin stand out even more. Heavy silver earrings tinkle lightly as she moves toward me. A scowl carves itself across her face when she sees my dress. "A little cold for that, isn't it?"

Her displeasure is heaped on my shoulders. I strike a pose in my boots and knee-length dress. It's not cold, but Mother uses that as an excuse to cover her own scars and hide who she is. She would wear jeans in the middle of summer on the equator. If she ever were to travel that far. It's why she applies so many lotions and creams, as if the right brew will erase her scars.

They haunt her but they don't scare me.

"Isn't that a bit revealing?" she says, lowering her voice as if we might be overheard. I know she'll never understand me, but still, I decide to try.

I pocket a few more stones and give her a smile, already backing up toward the door as she starts toward me.

"I like them, and the memory of not being trapped here," I say, holding out a leg so my scars can catch the late afternoon light. These silvery lines of tissue are a souvenir of the only time I ever left the island.

Mom looks away from me, closing her eyes as if she can remember every slice of the knife. The only time I was allowed to leave the island was when I had surgery; otherwise, the town views us as the strange Strand women alone on the widow's walk. I was small, still learning to toddle around on bones that didn't seem made for standing. My mother took me to doctors who split open my legs and wrapped my soft bones around metal. And I've lived with scars and the stretching of my legs ever since.

Mom said it was hereditary, not genetic. Elaboration was of course denied. Some topics were just off-limits. Just another thing that's strange about the Strand women.

"Where are you headed?" Mother asks.

I hold up a stone, a silent way of telling her where I'm going.

I want more than anything else to explore the city beyond our island's shores, but Mother shuts that down at every turn.

"Stay on shore, do not go into the ocean!" she calls after me. I give her a wave and head out. "I'll see you at home . . ."

Home is such a bendable word.

My mother contorts it to fit everyone else's ideals. I have no desire to pick up my mother's life, my family's legacy. I dream of how to get off the island and of the places I would go.

I will find a place where home does not bend until it breaks.

❀

The beach is mostly rock and crunches under my boots. Wind off the dark water whips at the loose strands of my hair. Whitecaps rush up from the waves and vanish just as they reach the shore.

Adjusting my stance, I take out a wishing stone and turn it over in my hand before giving it a good flick. It bounces over the waves, each bounce a wish—or so Mother tells the tourists. For me, each skip is a promise of adventure, of a place I will go.

Hiking the whole Via Francigena.

Seeing Lake Baikal.

Escaping my mother.

These rocks are a path out of this town, even if just for a moment. And even when they sink, they take my dreams into the ocean, who holds them close until I can collect them.

As the stone arcs for a fourth bounce, I reach for another.

But the stone comes flying back.

I duck, the rock sailing over my head.

Standing, I look out to the sea but find only waves. *This was nothing.* I pull out another rock, turning it over in my hand, gathering courage.

Again I toss the rock.

Once.

Twice.

And again it comes straight back at me. No cause in sight.

With no thought, I shuck off my boots and step into the surf, wading out until the cold water turns icy hot against my skin. My toes grip the sand and I watch for anything that might move. I do not fear the ocean—though Mother won't even come close to it.

Another rock, slick with the sea. I bring my arm back.

Once.

Then it too comes flying at my head. But there, between the waves—a flash of something. I reach out for the creature at the same time it lunges for me. Its skin is smooth and supple.

And the creature has fingers.

I grab on.

The creature fights back and jerks me from the comfort of the shallows. Below my feet the sandy bottom of the ocean falls away as I'm yanked out into open water. For all my bravery, I don't swim very well. My mother's fear of the water meant no swimming lessons. Between the waves and the creature's speed, I lose my hold. Set adrift, the current sucks me under, twisting me until I cannot tell up from down.

My legs and arms churn the water, searching for the surface. The sea will not take me today. With one last attempt, I reach for the sky, but even though I can see the glimmer of sun, my fingers still cannot scrape the air. It's too much effort and I stop fighting, letting the ocean pull me down.

That's when the creature's hand grabs me, pulling me close,

cradling me against a chest that feels human. We crack the surface with a splash. Sun slices into my eyes and I choke on water.

I land hard on the beach, rocks digging into my skin.

Salt stings my eyes, making it almost impossible to see, but I cough, trying to clear my lungs. Lack of oxygen makes the world spotty. Strong hands turn me on my side and smack my back, forcing the water from my lungs. My legs brush against scales. Skin against skin as someone traces my lips and the shadows under my jaw to check whether I can breathe.

A song that feels as old as the current fills my ears. I am tied up in its flow. Tears clear my eyes and I am face-to-face with a boy. His eyes are the blackness of the deep sea, thriving and unknowable. My heart slams against my chest, a scream caught in my sea-ravaged mouth. I try to wiggle free of his grasp, away from that liquid black gaze. Of all the things to crawl out of the ocean, this was not what I anticipated.

Where I expect to see legs, there is a tail, covered in rich black scales that glisten with a blue-green iridescence under the sun. His tail makes his skin look like the inside of a shell—pale white. There is not enough air. I have to be hallucinating.

His eyes run down my body, seemingly checking for injury. And that's when he sees my legs.

The change in his eyes, the press of his lips as he stares at my scars, makes me want to cower. My scars glisten in the sun, bands of bright, tight tissue that wrap around my doctor-made legs. The only thing more powerful than shock is shame.

I pull my dress farther down and tuck my legs under myself, suddenly understanding parts of my mother and why she hides her legs from the world. It's easy to ignore the townsfolk, their looks don't matter, but I deeply do not want him to look at me with the same derision. It's like breathing; this feeling is just automatic, as if my very cells recognize him.

His hands push mine away. "What have they done to you?" Melodies cling to his voice as if he was meant to sing instead of speak.

These are the same words my classmates use—but his are inherently different. My classmates' tones were malicious, their *what happened to you* meant to separate me from them, to convey that not only was I different, I was wrong.

The merman—and I am almost certain that's what he is— says it with something like sadness. As if he understands the very essence of me and my need to be beyond these shores.

Before I can stop him, his fingers explore the ridges of my scars, tracing their loops and sharp turns with reverence. A secret—about me—about my body—has been kept from me, burns beneath my skin with his soft touch.

"You're supposed to be—"

"You tried to kill me," I say. Anger fuels my outburst and I shove him hard, breaking whatever spell his beauty has me under.

His head snaps up and his dark gaze swallows me. I want to force him to explain who he is—what he is. But my statement knocks him back to reality and he looks around, his eyes settling high up on our house.

Then he is gone, without another word, back into the sea.

❧

I make my way back up to our house. Sea glass winks in the dying light, welcoming me home. It's all over our house, each Strand adding their own pieces to the ever-growing collection.

Pausing at the top of the hill, I look back to the ocean, wondering where the merman is now. I don't even know his name, just the song that wraps about my brain and leaves an ache in my chest. I can close my eyes and still see him, silhouetted against the sun, reaching for me as if he understands me—recognizes me on a primal level that feels unlike anything I've known. Somehow I already trust him and want him to tell me what he meant by *what have they done to you* . . .

I stumble into our kitchen, humming fragments of the merman's song, trying to hold on to the last moments with him.

"There you are." Mother's words stop as if she has stepped off into the deep ocean below. Her face pales. "Where did—" She clears her throat. "Aurelia. Go wash the sea off you."

I look down at my legs speckled with sand and flecks of shells and my dress still wet and stiffening as it dries. "It doesn't bother me."

But I still do as she says.

During dinner Mother is too precise with her movements, as if she's handling a bomb. I hum the song, determined not to forget it.

She slaps her fork down to the table. "Where did you hear that song?"

I open my mouth to tell her about the boy, about what I saw— but it all feels like sea-foam, effervescent and fleeting.

"You know it?" I ask, relief flooding me. I was worried the boy was a dream; mermen, after all, were only children's stories. A mermaid who gave up everything for love. Stories were mixed on how it turned out. From the schoolyard I heard love won out, but the fishermen on the docks reported something more sinister.

Mother focuses on her plate. She flounders for words. "It was— it's just something foolish—children used to sing—the words were cruel . . ."

"Kids usually trade stories on the playground. I always heard bits about a little mermaid," I say, feeling brazen for the first time in a long while. Normally I am so content to let Mother's words, her warnings, wash over me like waves on sand, but her brush-off doesn't hit the same.

"What have I told you about listening to that nonsense?" Mother asks, not expecting an answer. "Some people have too much time on their hands."

"I've heard a tale about—"

"Aurelia." Mom's hands slam onto the table, making the cutlery rattle. "Enough. You are too old for fairy tales."

I flinch. I couldn't say why, but it felt wrong, like the scars on my legs. Lies to cover up what was beneath it all. That wasn't good enough.

If she would not help, then I would find out for myself.

꙳

I race to the little library. The librarian is happy, if confused, when I check out a collection of Hans Christian Andersen fairy tales. Is it because she knows? Does the whole town know that my scars are more than scars? But whatever they know, they keep hidden; they've never been open to doing me or my mother any favors.

Later, curled up in my bed, the window open, the ocean waves singing to me, I flip through the book. The last page of "The Little Mermaid" shows a woman in silhouette, standing in the doorway holding a knife. She's meant to kill the prince with it and, in doing so, earn her tail back. I trace the knife—wondering if a fairy tale can be true.

The question is absurd, and yet I find myself drawn to the picture, to the story, trying to rinse fact from fiction.

Mother comes into my room, not pausing to knock. Her long hair flowing around her and her limp more pronounced than ever.

"I heard you went to the library today. I do not understand what has gotten into you."

I can't look at her, anger still too raw inside me. She got to decide what I knew. "I can't go to the beach and now I can't go to the library. What's next, school? Am I going to be confined to the house?" My fingernails press into the binding on the book, my nail beds turning white.

"Aurelia, whatever you are doing, it is enough." Her voice holds a plea as much as warning. *Please don't* forces itself between syllables, and fear laces it all together.

"What are we?" My voice is quiet, barely a whisper of waves against the rocks. I have always accepted her answers to my questions about the surgeries, about what is wrong with me, but I am owed answers now.

And I get silence.

It is Mother's best weapon. *Wait until Aurelia realizes there is nothing there, wait until she just goes along with it, wait until she learns that there will be no explanation . . .*

But this time I strike back. I turn the book around, showing her the story, the pictures.

"What were we?" I ask.

"We are human. Just like your grandmother before you and her mother before her . . ." Mother's voice wavers under the weight of her conviction. This truth, however, is stretched to the breaking point.

"And our great-great-*great*-grandmother?" I ask, finally meeting her gaze. Because what if my family's story didn't end the way Andersen wrote it? "Did she really throw herself off a boat?"

Mother's lips press into a fine line, her earrings tinkling as she shakes—whether with anger or fear, it's hard to tell. She looks at the book only once before leaving. Perhaps she wanted to stay on the island, feigning ignorance, being something we're not. The adventure I had always sought has been replaced by a desire to know more about myself.

Despite her wishes, I return to the sea.

※

I go back to the inlet, determined to see him again to either prove my sanity or live with madness. The dark ocean laps softly at the shore as if in opposition to my churning thoughts. He was real. Wasn't he? My pockets are heavy with skipping stones. One after another, I chuck them across the water. I run out of places to wish to see.

"Will you stop?" he asks, finally breaking the surface.

I march out into the ocean, to the very edge before the bottom gives way to the deep, ready to confront him. Even still, the water barely comes up to my waist. His song has filled my head, occupied every waking thought, and I want answers. "What did you mean?"

"I shouldn't have said anything." He keeps a healthy distance between us. If I want to force the truth from him, I'm going to have to go to him.

I step off into the open ocean.

The waves toss me back and forth as if they can't decide if I am to be kept or forced back to land. Fear rises in my chest as I push forward, wanting to know. Something has been hidden from me and no fear of the unknown will stop me.

At any moment, I expect him to fall back, to duck under the

waves and disappear. Allow me to chalk this whole experience up to an overactive imagination. Instead, he floats and I tread water.

"You asked what they did to me . . . who are they?" I ask, harder this time. "What am I?"

"Filthy humans." Anger turns his smile into a scythe, cruel and cutting, but he's confirmed something I already know.

"Without the doctors I wouldn't be able to walk," I say, suddenly defensive. I trace the line of a scar with my toe, feeling the sharp ridge.

He rolls his eyes.

"What am I?" I ask. Fear trips over my words but I can't hold them inside anymore. I want to know, need it like air.

He shakes his head. "We don't speak of it." He looks away the same way my mother does, as if there is something shameful in the truth.

"I'm a mermaid." It's the first time I've said the words out loud and they seem to cement something in my bones, and I wait for him to confirm my suspicions.

"Were." He flinches as if the word causes him pain. Sadness strangles his gaze as his dark eyes meet mine, his voice barely above the lap of the waves. The current seems to push us closer, urging us to explore, to touch worlds unknown to us.

"What does that mean?" I ask softly. I hold my breath, hoping for an answer.

His face is still as the sea on a clear day, but his eyes dart to the horizon, as if he's judging the distance it would take to swim away. I grab hold of him, relishing the smoothness of his skin against mine. Pulling us closer until our breaths mingle and I see the reflection of myself in his black eyes, I whisper, "How do I become a mermaid again?"

"How does one stop being a mermaid? You can cut off a bird's wings, but is it not still a bird?" His hands trace the top of my scar through my clothing—the one that curls around my hip—as if he can find the beginning of what was done to me.

I let out a low chuckle. My head swims trying to reconceive the world where mermaids, sea witches, and magic all exist. That a children's tale can truly hold the answers to my questions. And yet he can't wrap his head around medicine.

"I didn't think you were possible. For all I know, you might be a dream—I don't even know your name."

"Kuril."

"Aurelia," I reply.

Again and again, I returned to the inlet, ignoring my mother's warnings. I wanted to know more about what I was meant to be. Kuril would take my hand, I would fill my lungs with air, and he would show me a world that should have been mine. Ruddy-orange corals that twisted up toward the sky. Spiny sea urchins, their deep blue-black coloring reminding me so much of Kuril's eyes.

There was no more discussion of what happened in my family's past, no matter how I pushed.

He would always look toward the deep, as if he wanted to show me something that might hold answers to all my questions—but my lungs kept us close to the shore.

Wrapped up in a heavy blanket, my breath coming in puffs, I sit on the beach. Kuril lies next to me, his black tail and lacy fins warming under the early winter sun. His fingers make patterns on my skin, as if he could learn my life through touch. As if he too wants to explore me.

He looks up to the widow's walk that barely pokes out over the cliff's edge, and then back out to sea as if caught between a choice.

"Your family always walks there, but never takes the jump to join us."

✦

"What do you know about my family?" I'm not going to be distracted by the things I already know.

"Once, a mermaid left the sea. She made a pact with a sea witch, but—"

"And he didn't love her—yes, I know the story. Is there a way . . ."

"I found a way to change you back."

"How?" My hand stops on his heart, and it beats at a different cadence from mine. Skin against skin, feeling the ebb and flow of him.

His skin slick, the pads of his fingers trace up my neck, as if he could find the hidden seam of my gills. It lights a fire inside me. I shrug off the blanket and let him lead me into the water, to the world he knows so well. There, with the ocean's heart beating in my ears, I take a chance and kiss him. And on his lips, I taste salt and sea, taste a crispness that reminds me of air after rain. My ears pop and the world around me bends. Even with him breathing for me, my lungs seem to fold in on themselves, burning as they fight for something they already have.

I fight against the pull of the surface, wanting to stay below. Perhaps that is the fire, and my body is the crucible—going through this would make me stronger or purge me of the things done to me.

We crack the surface together.

He pauses, his lips a breath away from mine. "If you can return the knife to the sea witch, she will give you your tail back."

I hold on to him, hope lapping at me with every brush of the waves. It is as if the ocean had sent Kuril to give me a wish I could not imagine for myself.

❁

There is only one room in the house that is off-limits. It is only on rare occasions that I am allowed to cross the threshold.

If she has something to hide, it will be here.

Shadows collect in my mother's room as I go searching for the knife. Her room is musty and smells of earth and dried things. Mother refuses to open her windows and let in the one thing she hates.

I stand there in the doorway, wanting to take this next step but afraid of what it will really mean. I have dreamed of leaving this house, this island, so many times, and now, once again, a knife is the thing to pull me from this place. This time I do not anticipate coming back.

I won't end up like *her*, so I step inside.

One choice and I'm thrust into action. Pulling out the drawers of Mother's dressing table, I upend bottles of powders and potions to keep her scars soft and pliant, and toss aside shells and sea glass. Mother may hate the ocean, but she can't escape it either.

Where is the knife?

The mantel is decorated in dying flowers and old photographs. A line of every Strand woman, some in color but the oldest ones in fuzzy black and white. There is even one so old that it is just a sketch. Upon a closer inspection, I see what Mother had insisted was a fan is a knife—bowed and oddly shaped, but there's a highlight to bring out the sharpened edge. Another one of Mother's lies.

And that's when I know what I'm looking for.

Below me a door slams. Panic hits me hard and fast—Mother's here. Somehow, she must know.

I grab the dying hellebores, petals scattering as I rip the flowers from the vase. My rampage catches the edge of the drawing and sends it crashing to the floor. The old frame shatters, the back matting coming loose and exposing something bone white.

"Aurelia." Mother's voice carries up the stairs, wild like the wind. It's meant to whip me into compliance, but she can't stop me now.

Crouching over the ruins of the drawing, I push aside the backing and pull free the knife. It's small, barely the size of my palm, but still sharp enough to pierce a prince's heart. My pulse beats in my ears, because I feel like I'm holding the answers in my fingers.

"We cannot go back. It's dangerous . . . you don't know . . ." Mom says from the doorway. She's bent over, leaning heavily on the jamb. The race back here couldn't have been easy on her legs. Her voice is a harsh rasp, like the ocean against rocks.

I hold the knife against my chest, anger and hurt warring inside me. "Why not trust me? Why not let me decide for myself? Why is it that I always have to do what you say?" I expect anger; it has boiled inside me long enough. But instead, my words are sad—I feel betrayed by my mother's lack of trust.

"Because I know best."

"How was this better? We don't belong here and nothing you do can change that. What good could come from not telling me?"

"I never wanted you to live with what you might have been and to know you could never be that." Her eyes stray to the doors and beyond that, the ocean. And in that moment, I realize she doesn't hate the ocean, she wants it more than anything. "I loved you so much I wanted to give you the life I never had."

And that's what kills me. That in all of this, what my mother wanted for me became her biggest transgression. I want to feel the world as I am meant to, not through the oil slick of her love. It's a coating that's slowly killing me, weighing me down, reshaping my body to fit some idea of who she wants me to be.

I shake my head, not wanting to hear another word. She can choose this half-life on land, but I want to test my luck, to undo this curse that binds us here.

"You kept this from me!"

"I gave you a better life, free of the shackles of our ancestors. We are not them anymore." She blocks the door as if that will stop me. "It was so long ago . . ."

Instead of sprinting for the door, I turn and race through the French doors, hurtling across the widow's walk. It's not the titanium in my bones that gives me strength but my own courage as I pick up speed and leap off the end of the balcony. I will risk what others could not—would not.

Water rises to meet me and all I can think is, *I'm home.*

THE DARK CALLS

Preeti Chhibber

There's a cold spot in the water, and Bijal shivers once. The skin of her arms puckers. She rubs her palms against them. Her nose scrunches as she frowns, running a finger along the inside of her wrist. The tiny bumps there unpleasantly remind her of the underside of a yeti crab. The sea is dark as ever.

Ahead of her, she can see exactly where the sand ends, breaking into nothing but open water with a clean, sharp edge. Bijal isn't sure why she keeps coming back here. She flips her tail and swims forward, ignoring the slight bubble of guilt inside her, and peers over the end of the seafloor and into a wide darkness below. It's a huge expanse of nothing, and even with her eyes, accustomed to seeing in low light, she can't discern anything. She's not technically supposed to get so close to the ravine—no one is, not really—but there's something about it that intrigues. It's like an itch inside of her, begging for her attention. Bijal hums, thinking of an old warning rhyme she'd learned from her father. "The deep dark calls, you answer with your blood," she sings to herself. "The deep dark pulls, and asks for you by name. The deep dark waits, knowing that you'll answer. The deep dark is there, waiting to be claimed."

The chasm had been there longer than she'd been alive, longer than her mother had been alive, and her mother's mother. That meant generations of warnings, of fear—but Bijal never understood *why*. Her mother said, don't go near the break. Her mother's mother said, don't go near the break.

She'd asked why once.

"Because."

"Because *what*?" She'd swum in circles around Ma, who was trying to harvest the heavy conch fruits from their garden, until her mother had tweaked her tail and pulled her down, glaring at her with pitch-black eyes.

"*Because* it's dangerous."

"But *who* decided?" Bijal asked, voice plaintive. Her mother paused her ministrations, fingers stilling. But her ink-blue tail twisted back and forth, made evident her anxiety. Bijal watched her mother's scales reflect the soft glow of the wide, intersecting lines of bright white lights dotting up and down her fin. She saw the glow flatten as the scales shifted to hard, tough skin at her mother's waist.

"Because tradition. Because history. Because *we say so*, Bijal. Now, ja, go away from here."

A bright something flashes in the corner of Bijal's eyes, interrupting her thoughts, and she turns to see an angler fish go over the edge and swim down, its tiny light guiding the way. She follows the small dot with her eyes until it shrinks farther and farther into nothing. And then she lets out a light groan. Digging her fingers into the sand, she watches the brilliant, thin blue and green lines on her skin disappear into the grains. Suddenly there's a sharp and bright blossom of pain in her finger and she snatches her hand back. She sucks in her teeth, a rush of briny water flowing over her tongue as she lets out a curse.

"*Ish.*"

A bubble of green blood expands on her pointer, and it starts to lift up and fade into the water around it. There's movement in the sand below and a tiny, spiky sea spider pokes out of the hole she'd made, glaring at her for disturbing its rest. Or she assumes as much.

"Sorry," she mumbles, rubbing her thumb against the small cut, thankful for the salt in the water that will heal it quickly. Then she shakes her head, once, and groans. "What am I even doing here?"

She pauses and then chokes out a laugh, "Who am I even *talking to?*"

The valley below her rumbles.

"What the——" Bijal swims backward hastily, pushing her fin against the stillness as hard as she can.

"*Bijal.*" A voice wafts its way up and into her ear, or maybe into her mind, she can't tell. It's soft and slippery and feels as amorphous as the cloudy jellies that float through the halls of her home.

A current pulls her forward, toward the drop, toward the dark. She doesn't resist. She can see the stream of it as it takes her closer and closer to the open water. To the dark. Distantly, some part of her wonders what she's doing and why she's letting it pull her away.

"BIJAL!" A voice shatters her trance, and she fights hard against the grasping current, shooting in the opposite direction. "BIJAL, WHERE ARE YOU?"

But Bijal doesn't respond, shaken by whatever just happened.

"Bijal?" The other voice is closer now, and before she turns around Bijal knows her sister, Kavita, has found her.

"Hey," she says, eyes cutting to the side to take in the other girl, surprised that her sister was looking for her. Kavita's long dark hair is a cloud around her face, her fin a deep black, just translucent enough to see the bones that make it work. Like the rest of their family, and decidedly unlike Bijal, the lights that run along Kavita's fin and up her spine are a bright white. Her brows are furrowed as she looks at Bijal.

"Are you okay?" she asks, voice laced with an uncharacteristic hesitance. It's strange enough to hear that Bijal paints a smile onto her face, before nodding with feigned enthusiasm.

"Yeah, definitely. I was just watching an angler fish dive."

"Okay . . ." Kavita looks toward the gulch over Bijal's shoulder and shudders. "Why do you go near that place when you know we're not allowed? It's creepy and dangerous."

"It's fine. I'm fine." Bijal hears herself say the words, even though she isn't sure they're true. But she doesn't want to worry her sister; it's not right. The voice was probably nothing, anyway. Just her imagination.

"Kavita! Come, have one more seaweed wrap."

Bijal watches her sister protest, covering her plate with her hands to stall her mother's insistence on adding more food. The lines in her skin glow brighter as Kavita gets more irritated, flashing a brilliant white and highlighting the dishes resting on the table in their small home. "Ma, I am not hungry, please stop feeding me."

Bijal looks down at her own plate, slipped and locked into place in a divot on the large stone table. There are five seaweed wraps rolled up tightly under the curved dome covering half the plate, just the stubs of green edges peeking out and waiting to be pulled and eaten. A clamshell sits broken open and empty next to one still tightly closed. She thinks the mollusk must know it's on a plate and shoots it a sharp-toothed grin. Bijal toys with the top of its shell while their mother continues nattering at Kavita.

"Fine, what do I know?" she says, bristling. "And you . . ." She turns on Bijal, glaring at her still full plate. "Is this not good enough for your—"

Kavita lets out an aggrieved squeak, interrupting before their mother can really get on a roll.

"I didn't say that it wasn't—"

"You may as well have . . ."

Bijal tunes them out, far too used to these arguments about nothing. Instead, she thinks back to the voice she couldn't possibly have heard. Her mind is stewing with the idea that if Kavita hadn't shown up and yelled for her, Bijal isn't sure what might have happened. It's perplexing, and a little unsettling. She shivers, short and violent. Her arm jerks, knocking against her plate. Two of the wraps get loose from their cage and begin floating up slowly, toward the rocky ceiling. She stares at them without seeing, mind stuck in the accident of her sister's interruption.

A dark hand darts out to grab one of the wraps, cutting into Bijal's vision and startling her.

"Eh! Pay attention, we don't want a mess on the ceiling. It attracts those terrible keeda." Her mom is holding the wraps in her fist, squeezing them, and for a second Bijal thinks they'll burst, making an even worse mess than the one her mother is worried about. Using their fine mesh net to get minced seagrass out of the kitchen water is not something she wants to spend her evening doing. But her mother relaxes her fingers and lightly shoves the wraps back onto Bijal's plate, into the curved space to keep them stationary until she's ready to eat.

"Sorry, Ma," Bijal says, flinching when her voice sounds anything but normal. Her mom gives her a suspicious look but doesn't comment on it.

"Clean up the kitchen when you've finished," she says instead, and Bijal relaxes. She's not as open as she once was with her family, but she knows her mother can still read her when she wants to. "I'm going to join Papa after this. We'll both be back tomorrow. You could probably use a break from *me* anyway." Her mother mutters the last part quietly, but Bijal can hear it as she gets farther away. Kavita rolls her eyes and moves to pick up the rest of the food so it can go back into the coral storage.

"She needs to relax; I hope Dad comes back soon so she can put some of that suffocating attention back onto him. The person who *chose* to be around it."

Bijal keeps her mouth closed. Kavita needs to do this sometimes—to vent and get her frustrations out. Bijal's always been more passive—*no, not always.* The thought breaks into her head unbidden, and Bijal's lips turn down into a frown.

"What are you doing with your face?" Kavita asks, and then without waiting for Bijal to answer, goes back to what she'd been saying. "She just—*argh!*"

Bijal shrugs noncommittally and starts pulling at some of the other dishes, slipping them off their anchored positions, and then flips her tail, following in her sister's wake. Together, they deal with the leftovers. Extra wraps go back into a loose net tied to the bottom of the coral storage, and the empty clamshells get put inside a bisected, hollowed-out conch to be used later. The conch's insides glow iridescent in Kavita's white light. There's a light snapping sound behind her, and Bijal feels a slight vibration in the water. She turns around to see the other clam, alive and dropping down to the sandy floor. She watches as it burrows into the sand. She hadn't noticed it was missing.

"Ugh, are you going to get that?" Kavita asks, looking with mild disgust at the place the clam dug. Bijal's shoulders lift into another shrug.

"If it gets away, I guess it deserves it."

"You can tell that to Ma when there's a nest of them."

Bijal laughs at her sister.

"I don't know if that's how a single clam works, Kav."

"Whatever." Kavita's voice is still angry, and her movements doubly so. Her lights are pulsing, and Bijal thinks that they're *loud*. Kavita closes the coral storage basket hard enough that a small piece breaks off and drifts slowly to the ground. "*Argh*," she says again, and Bijal can see Kavita's pointed teeth flash brightly, a white shock in the seam of Kavita's dark mouth.

"Ma's just showing you she cares about you," Bijal says, placating her.

Kavita's shoulders tense and her tail stills, the dark scales oscillating with the pulsing lights of jellyfish floating along the edges of the room. Bijal waits for her sister to respond, waving her hands against the pressure of the water, and watching as the movement distorts the image of the kitchen counters, of the long black threads of seaweed wafting up from the floor, of her sister's back.

"*Bijal* . . ."

Bijal's head snaps to the doorway to her right, the one leading outside. Unthinking, she starts to slip along toward the exit.

"I *know* it's because she cares . . . I just wish she'd back off sometimes," Kavita says and brings Bijal back to herself. Her sister looks furious, but Bijal can see the uncertainty underneath. Kavita loves their mother's overwhelming love. She'd told Bijal once that it was proof that they were wanted.

Bijal had responded, "You don't think it's just proof that she's afraid of losing us?"

"What's the difference?" Kavita had asked.

Bijal hadn't been sure how to answer. And she's not sure what to say to Kavita now. So she doesn't say anything at all. She twists her hands back behind her and pushes forward, gaining momentum and swimming out of the room.

She doesn't feel guilty for leaving. Kavita will be fine, as ever. Besides, there's a weight in Bijal's body, and a heaviness to her eyelids. It's time for rest. Leaving Kavita, she floats toward the back of their house, where the bedroom she shares with her sister is tucked away. It's large and open, in a way that suits Kavita more than Bijal. They have sleeping hammocks on opposite sides. Kavita's side is a mess of things—jewelry, strange and shiny odds and ends she's found, and gifts from her friends. Bijal's is calmer and more austere. A single smooth obsidian rock, rescued from an angry squid years earlier, sits next to her hammock. She stays close to her corners, pushing against the sea so she's horizontal and on her side, nestled tightly into the seaweed-sewn fabric.

***

Bijal wakes up back at the edge of the canyon. Her fingers are gripping at the jagged cliff, and she has to try to make her hands move. There's a deep pounding in her head, and her heart races. Thoughts are frantic, rushing, no spaces between them, like it's all one long word. *How-did-I-get-here-what's-happening-I'm-scared-I-need-help-who-is-he? Who* is *he?* Her heart hammers, blue and green luminescence stutters all along her skin. She is not alone.

Next to her, there's a boy. Her mouth opens to scream, and she pushes her fin as hard as she can to swim away, but the boy's fingers are against her hip, gripping tightly and keeping her from leaving. If she pushes too hard, her fin might tear. She doesn't want to get hurt.

"Please let go," Bijal tries, keeping her sleep-rough voice as even as she can. He doesn't say anything in response, but he lets go of her and pushes back, giving her the space she'd attempted to gain just a second ago.

She finally has the wherewithal to look at him. His skin is like hers, deep black, but where hers peters off into her tail—strong and scaled and dark gray, with spots of blue-green brilliance—his goes into one long black slippery point, like the end of an eel. She's never seen anything like it. His hair is a shock of white, floating this way and that in a chaos of curls. It's at odds with the thinness in his face. His bones are prominent, his mouth hungry in a way that unsettles her. His gaze is stoic, and Bijal isn't sure if he's blinked even once since she woke up.

How did I get here? she thinks again.

"I have to go home," Bijal says. It doesn't matter who this strange boy is. She should get home. The sea around them is empty and still, and it's discomfiting. There's a burning in the muscles of her fin as she starts to swim away again—it's so much more difficult than it usually is. The water feels *thicker*. The boy starts toward her and holds up a hand as if he's asking her to stop. And suddenly there's an invisible *something* blocking her way. She glances back at him, awed and terrified. She's never seen anything like this.

Shivering, Bijal twists her fingers together. The gills that run along the edge of her forehead strain and stutter in a way that makes her understand she might be on the verge of a panic attack.

The boy swims closer. Bijal throws out an arm. She can feel the reverberations in the water around them at her movement.

"No," she says. "Wait."

He stops short and tries to say something. Or, she thinks he's trying to say something. His lips are barely parted and there's no real sound, only a soft, muffled vibration of . . . gurgles coming out of his throat. Bijal's nervous energy needs to go somewhere and she starts swimming in small, tight circles. The boy's eyes are wide, and he backs away farther, swimming painfully close to the edge of the cliff. Bijal isn't sure what to make of him, but with his retreat, the water behind her is open again. Unwilling to miss her chance, she turns tail and takes off. She doesn't stop until she's under the overhang of their cave. And then she hesitates.

It's quiet, which means she can't have been gone long enough for it to be waking hours already. She looks back at the expanse behind her; it's still deep black, no telltale pricks of light dropping down. There must be time yet before the copepods make their migration back down from the surface, calling for the start to the day. Bijal swims into her family home, turning down into the carved hallway leading to her shared bedroom. Pausing at the long strands of grass covering the opening, she stalls. She knows she'll go in and find Kavita tangled up in her hammock, maybe even flipping around with the excitement of whatever dreams were running through her head. She wonders briefly if she should wake up her sister and share what had just happened—but then she remembers Kavita's fear and confusion when she found Bijal at the canyon earlier.

Bijal isn't entirely sure what to make of it herself just yet. That boy . . . *Who was he?* she thinks again, imagining his strange and pointed eel-tail, and his terrifying eyes. Now that she's home and calm, with her heart at a steady rhythm . . . Bijal grins to herself, small and secret. There was something exciting in how he'd unsettled her. Something new.

Flipping over so she's horizontal, she lets her body float up with her back toward the surface, looking down at the floor below her. The pointy rocks of the ceiling poke into her back, but Bijal rests against them, enjoying the way they press into her skin. She wonders if that boy was the reason they weren't supposed to go near the canyon. Was he the one calling her name? But she immediately dismisses the question, running through their interaction—he was more confused than aggressive; she was sure of it. She'd let her own panic get in the way. Curling her hands into fists, she groans, furious with herself. Finally, something interesting happened to her, but she'd panicked and run home like a child. Bijal pushes off the ceiling and slips in through the curtained tendrils of braided grass to find Kavita just as she'd expected, her sister's arms wrapped tightly around herself, fingers tangled in the woven fabric of her hammock.

She bends down at the waist and whispers into the water above her sister's ear, "I met a boy at the canyon."

Kavita doesn't wake up.

🐚

Bijal's parents come home early, just after the sweet spots descend. She knows because she hears them swim in after they've finished watching the bright copepods dance down from the surface. Not long after, her sister quietly pushes out of her corner. Kavita doesn't look in Bijal's direction, stopping only to examine her own reflection in the sea glass, pinching at her dark cheeks and biting at her lips to make them swell just the smallest bit. Then she turns and swims through their doorway toward the main room. Bijal counts down in her head then, and just as she hits one, hears the muffled sounds of surprise from her mother and outrage from her sister.

By the time she makes it out and up, her sister is long gone. More and more, Bijal is convinced Kavita needs the active proof of care and incites it whatever way she can. It seems so draining. Her mother is already cleaning, picking crustaceans off the jagged ceiling one by one and dropping them into a bag. She tells Bijal to join her once she's finished breakfast.

Bijal spends the day helping her parents with the chores Kavita was supposed to do as well as handling her own. It's not thankless work, and spending time with her family is fine, even if it's while scraping krill off the sides of their home or bringing seagrasses in from the garden. Her father takes the shards of glass from Bijal, humming in appreciation at the pretty colors she'd salvaged, before placing them carefully away in one of his pouches. Bijal touches her father's shoulder.

"Pa?"

"Hmm?" her dad asks, still looking down at the pouch, struggling to tie the strings together.

"Do you remember the song you taught us when we were little? About the canyon?"

"Maybe," he says, distracted and voice laced with tiredness.

"'The deep dark calls for you by name?'" she asks in an exaggerated baritone, trying to lighten his mood. The corner of his lip pops up in what could possibly be called a smile.

"Oh yes, the folk saying." He whips his tail back, and his wide fin clears the excess sand from the front of their cave, leaving it smooth and even. Something small scuttles by but it moves too quickly for Bijal to focus on it.

"What did it mean?" she asks.

"Probably to be careful of a place you can't safely explore. Plenty used to be hurt down there, so they say."

"Not since I've been alive. Or you, I bet."

Her father shrugs, looking at a school of krill winding their way over the cave. "Sounds like the rhyme worked," he says.

Bijal pokes him with a spiny seashell and he yelps.

By the time it's come around to resting hours again, she's ready to be *done*. Too tired to think about anything, she swims straight into her room and then digs into her hammock. Her eyes close. She barely feels the voice in the back of her skull, running along the veins that go bright.

"Bijal . . ."

She wakes up suddenly when someone pokes her shoulder.

"Kavita," she says sleepily, "leave me alone." But in that small moment between sleeping and waking, Bijal distantly realizes she's moving. She's floating up. The hammock's not holding her down and in place like it should. Then there's a soft hissing sound, and a word—thin and reedy—hits her ears.

"Who?"

Bijal yells out in surprise. The lights running up and down her arms go brighter than ever in a chorus of blues and greens, and there's a loud cry as the boy rushes backward, his long tail whipping this way and that to get away from her. Bijal goes dead still, counting beats against her fingers until her heart stops pounding so swiftly.

She's back at the edge of the canyon. Again. She's surprised to see fear on his face when she finally looks up at the boy again. He's floating closer to the edge, like there's . . . comfort there for him.

"Where did you come from?" she asks, searching for calm, battling against a learned uneasiness settling into her stomach.

He points over the edge of the canyon. She inches forward, trying to keep her mother's voice out of her head. Something drew her to it, that much she knows.

"Why are you here? Are you the one saying my name?" she asks, curious. "I didn't think you were, but—sorry." She stumbles, and then waits for him to answer her questions.

He's watching her warily now, but swims back in her direction.

"Darktripper," he says, pointing to himself. "I'm . . ." He hesitates briefly and then continues, "Visiting. Difficult to get used.

66

Pressure. Here." He pauses. "Not call. You," he says haltingly, gesturing to his throat.

Her eyebrows come down over her eyes, and the gills at her hairline stretch.

"You're from there?" She points to the canyon and he nods. She's not sure what to think. She knew fish must live down there, and maybe some other animals—but, merfolk? The deep dark and the light above . . . She'd tried swimming upward once, as a child, despite her mother's rules against it. The brightness had hurt her eyes so badly she never tried again. It always surprised her how her parents feared the light above and the dark below in equal measure. But at least with above, she'd experienced it. She understood it.

She's never seen anyone like him before, though. There's something . . . enticing about him. He's back within arm's reach now. Bijal leans into her curiosity. Her hand reaches forward to run a finger along his skin. He flinches backward before she can make contact and opens his lips in surprise. The two rows of teeth inside are pinpoints, longer and thinner and sharper than her own. The electric lights on her arms go bright and blood rushes to her cheeks. His jaw snaps shut, and his eyes search her face. She's not sure what he's hoping to find. "Sorry, sorry," she says again, realizing her error, and then, "Can I?" And gestures to his arm.

Slowly, she reaches forward again, and this time he doesn't move. She's not surprised to find that when she touches his skin, it's rough. What *does* shock her is the luminescence that springs to life under her fingers. It's colors she's never seen before—ones she doesn't have names for. She gasps.

"Red," he says. "Purple." His teeth don't seem so harsh in a smile. "Show me again," she says, grinning.

That's the beginning for some things and the end for others.

His name is Dhvant. Bijal no longer waits for her body to take her there on its own—she doesn't just wake up there, she makes a choice. Whenever she can get away. Her home with its rough ceiling and small squabbles seems smaller than ever. Once, her sister suspiciously asks her where she's coming from, but Bijal just hums something inarticulate and asks Kavita about her day instead. A suitable enough distraction, it turns out.

There's a kindred spirit inside Dhvant, and Bijal can't believe this has been missing from her life. He's *curious*. They spend hours together on the edge of the deep. Dhvant, used to the pressure now, but his voice still thin and cracked, tells her about the ocean below them—fish she's never heard of, with soft, silky skin. A world where so much is learned by touch and feel and instinct. Where there are entire schools of thought she's never considered, new roles she could see herself playing; he uses words like *adviser*, *creation*, *building*. It sounds magical and mysterious. He says he lives in an obsidian castle, and Bijal thinks of her rock. She thinks of fate. She tries to tell him about her own life but knows that there's not much to share.

"Bijal!" her mother calls one morning. "Kavita! Come look!" Bijal disentangles herself from her hammock and blinks blearily into the room around her. Her sister groans and mumbles something but follows suit a second later. Together, they swim toward their mom's voice. She's floating outside with their father. They're both looking up. The copepods are descending—and multiplying. The season is turning. It's a gorgeous sight, blackness with twinkling blue and white, but it's one she's seen at the turn of every season for her entire life.

Bijal yawns.

"Not excited for the new crops or the changing of the season?" her father asks, lightly joking. Bijal gives him a half smile.

"It's fine," she says.

"It's beautiful," Kavita says next to her, and Bijal can see she has their mother's hand gripped tight in hers.

Eventually, Bijal and Dhvant start building meaning into words—and meaning into hours together. They find a massive shock of something round and shiny that shows reflections of their lights when they glow. She catches a thin lantern fish for him, and he makes a necklace of its bones and teeth after they've eaten. She wears it everywhere.

Later, after swimming home from Dhvant, she finds her family already at dinner. Her father, mother, and sister laughing with each other. Kavita has a long piece of grass pressed against her upper lip in an impression of their father. There's no space between the three of them, where Bijal isn't. She smiles.

🐚

"*Bijal . . .*" Something calls her name again, and when her heart beats, it's in anticipation. It's the first time in a while she's heard it, since she started spending time there on her own. It must be important. Bijal waits for her sister to roll herself tightly into her hammock, and when the house is quiet, Bijal takes off into the quiet of the sea.

Dhvant is waiting for her at the edge of the gulf. He looks as if he's on the cusp of an action, but she isn't sure what it could be. She plays with the edge of the necklace he'd made her, and hisses as she presses too hard on one of the sharp, needlelike teeth. A bubble of green blood appears on her finger and Bijal has the strongest sense of déjà vu.

"*The deep dark calls, you answer with your blood . . .*" Dhvant says.

"Why did you say that?" Bijal asks, even as she guesses. Dhvant shoots her a look but doesn't answer. He swims down to the floor and rests against the edge of the chasm, looking down below. She waits a beat and then joins him.

"You can hear it?" he says, in that strange, tinny voice she'd come to love listening to. "The dark below? That's who was calling your name?"

She nods.

"Why don't you listen?" he asks. And she's surprised to realize he means exactly what he asks, there's no intent behind the question. He's genuinely curious.

"Why should I listen?" she asks, instead of answering.

"Because it wants you enough to ask," he says in return. Then he pauses. "Will you come with me?"

Bijal pushes her fin down, reaches out her arms, and swims toward the break.

The deep dark calls, you answer with your blood
The deep dark pulls, and asks for you by name
The deep dark waits, knowing that you'll answer
The deep dark is there, waiting to be claimed.

RETURN TO THE SEA

Kalynn Bayron

"We all return to the sea and we have our own traditional practices, things that you only have access to if you're in community with us." As I said the words, it was as if the air had been sucked out of the classroom. I knew my presentation on mermaid history and advocacy in conservation spaces for Mr. Keller's senior AP History course would make some of my classmates uncomfortable, especially the ones who cosplayed mermaids when it suited them, then cast our identities aside when it wasn't fun anymore. "Especially when we're talking about sea life conservation," I continued. "A lot of wildlife conservationists are so busy trying to speak *for* us that they stop listening *to* us. We are the stewards of the sea."

A hand shot up.

"Yes?" Mr. Keller asked, slight twinge of annoyance in his voice.

"Just because some of us aren't mermaids doesn't mean we

can't appreciate sea life," Katie said. "We can be advocates the same way you can." Katie had an unhealthy obsession with mermaid culture, to the point where she claimed one of her great-grandparents was one of us. She couldn't even swim.

"I mean, that's true," I said. "But you should be listening to the people who are already involved instead of trying to talk over—"

"You don't know everything, Keisha," Katie said, her eyes narrow and angry. "Just because you're one of them."

"Seems like she does," a voice chimed in.

Everyone turned to the girl at the back of the class who'd made the comment. She was new and I hadn't heard her say two words to anyone until that very moment.

Katie whipped her head around and stared at the girl. "What?"

The girl kept her eyes downcast. "I . . . I mean, it seems like somebody who's a mermaid probably knows more about what's helpful than you do."

Katie turned back around, and the look on her face was so good—a mix of embarrassment and confusion—I was tempted to pull out my camera and take a picture.

"You can appreciate something without having to take ownership of it," I continued. I kept uncomfortable, but unwavering, eye contact with Katie. "And yes, you can advocate for sea life conservation if you're willing to listen."

"To you?" Katie asked. "Why?"

The girl who'd spoken up leaned forward on her desk. "You could listen to scientists. To people actually in the field doing the work. They'll tell you the same thing."

A swell of annoyance rolled over me. "Or you could just listen to me because this is my life and my people we're talking about here." I turned to the girl. "I don't need to consult with some scientist who looks at me like I'm some kind of specimen." Rounding on Katie, I narrowed my gaze. "You don't get to have access to us and our cultural practices just because you want to. You have to be respectful. You have to be willing to listen when we tell you you're doing it wrong."

Katie blinked a few times, then tilted her head to the side. "You're so sensitive with all your 'we return to the sea' shit. You're not the only ones who can say that. You don't own the sea."

I took a step toward her, and Mr. Keller stood and moved between us. "Thank you, Keisha. Your presentation was great and we're all very appreciative that you were willing to share your knowledge with us." He turned to Katie. "Use that language in my class again, and it'll be detention for a week."

Mr. Keller stood in front of me, his lips pursed, a silent plea for me to retake my seat. What I really wanted to do was drag Katie out to the ocean by her hair and toss her to some ravenous shark as an afternoon snack. There was no winning with people like her.

I reluctantly took my seat next to my best friend, Alex, and he leaned over to me.

"Katie has wanted to be a mermaid ever since she saw *The Little Mermaid* when she was, like, four. She could never." He puckered his lips overdramatically and winked at Katie, who was staring at me like she wanted to fight me. "Anyways, we have bigger issues than Katie being a culture-vulture."

"Like what?" I asked.

"Like how the new girl has not stopped staring at you since you got up to give your little presentation."

I glanced across the rows of desks at the girl with waist-length braids and big brown eyes. I quickly looked away and slid down in my chair. "Do I have something on my face?"

"Nah," Alex said. "You're just cute." He grinned wide.

I rolled my eyes. "Please. That's not what this is."

Alex shrugged and tossed a piece of balled-up paper at me. "Keisha, not tryna be rude, but you can be really oblivious some- times. Remember last year when that girl—what was her name?"

"Loni," I said, as the most embarrassing memories of my entire high school life flashed in my head.

"Loni!" Alex said. His smile shifted into a pained grimace. "She was writing you love letters and sending you flowers and shit. Full-on romance-novel behavior and you didn't even clue in on it until I said something."

I could feel the heat rising in my face. "Not true. I understood what she was tryna do after the whole lunchroom serenade thing."

Alex's eyes grew wide. "Oh my god, I almost forgot about that!" He put his face in his hands. "I can't. You know how obsessed with someone you gotta be to write a song and sing it to them in public?"

The song wasn't terrible, and Loni was nice. I absolutely picked up on the fact that she was a little obsessed with me at one point, but I wasn't interested. Now she was dating a girl in my gym class, so it seemed like everything worked out for her in the end.

Alex glanced at the new girl and then back to me. "She's still looking."

"Are you sure it's an I-want-to-date-you look and not a I-want- to-fight-you look? I didn't exactly take what she said lightly," I said. "You'd be surprised how similar those two things are."

"I don't know," Alex said, grinning. "Maybe she wants to fight. Maybe she wants . . . something else."

I playfully punched him in the arm. "Stop." I shook my head. "What's her name again?"

Alex's brow arched up and a little smirk crept across his face. "So, you're interested?"

"Absolutely not," I said. "I'm just . . . curious."

"Her name's Yasmine."

"Right," I said. Maybe I was trippin'. She'd pissed me off with her question, but in that moment, Yasmine sounded like the most beautiful name I'd heard in a minute.

The rest of the day dragged by. At the end of seventh period, while everyone else was heading off to their last classes, I went to my locker so I could drop off my stuff. I had a pass to skip eighth period on the days I worked at the marina. Monday through Thursday I was halfway to work while Alex was languishing in social studies, and since summer was almost here, swim lessons in the waters off Catalina Island were ramping up and I was sure my boss was going to ask me to pick up a Saturday shift any day now.

As I shoved my books into my locker and slipped on my backpack, I caught sight of the new girl, Yasmine, as she zigzagged her way through the crowd. Her gaze flitted to me and I thought she would turn around and go the other way, but instead, she made a beeline toward me.

I shut my locker just as she approached and we stood awkwardly facing each other in silence for a full five seconds. Flashbacks of Loni popping up on me cut through my brain.

"Hi," she said softly. "Hey. Sorry to bother you. I . . . . I just wanted to tell you that your presentation was really good. I agree with everything you said."

"Really?" I asked. "It felt like you were tryna tell me I should listen to scientists over my own actual experience."

"No!" she said a little too loudly. She looked down at the floor. "Sorry. That's not what I meant. I just . . . I was trying to back you up. Everything you said was right."

She was so soft-spoken, and I felt like I didn't even know her well enough to decide if I cared about what she thought or not.

Yasmine chewed at her bottom lip. "Also, I . . . well, I just—" She stopped short, like she forgot what she'd meant to say.

"I'm Keisha," I said, saving her from having to make an introduction, because she was clearly nervous. "In case you were wondering."

She clasped her hands together in front of her and looked down at the ground. "I know. I . . . I'm sorry. I should've introduced myself. I'm Yasmine. Everybody calls me Yaz."

"Nice to meet you," I said. I had no idea where this was going and I glanced at my phone to make sure I could still get out to the island on time. "I'm on my way to work. Did you need something or . . . ?"

"Oh. No. I—where do you work? I could drive you."

I tilted my head and, hard as I tried, I couldn't keep myself from smiling. "That's nice of you, but I can't get there by car. I work on Catalina Island, at Middle Beach."

"Oh," Yaz said. "Right, okay. I work at the Marine Conservation Center in Newport Beach. Do you know it?"

I nodded. "They do good work there. That's kind of what I was saying in my presentation."

"Right," Yaz said, keeping her eyes down. "I'm on my way there right now. They gave me this pass so I could work."

I held up my own pass. "Get-outta-class-free card."

"Not exactly, right?" she asked. "We have to get a note from our jobs and we get school credit for it so . . . sorry. I'm rambling. You know that already." She pulled at the end of one of her braids, her big dark eyes darting from my face to the floor and back again. "Do you . . . do you wanna come by?"

I couldn't help but smile. She seemed sweet, if not a little awkward. "Right now?" I asked.

"If that works," Yaz said.

"I don't think I'll have time," I said.

Yaz looked severely disappointed. "Okay, well, I just thought maybe . . ." She trailed off and her gaze became glassy, like she was tearing up. "I . . . I'll see you later."

She turned and headed down the hall without another word. I collected my things and was on the bus before I realized that the only thing I could think of was the disappointment in Yaz's eyes. She'd seemed almost sad.

I checked the time on my phone again. The swim to Catalina Island was a solid forty minutes. I was hoping to catch a current and cut my time in half.

But first, I'd stop to see Yaz after all.

I hopped off the bus directly across the street from the Marine Conservation Center. It was a big glass building that reflected the clear blue sky like a mirror. A sculpture shaped like a giant piece of coral sat right outside the entrance. Inside, people in twos and threes wandered around in the main building looking at exhibits as a video of Marine Conservation Center staff tending to wounded manatees played on a large screen on the rear wall. Small children darted between display tables, their voices echoing off the panes of glass.

Near the rear of the building I caught a glimpse of Yaz. She sat on a bench in front of a giant tank filled with colorful fish.

"Hey," I said quietly.

Yaz jumped up and spun around. "Keisha?"

I grinned at her. "You asked me to stop by, so here I am."

"Thought you had to work," Yaz said.

"I do, but I usually leave out of Newport Beach anyway, so yeah." I didn't want to tell her that the image of her face, the sadness that seemed to linger in her eyes when I said I wouldn't have time, hurt my heart.

I approached the fish in the tank and they coalesced into a big undulating mass. Yaz stood next to me and stared into the tank.

"It's me," I said.

"What do you mean?" Yaz asked.

"Fish tend to sense the presence of mermaids whenever we're close by."

Yaz nodded, and her gaze flitted to me and then back to the tank.

"I don't have a whole lot of time," I said. "But I wanted to stop by."

The corner of Yaz's mouth pulled up and a little dimple appeared in the apple of her cheek. My heart ticked up.

"Right," Yaz said. "Yeah, I just, I wanted to show you something."

Her tone was low and serious. I wondered if maybe I'd misread her. "Okay," I said.

"There," Yaz said. She gestured toward the tank and then gently put her hand on my bare shoulder. A ripple of warmth coursed through me, but I focused on what she was showing me.

In the tank, hidden among some of the marine foliage that swayed in the crystal-clear water, was a massive sea turtle. His gnarled shell, like a giant upturned bowl, was at least three feet across.

"Oh wow," I said, stepping closer to the tank. The other fish flitted off and I stared through the water at the ancient creature.

"He's gotta be old," I said. The way he bobbed in the tank, letting the gentle currents created by the pumps and filters rock him from side to side, seemed off. I wanted so badly to stick my arm into the water, but the tank was higher than the top of my head and sealed up tight. If I had direct contact with the water, I could communicate with him and figure out what the issue was.

"He's old," Yaz said. There was that sadness in her voice and in her eyes again.

"Is that what you wanted to show me?" I asked. "I mean, he's beautiful but—"

Just then, a group of preschoolers pushed in front of us and began tapping on the glass with their grubby little hands. Yaz blinked, then moved toward them.

"Aht. Aht," she chided. "Please keep your hands off the glass. The fish don't like that."

The children's teachers ushered them back and Yaz sighed.

I glanced at my phone. "I'm sorry," I said. "I really have to run. See you tomorrow?"

Yaz nodded, but that troubled look in her eyes stuck with me the rest of the afternoon.

Lifeguard headquarters was on Newport Beach Pier, and the staff there allowed me to stash my backpack and phone in one of their employee lockers on the days I had to work. I'd lost more phones and backpacks in the water than anyone should, and my mom had warned me to be more careful. I stashed my phone and bag and made my way to the shady area under the pier in the early afternoon hours.

I let my bare feet sink into the warm dry sand, making sure not to let the salty seawater touch the exposed skin of my legs until I was ready. The change was always quick, and I tried to time it so that I'd be fully submerged before it was complete.

I stripped off my shirt and shorts. Anybody who'd been looking would have seen a naked chick on the beach, and while their sensibilities may have been offended, mine were not. The movies showed mermaids with long hair covering their breasts, but those images were conjured from the imaginations of people for whom naked breasts were taboo. I kept my coily hair short to eliminate drag in the water, and if my titties happened to be out because of it, so be it. I had to be completely disrobed; the change would otherwise rip my clothes apart, and I did not have the money to be buying new shorts and T-shirts every week.

I shoved my clothes and my red bikini top—apparently titties out at work wasn't the vibe my boss was going for—into a watertight bag and looped the strap around my body.

Stepping into the water, I felt a familiar tingle make its way up my leg. The salt water spurred the change, and it was like an awakening every single time it happened. I lived for it, and the older I got, the more I understood why some mermaids chose to stay away from the land on a more permanent basis.

The prickly feeling made its way through me. Brown and green scales began to form across the skin of my legs and the rounded slope of my belly as I sank lower in the water. I bobbed there for a moment as the gills along my rib cage opened and closed, cycling water through my lungs and filtering out the usable air. My ankles fused together and the fin at the end of my tapered tail unfurled.

People who had seen me change always asked the same question, was it painful? It wasn't. The only way I could describe it to them was to say it felt like that stretch you do first thing in the morning that sends shivers through your entire body.

After a moment, the change was complete and I felt more alive than I had all day.

A little girl with her hair full of knockers and a bubblegum-pink swimsuit waded in the water nearby. She watched with wide eyes, a tiny smile on her lips. She waved and I waved back.

"So pretty," she said in a high-pitched little voice.

I swept my hands through the water, sending a current pulsing out of me. It rippled through the water and beckoned to all mild-mannered sea creatures in the immediate vicinity. The first to answer the call was a swarm of seahorses in an assortment of teals and greens. They bobbed in circles around the little girl and she giggled until she could barely stand. I ducked under the gentle ebb of the water and swam to Catalina Island.

🐚

Late afternoons always brought warm tides close to the shore. It was for this reason that swim lessons for beginners were held around 4 P.M. at Middle Beach in an area that was sectioned off by long ropes affixed to orange buoys. I arrived five minutes to four and saw my boss, Marilyn, waiting on the beach, her arms crossed hard over her chest. She did not look happy.

I swam up and poked my head out of the water. "You look mad. Whatever it is, I just got here, so it can't be my fault."

The corner of her mouth lifted. "Don't make me laugh. I'm trying to be pissed off right now."

"Why?" I asked as I removed my swim top from my bag and tossed it onto the beach.

Marilyn sighed. "Cassie called out sick and Ben is still healing from that propeller strike. I'm so sorry, Keisha, but it's just you today."

My heart ticked up a little. Usually, Cassie, Ben, and I worked in tandem to calm the tides in the swim area and keep out any predators that may have been lurking in the shallows. Initially, we'd keep the water flat calm while the swimmers became accustomed to the sea. But the sea was not always gentle and forgiving, and that was a lesson worth learning. So, over time, we allowed gentle currents to sweep through, eventually removing ourselves from the area completely and letting the new swimmers navigate the full might of the ocean.

But if Ben and Cassie weren't there, it would be only me between the ocean and the fresh batch of students. I took a deep breath and gazed out over the gently rolling waves. The salty breeze dampened my face and I slipped on my swim top beneath the cover of the blue-green water.

At four o'clock, Marilyn ushered six new swimmers into the waist-deep water as I swam back to the line of buoys. The current was swift and there were schools of fish darting in and out of the shallows. I concentrated on the feeling of the water sweeping past the sensitive scales on my tail, felt the pulse of the ocean in my bones. I willed the sea to calm, and it obeyed unquestioningly. Alone, I was able to extend this effect about twenty feet in front of me. The swimmers and their instructors cheered and splashed around in the water as my body hummed.

The sun slanted down, the hottest part of the day over, leaving only the ambient warmth in the air and in the water. As I let the water lap against my back, I leveled my gaze at the shore. Standing there was Yaz. I'd had her face in my mind all afternoon and had to blink twice to make sure I was seeing her clearly. She had changed out of her work uniform and was now sporting a pair of cutoff jean shorts and an oversize orange tank top, the strings of a blue bikini top peeking out. Her smooth brown skin drank up the sun and she'd piled her long braids high on top of her head. I felt like I was seeing her for the first time, and all I could hear in my head was Alex's voice . . . "*So, you're interested?*" She waved and I smiled at her.

She sat in the sand until the swim lesson wrapped up. When the kids were safely back on shore, I let my body relax and the waves rolled back in. Before I could swim to meet her, Yaz had kicked off her flip-flops, stripped down to a teal two-piece, and was wading out toward me.

"Hey," she said as she stood in the now chest-deep water.

"How'd you get out here?" I asked.

She smiled. "The ferry."

"It's like seventy bucks to get out here that way."

Her eyebrows pushed together. "It's kind of important."

I tilted my head. "You know, I could tell something was up when I was at your job."

She pressed her lips together. "I wanted to say something about it then, but . . ." She trailed off.

"But what?" I asked.

"I know you're a mermaid," she said.

I flicked my tail, splashing her a little but not enough to get her hair wet. "Ya think? I thought that was established already."

She smiled, but her eyes were sad. "I just—I was trying to tell you earlier. I . . . I love . . . sea creatures."

"Ummm, the fuck?" I pictured myself smacking her with the broad side of my tail. The way she said *creatures* made my skin crawl. Memories of kids taunting me for what I was, calling me names. *Sea creatures* felt a little too much like an insult to me. "You paid all that money to come out here and insult me?"

"No! I—that came out wrong! I'm so sorry. I—you're not a creature. I wasn't talking about you. You're beautiful and I think your job is amazing and—"

She stopped and took a deep breath. I waited for her to continue. She kept looking down into the water and pulling at her neck. A part of me felt bad for her. She was clearly nervous and trying to tell me something that she couldn't seem to get out. "Breathe," I said. I had no idea what she was trying to tell me, but it was pretty clear that her sea creature comment had been an unfortunate slip. "What are you trying to say? What's so important?"

"I'm in the marine biology program at school," she said. "I don't know if you knew that."

"Okay?" I said, still confused.

"I'm gonna go to college for it," Yaz continued. "I've been at the conservation center for three years. I used to take the bus from West Covina when I lived over there."

"Damn," I said. "How long is that commute?"

"Too long," she said. "When I first signed up to volunteer, we were doing a beach walk and found this turtle. He was injured, so we took him in and he got better for a while. He's so smart. He's beautiful and—" Yaz's eyes filled with tears and she sniffed.

"The turtle in the tank," I said. "That's what you wanted me to see?"

She nodded. "Now he's sick."

She was clearly broken up about it. Her trembling lip put an ache in my chest. "I'm sorry."

She wiped her tears away with the back of her hand and tilted her face to the bright blue afternoon sky. "The medical staff has run tests but he just keeps getting worse. They don't know what to do and, well, I know that some mermaids can communicate with other things that live in the ocean."

I sighed and air hissed out from between my ribs. "You want me to see if I can find out what's wrong with him?"

She nodded and her eyes became glassy again. "I'd do anything for him. He's been through so much. I just want to help him and I don't really know many other mermaids."

"You don't really know me either," I said. It wasn't the first time somebody had asked me to diagnose their marine pets. I didn't believe that ocean-dwelling animals should be kept in captivity at all, so most of their requests were met with some choice words, but I couldn't bring myself to cuss out Yaz. The conservation center took care of sick and injured marine life and they had nursed more than a few of my people back to health after run-ins with propellers or great whites.

"I'm sorry," Yaz said. "I don't know what else to do. I was gonna ask you earlier but I got kind of caught up in trying to spend time with you. I didn't want you to think that was the only reason I asked you to come to my job."

"What was the other reason?" I asked.

Yaz stared at me, and while there was still sadness, there was something else too. "Just to see you. To spend some time with you away from class and people like Katie, who irk the shit outta me."

I laughed and Yaz smiled warmly. "I'll see him," I said. "Maybe

I can help. But I need access to the water. I can't do anything outside the tank."

Yaz's face lit up, and before I could stop her she threw her arms around me and squeezed me tight. Her skin smelled like cocoa butter and sunscreen. She was warm and I found myself liking her embrace a little more than I thought I would. She quickly stepped back, almost losing her balance in the push of a small wave. I reached out to steady her and she gripped my arm.

"Thank you," she said, her bottom lip quivering. "Can you come by on Friday? He'll be in a shallow tank for testing. I'll take you. Maybe right after school?"

"Yeah, okay," I said. "You're driving?"

She nodded. "Just please don't judge me when you see my car."

I smiled. "I promise I won't."

"I lied," I said to Yaz as we walked to the student parking lot after eighth period on Friday. "About not judging your car."

"No. You promised," Yaz said. She clicked the key fob, and the locks popping open sounded like a shotgun blast.

"The hell?" I whispered as I took in the state of her beater. It was a kaleidoscope of colors, and not because she'd painted it that way. The car literally looked like it was cobbled together from mismatched parts of other vehicles. The driver's side door was yellow, the hood was red, and the roof wasn't painted at all.

"My dad owns a scrap metal yard," she said. "We never run out of car parts."

"Right," I said as I slid into the passenger seat. I had to slam the door three times to get it to stay closed, and as Yaz climbed in beside me, she grinned.

"Seat belt," she said.

I quickly grabbed it and pulled it across my chest. "Are you sure it's safe?"

"I mean, sure." She shrugged. "It gets me where I need to go."

"That's not a real answer," I said.

She started the engine, which low-key sounded like a jetliner about to take off, and as we drove to the Marine Conservation Center, I prayed that the whole thing wouldn't blow up before we got there.

"The radio doesn't work but the tape player does," she said.

"That *what* player?" I asked. "They still make cars with tape players?"

"Ask me what year the main part of this car was built," she said, grinning.

"Nah," I said. "I don't need to know." I manually rolled down the window to let the warm air waft through as Yaz hit a button and Janet Jackson's voice echoed out of the speakers.

We arrived in the late afternoon and Yaz pulled into a parking spot at the back of the building. After Yaz's car rumbled to a stop, we got out and went inside.

Yaz led me through a series of hallways and locked doors, and finally down a short flight of stairs. We emerged into a warehouse-like room filled with tanks and open pools that were off-limits to the general public. Near the back was a small tank that was separated from the others by a folding screen.

"He's back here," Yaz said.

I stepped around the screen and saw that a small shelf had been lowered into the water, and that the large, frail-looking turtle lay atop it as a staff member scooped water over his battered shell. He barely moved. His eyes stared into nothingness.

"Oh man," I said. I hadn't expected him to be in such rough shape; he'd deteriorated a lot since I last saw him. It was clear that the situation was dire.

"Hey, Yaz," a staff member said.

"Hey, Mark." Yaz's voice was choked with sadness. "Any improvement?"

Mark shook his head and ran his hand over his mouth. "I think he's taking a turn for the worse."

Yaz mounted the platform and put her hand on the turtle's shell. He moved his head from side to side, opening and closing his mouth.

"He's happy to see you," I said to Yaz.

Mark looked me over and raised an eyebrow. "Uh, how do you know that?"

I approached the tank and put my hand in the water. What I could do was not some trick or supernatural ability. It wasn't like I could read the turtle's mind. The water served as a conduit for the nearly imperceptible vibrations sent out by turtles and the members of their home groups to communicate. Lots of sea life communicated in this way and I was no different.

As I dipped my hand into the water, a scattering of luminescent brown and green scales rose to the surface of my forearm. Mark glanced at me.

"Oh," he said. "Right. That makes sense."

Sea turtles were some of the most respected and beloved creatures in all the ocean. Even human beings understood that, for the most part. But merchildren were taught from the time we're nursed in the kelp that they are to be protected, revered. As I felt his weakened call go out into the water, I was taken aback. I turned to Yaz.

"He's pushing sixty," I said. "For some sea turtles, that's like living to be a hundred." I ran my hand along his shell and he opened his eyes to look at me, like he was trying to let me know something. I understood. I put my other hand on Yaz's and held it tight. "Yaz, I'm so sorry, but he's come to the end of his journey."

"What?" Yaz slipped her hand out of mine and leaned back. "No. No, if we can find out what's wrong, we can save him."

I shook my head. "He doesn't want to be saved. He wants to go home."

"Home?" Yaz asked.

"The ocean," Mark said.

I glanced up at him and tears filled his eyes. Yaz began to sob and I had to bite back tears myself.

"The bosses here won't let that happen," Yaz said, looking down at the turtle. "I'm so sorry."

"Won't let him go home to the ocean to die?" I asked. For all their good work, it seemed unnecessarily cruel. I turned to Mark and some silent understanding passed between us. "What time does this place close?" I asked.

"We're open to the public until six," Mark said. "Staff is here in some capacity twenty-four seven, but I'm on duty tonight from nine to midnight . . . alone."

I took Yaz's hand in mine and held it firmly. "You care about him." I gestured to the turtle and lowered my voice to a whisper. "You can help him. *We* can help him by doing this one last thing." A knot crawled its way up my throat. "He belongs in the ocean."

Yaz nodded as tears streamed down her face. "I know."

I turned to Mark, who was sobbing quietly into the collar of his shirt.

"We'll meet you at the back door at ten," I said. "Then load him into the car and take him to King's Cove."

Mark nodded and then set his hand gently on Yaz's shoulder. "I'm sorry, Yaz. I know how much you care about him."

Yaz only nodded as she backed away from the tank and stood watching the turtle as his eyes closed and his breathing became shallow. I took her by the elbow and led her back to her car, where we sat quietly for a long time.

Yaz finally broke the silence with a heavy sigh. "Where's King's Cove? I've heard of it but I don't think I've ever been there."

"It's special for us," I said. "There aren't many places left that are just for us. People are constantly crowding in on our spaces, but not at King's Cove. It's a protected place." I looked down at my lap. "I just want you to know that I see the way you loved that turtle. Caring about another being like that—it takes a special kind of person."

She leaned back against the seat. "I just wanted him to get better so we could set him free."

I nodded and reached out to take her hand again. This time she squeezed it back and I turned to look into her big brown eyes. "We can still set him free. I know it's tough, but I'll be there with you every step of the way, okay?"

Yaz turned to me, her eyes searching, her hand trembling. "Can I ask you something?"

"Yes."

"Why are you helping me do this?"

"I thought you wanted my help," I said.

"No, I do. But I see how people like Katie are. I wouldn't blame you if you told me to fuck off."

"You're not like her," I said. "I'm inviting you to be with me in King's Cove. People like Katie don't even know about it because their interest in mermaid culture is surface level. She doesn't give a shit about our practices or sacred places. She wants to dress up like a mermaid and discard the costume when she's moved on to the next thing. I don't get to take the tail off. Ever."

"Why would you want to?" Yaz asked. "It's beautiful."

I smiled at her and we stayed in the parking lot, holding hands, until the sun set.

At ten, Yaz pulled her car around to the rear entrance of the Marine Conservation Center. I was glad Mark was alone, because there was no sneaking off in Yaz's car. It was entirely too loud.

Mark met us at the rear door. He'd transferred the turtle to a rolling exam table and wrapped him in a damp towel. We carefully loaded him into the back seat of Yaz's car.

"Really appreciate your help," Yaz said to Mark.

He nodded and gave her a big hug as I climbed into the back and cradled the turtle halfway in my lap. I gave the directions and Yaz steered us to King's Cove. Forty-five minutes later we were lugging the hundred-pound turtle out of the back seat and down onto the sand.

King's Cove was surrounded on three sides by steep, tree-covered hills. The nighttime sky was black and dotted with hundreds of stars, not a cloud in sight. The low rush of the water as it lapped at the shore was soothing, as was the warm breeze. The salty sea air stirred something in my bones, a feeling of belonging.

Yaz removed the damp towel from around the turtle's shell and scooted him toward the water. I kicked my shoes away and stripped off my clothes. Yaz looked, but in a way that conveyed only tenderness. I waded into the water and allowed the transformation to take place. As my body hummed in the salty water and as my tail took shape beneath the nighttime waves, I sent out a call, a little ripple in the water. Soon enough, the entire cove was alight with soft green bioluminescence.

From the water, I scooted back into the shallows and helped cradle the turtle as Yaz moved him into the water beside me. She laid her head atop his shell and let her tears mingle with the seawater.

"Come on," I said.

I held out my hand to her and she took it. Pulling her close to me, we floated the turtle out to chest-deep water. The dark night and muted green light, the stars above, all gave the feeling of floating in an endless expanse. Not alone but connected to all of it. I set my hand on the turtle's shell and felt what little life remained.

"It's time," I said to Yaz.

I stirred the water around us and a gentle current formed, trailing the bioluminescent algae out into the deep water in front of us. I carefully put the turtle into the low tide just as the last of his extraordinary life slipped away from him. I could feel it as it went. The ocean carried him softly away and I interlaced my fingers with Yaz's under the blanket of twinkling stars.

"Thank you for bringing me here," Yaz whispered through a torrent of tears.

She put her head on my shoulder and I rested my cheek against her hair. "He came from this place," I said. "Now, he'll return to it."

Yaz and I stayed in the water near the shore as the soft green light around us faded. Things were as they should be.

THE DEEPWATER VANDAL

Darcie Little Badger

As Cassia and Justice walked through the dockyard, they passed boats in various states of repair. Big boats, little boats, boats with paddles, boats with smokestacks, and boats with steam-powered engines. The vessels probably had more specific names, like schooner, yacht, or dinghy, but Cassia couldn't identify them. For most of her life, she'd been raised inland, far away from the waters that had destroyed her father and nearly killed her, too.

At the end of a narrow pier, they stopped in front of a sailboat; the name *EXPLORER IV* was painted in red across its bright white hull. "Well," Justice said, "what do you think?" Over the past two days, he'd detailed and cleaned the hull of barnacles. Even the sail, which was folded like an accordion, seemed crisp and new.

In actuality, *Explorer IV* was fifteen years old, the last gift Cassia received from her father, Liam, who'd planned to teach her how to sail. When she was older, when he was richer.

He never got the chance.

"I know men who'd buy the boat as is," Justice said. The red-haired fisherman patted Cassia's shoulder, his calluses scratching the linen of her long-sleeved tunic. She had calluses, too, but they were along her upper palm, where she held her gardening tools. "Take the money. Get an education."

He'd been discouraging her plan all day. It was risky, silly, like something from a tall tale. The Deepwater Vandal might be less homicidal than other mermaids, but she was still dangerous, wretched, untrustworthy. And yes, he was absolutely right. Yet if Cassia turned back now, she'd always wonder if a risk could have saved her father.

"I'll sell the *Explorer* when I return," she promised.

"Your choice." With a sad smile, he took Cassia's hand and helped her onboard. The ocean sloshed against the dock pilings and rocked the *Explorer IV* side to side.

"I can take you to where the Deepwater Vandal was last spotted," Justice said, busying himself with sailing tasks. "However, if that punk sea-born doesn't appear tonight, we leave. No second, third, fourth attempts. This isn't a wild-goose chase."

"Understood."

Slowly, they drifted out of the dockyard, past a seal-covered jetty, and into the open sea. The sunset darkened from peach to fiery red. Although Cassia had chewed on ginger candy to calm her stomach, she felt queasy, but perhaps that was due to anxiety, not the waves. She'd done months of research for this moment, but stories and books could be misleading.

Cassia reached into her deep vest pocket and removed a jingling doe-leather pouch. Inside were coiled chains of gold, each collected from the ocean during her father's early dives. They were the last of her inheritance, aside from *Explorer IV*, and Cassia had promised her mother that she'd use every gold link to study botany in the Gleaming Academy, but Justice had been invaluable help, missing days of work to support her tall-tale plan. "Thank you for everything," Cassia said, offering him a gold chain. The metal felt gritty, its surface rough with salt.

"Keep it."

"But——"

Justice's low voice interrupted her complaint. "When I was only twenty, I begged your father, Liam the Daring, to hire me as a deckhand. I'd mostly worked on merchant vessels. Thought treasure hunting would be an interesting experience."

"Was it?" she asked.

"Too interesting. We were trawling for jewels in the drowned city of New Mariel when a storm appeared. It was as if somebody had torn open the sky and let chaos billow through. A massive wave—fifty feet high, they say!—capsized us. Happened fast. I'd been sifting through our catch, extracting diamonds from silt, and was trapped inside the sinking vessel. Everything went upside down and dark, with water rising past my knees, waist, shoulders. Couldn't find the exit. Could barely breathe, my face pressed against the floor-now-ceiling so I could suck air from a bubble trapped within the room. The moment I thought, 'I'm dead,' I felt a hand squeeze my arm. It was Liam. He'd returned to the ship to lead me to safety. All this with no light, no diving equipment." He sighed. "I owe your family a great debt. I just wish . . ."

What did he wish? She'd never know. He buried the answer in

another sigh before patting the spoked wheel and commenting, "The Deepwater Vandal is going to destroy this poor boat."

Cassia smiled. "If I'm successful, she'll sail it instead."

After reaching their destination, Justice set the self-steering vane and retired to his bunk belowdecks, reasoning that the Deepwater Vandal would prefer a quiet target. For her part, Cassia huddled under a blanket near the wheel, clutching a small satchel of herbs, breathing the scent of sage and lavender, thinking of her mother's garden at home. She focused on the rhythm of the gentle waves, listening for out-of-sync splashes or scrapes against the hull.

Thump!

While turning toward the sound, Cassia threw off her blanket, and for a split second, she saw a figure standing near the flagpole on the bow, a short, muscular woman with shark-gray skin and a crown of bone-white coral. The sea-born mermaid clutched the sailboat's flag, which was defaced with violet handprints. Did that mean she'd already finger-painted on the ship's hull, undetected, repainting the perfect canvas with graffiti? Or had she boldly started with the flag?

"Are you the Deepwater Van—" Cassia began. But before she could finish her sentence, the sea-born woman snorted with amusement, dropped the flag, and dived overboard.

"Wait!" It had happened too quickly! What good was a lure if the target broke free? Cassia sprinted to the rail and leaned over, seeing no sign of the sea-born in the black water.

"Please stop!" There'd be no second chance, no better choice: Cassia jumped into the ocean, her linen nightdress billowing. As she was engulfed by the water, terribly cold and bitter with salt, she screamed, "Help!" into the darkness. Her garbled scream bounced around the air bubbles streaming from her mouth. *HeEhEeEElp!* Fighting the urge to suck a lung full of water, Cassia kicked her legs and surfaced. She gasped twice, bobbing alongside the *Explorer IV*. She was a practiced swimmer, but the ocean was much rougher than the lake behind her garden. Colder, too. Bitterly cold.

Suddenly, an arm snaked around her chest, holding her above the waves like a flotation ring with claws.

"Why'd you do that?" The Deepwater Vandal had a gravelly voice, and her breath reeked of wet mud dredged from deep places.

"I w-was looking for you," Cassia explained, failing to rein in her shivering.

"This must be important if you'd risk death for my attention."

"It is. C-can you help me find another sea-born?" Cassia asked. "A leviathan known as the Ship Eater."

The Deepwater Vandal made a series of choking sounds. It took Cassia a moment to recognize them as laughter. "Why are you looking for that violent creature?"

"Because," Cassia said, "he . . . he's . . ." Her teeth chattered between words. Even during the coldest winter, she'd never shivered uncontrollably. It was becoming difficult to breathe, her chest constricting and seizing in the cold. Cassia clutched the Deepwater Vandal's arm, but their closeness only aggravated the chill. It was as if the sea-born radiated the iciness of a deep abyssal trench. Cassia felt the first true surge of terror. She could die like this, freezing in the arms of a sea-born mermaid.

"He's my father," Cassia sputtered.

The sea-born's laughter ceased.

"I'm sure you're aware," she said, "that there's only one way to become a sea-born."

"Yes." The ocean must steal your greatest love, destroy your spirit, hollow you out. Consume and change you. "The ocean has to break you," Cassia said.

"I'm curious." The Deepwater Vandal's voice softened, becoming almost kind. "If the leviathan is your father, what did the sea take from him? What could possibly be more precious than a daughter?"

"If you help me, I'll explain everything."

"Ha!" Fluidly, the Deepwater Vandal grabbed Cassia by the arm, hoisted her onto the *Explorer*, and dropped her onto the deck. Then the sea-born paced, her broad webbed feet pattering against the wood. She wore tight shorts and a belt attached to several waterproof bags, no doubt filled with implements of mischief, and her chest—covered by a thin, horizontal strip of cloth—was smooth, like a shark's belly. Some sea-born people grew tentacles, fins, or alien extremities with no basis in the natural world. Not the Deepwater Vandal. Her body was still mostly human, although it seemed to change subtly, its shape and color never perfectly constant. Seawater dripped from her coral crown, running down her sharp cheekbones and pointed chin. Up close, Cassia could tell that the dead coral grew directly from her head, similar to antlers on a buck.

"The Ship Eater, your father, lives somewhere in the Tethys," the Deepwater Vandal said. "I just don't know where, exactly."

"But I thought your kind can sense each other?"

"Sorta," she grunted, shrugging. "I could track him, but that may take years. The Tethys is big, to put it lightly. Luckily, there's a sea-born gal who knows everyone in the nine seas." She smiled, and her teeth were long and thin, like the bristles on a comb, the baleen of a whale. Cassia could've sworn that they'd been small and sharp just a moment ago. "A real busybody. The Maelstrom Siren of New Mariel. She trades odds and ends for information."

From across the ship came a sharp intake of breath. Cassia turned to see Justice standing in the shadows, fully dressed in his wet suit and boots. A bright orange throw ring was propped against the wall of the cabin, ready for deployment. "I . . . didn't think your plan would work." The ring slipped from his fingers.

"But it did. She'll help me, Justice."

"I will. On three conditions." The Deepwater Vandal's eyes shifted from black to bioluminescent, two circles of pale, glowing blue that leveled on Cassia. "One. At sea, I may tell you a story. You must remember my story and share it with the people on land. Two. My orders could mean the difference between life and death. Always do as I say. Three. And this is important . . ." Her eyes flickered out. "Do not let the sea consume you."

BEFORE THE STORM

Two nights later, after returning Justice to land, Vandal steered the sailboat toward the dark horizon. That's when she shared the bad news.

"Soooo, here's the thing about the Maelstrom Siren. She can't know that I'm helping you. We have bad blood. In other words, you gotta be the one to make contact."

The deck was lit by several wave motion–powered electric lights. In their yellowish glow, Cassia could see every detail of the Vandal's hands on the wheel. Earlier, there'd been translucent webs between each digit. Now, the webs were gone, leaving strong, five-finger hands with neither nails nor claws. At first, the changes had unnerved her, but now she sought them out, playing a game of "spot the difference." Entertainment on the ship was hard to come by.

"Wait, what?" Cassia exclaimed. "I'm human! A human in her territory! Won't the siren try to murder me?"

"Nah. You're seventeen. She doesn't mess with kids or teens."

"That's . . . good to know." Cassia sat cross-legged on the cockpit bench. "What'd you do to piss her off anyway? Write a naughty poem on the side of her underwater house?"

"Pfft. No. I only pull that nonsense with humans."

"Like the mural you painted on that freighter—"

"Which one?"

"From Barrels Dock. You covered it with ten thousand handprints. How are you so sneaky?"

In the dim light, it was difficult to be certain, but Vandal seemed to beam with pride. This time, her teeth were flat and stubby. "Practice."

"I bet."

"I'm surprised my reputation didn't scare you off, Cassia."

"I researched you for months, collecting stories from fishermen and lighthouse keepers."

"Creepy."

"Cautious," Cassia corrected. "This world's full of dangerous people, but by all accounts, you're a menace, but you've never killed anybody. Which . . . is surprising, honestly."

"Oh?" Bright red gills, as fine and frilly as betta fish fins, flared behind her ears and then vanished.

"Well, yeah. You've lived centuries, and like I said, the world is dangerous. Isn't bloodshed hard to avoid?"

The smile returned. "Ah." She turned her head to look down at Cassia. "Here's the thing . . ."

For one second, a veil fell, and Cassia saw Vandal as her real self, a million bodies in one shell: eyes, teeth, tails, and grasping tentacles, gasping, thrashing, suffering. A bitter smell—the scent of a fishing pier, the fear and blood of nets full of fresh, dying catches—spilled from every pore of the writhing form. Cassia recoiled, her back smacking into the hull, and even after Vandal's body had returned to its disguised state, she was keenly aware of its reality. So many bodies, all trapped in the agony before death.

"With this body," Vandal continued, unfazed, "people of the world can't hurt me anymore. I'm strong. There's no need to kill."

Cassia took a deep drink of ginger tea. "I . . . gotcha." A lie. From her experience, those with power were—if anything—more likely to cause death.

"Do you?" Vandal snickered and scratched the skeletal crown on her head. That was the only part of her that never changed. Perhaps it couldn't change. "Go to sleep, Cassia. Only one of us should be nocturnal."

She'd expected danger and beauty at sea, but as the days passed in isolation, Cassia was mostly bored. Vandal, who slept underwater by day, did all the fishing, boat maintenance, and sailing at night.

Cassia missed her garden's neediness. Every day, there'd been new weeds to pull, pests to remove, leaves to trim, plants to water, food to gather—skills her mother taught her, which were useless out here. This was her father's world, always had been, and she didn't know how to survive in it, much less appreciate it.

"We'd get to the drowned city more quickly if I knew how to sail," Cassia said. "Could you teach me?" It was early evening, dinnertime, when her schedule and Vandal's briefly overlapped.

"Nope."

"But . . ." She picked at a piece of dried apricot. "Maybe I could observe you quietly? I'm bored."

"The less you know about boats, the better," Vandal grunted, scratching at a patch of silver scales behind her ear. "Trust me. You have a home on land, right? Far away from all this water?"

"Yeah. A house in the forest. Mom grows herbs and vegetables." She crushed the apricot between her teeth, swallowed. "I'm going to study in the Gleaming Mountains, learn how to make enchanted medicine with plants. Actually, Mom thinks I'm on the way there now, after a brief visit with friends."

Vandal turned, and her eyes were a dull shade of gray, the same color as her skin. "Why did you lie?" She shook her head once, sharply. "Deceiving your family . . ."

"I'm doing this *for* family," Cassia exclaimed, clutching the bag of herbs in her pocket. "My father's been gone almost fifteen years! Anyway, if Mom knew my plans, she'd get sick with worry. Mom's terrified of . . . of your kind."

"Wise woman," Vandal snapped. "A sea-born has never regained their humanity. What makes you think the leviathan will change back into the man you loved?"

"I have compelling reasons."

"Which are?"

"I'll explain after we get info from the siren." Vandal might abandon the mission if her curiosity was sated too soon.

"Ha," she snorted, amused. "Fine."

The next morning, when Cassia stepped onto the deck, she

found a driftwood-bound sketchbook propped beside a box of watercolors, pencils, and brushes. Vandal had included a simple note: FOR THE BOREDOM.

Sitting on the bow, her face cooled by the wind, Cassia painted flowers in every color but blue.

THE MAELSTROM SIREN

A few days later, Cassia was working on a self-portrait when Vandal vaulted over the starboard rail. In the midafternoon sun, her skin shifted from gray to white, and barnacles sprouted down her back. "We're close," she said. "Change into your wet suit and goggles."

"Finally!" After dropping her paints, Cassia scurried below-decks to gear up. Within minutes, she was back and ready to swim. "Not that I'm complaining, but shouldn't we be near an island?"

They'd planned to navigate into the drowned city, find solid ground, and drop off Cassia.

"That's not going to work anymore," Vandal explained, while securing a bright yellow life vest around Cassia's torso. "The siren's nearby."

"Shoot, can she sense that you're here, too?" Cassia leaned to adjust one of the pant legs of her black wet suit. It covered her, ankle to wrist, with a mock neck ending below her chin.

"Nah. I'm older, stronger," Vandal said. "More sensitive to her power."

"What does it feel like?" she wondered aloud. "Heat?"

"Sometimes, a pull. Desire. Other times, a repulsion. Disgust. We are like polar molecules." She grinned, baring a hundred needle-sharp teeth. "In any case, I shouldn't get too close." With that, Vandal handed Cassia a pair of binoculars. "Tell me when you see islands on the horizon. At that point, you'll need to swim."

Cassia trained the binoculars on the silver line between the water and the sky. Before long, she noticed a smudge of black. "There! Land!"

Vandal handed her a waterproof backpack. "I put supplies in there," she explained. "Water, bandages, flint. Stuff you may need. Ready?"

"Uh." Cassia raised a shaky thumbs-up and smiled. That must've been enough reassurance for Vandal, since the sea-born woman patted her on the shoulder and then shoved her into the ocean.

To Cassia's relief, the surface ocean was bathwater warm. She alternated between a backstroke and breaststroke, taking quick breaks when fatigue burned through her arms. As she neared the island, Cassia saw that it was a mound of concrete and metal garbage piled on a high, flat base. There were similar structures behind it, the remnant skyscrapers of New Mariel. She paused, her heart galloping, and looked down. Below her feet were vague shadows of a city. Tufts of coral grew on underwater rooftops, and fish swam through dark windows.

Then a sparkle of quicksilver scales caught her eye. A tail, long and bright, vanished behind the reef.

"Hey!" Cassia called. "Are you the Maelstrom Siren?"

Suddenly, the temperature dropped, as if dense, cold water had been thrust toward the surface. Trapped on the crest of a freak wave, Cassia rushed toward the man-made island, her speed and height increasing rapidly. Although she kicked and thrashed, Cassia couldn't escape; cursing, she tucked her chin and covered her face, bracing for impact against piles of garbage.

When the wave broke, Cassia slammed into a rusty metal cabinet and dropped hip-first on the barnacle-crusted concrete. Wheezing, she crawled into a sitting position. Thank the creator: Her body felt bruised, but not broken. As Cassia caught her breath and let the pain subside, bubbles popped in the nooks and crannies of the stinking island, and a little green crab scurried sideways across her hand.

"People call me a siren," sang a resonant voice, powerful and sweet. "But my name is Liberty. What's yours?" Turning, Cassia saw a woman sitting on the hood of a rusty red car. Her skin was a tie-dyed mix of pinks, blues, and yellows, like the patterns on a tropical reef fish. Instead of hair, the siren had a cap of brilliant silver scales; they matched her splendidly bright tail. However, despite all the colors and flash, Cassia was drawn to the siren's eyes, which were a profoundly human shade of brown.

"Cassia," she responded. Then she hastily added, "I'm only seventeen." That made Liberty smile. Slowly, slyly.

"Nearly an adult," she sang. "What are you doing in my city, alone?" Her eyes flicked from Cassia to the horizon, where the *Explorer IV* was a bobbing dot of white.

"Looking for my father. He's a sea-born, like you."

That seemed to disarm Liberty, since her voice lost its musicality. "Your father?"

"People call him the Ship Eater," she said. "But his name is actually Liam. Almost fifteen years ago, in the North Tethys Sea, my father was on a treasure hunt with a crew of ten. They were searching for the sunken tomb of the Green-haired King. In the middle of the trip, he . . . received bad news from land, which caused him to transform, sinking the ship and drowning everyone aboard, except the old cook."

Liberty leaned forward, propping her sharp chin in her blue hands. "It must have been heartbreaking news."

Cassia looked away. "Can you tell me where my father lives?"

"Yes. But how did you know?"

"I . . ." Cassia couldn't mention Vandal, but she was afraid to lie. Some sea-born could hear your heartbeat and smell the tang of anxiety, like living lie detectors. "You're powerful," she said. "Powerful sea-born can sense each other, right?"

"Correct." Liberty casually pinched a whelk off the ground and popped it into her mouth. The snail's shell popped between her teeth with an audible crack. "However, I won't teach you where the leviathan lives."

"But he's my father!" What could she possibly offer a woman who reigned over New Mariel? Treasure hunters risked their lives to dive for its riches. When the city drowned, the water level had increased so quickly, merchants had fled without their inventories. "Do you want payment? A gift? I have gold . . ."

"No," Liberty sang. "No price on earth could tempt me to send a youth into danger."

Cassia rubbed her aching hip, and Liberty had the decency to look contrite for causing the injury. "I thought you were a thief," she explained. The water around the island swirled, as if stirred by an invisible hand. "I'll carry you gently this time. Go away. Sail back to land. Your father is as good as dead; it's a difficult lesson, but you'll learn in time."

With seconds to spare before the water pulled her back to the *Explorer IV*, Cassia scrambled to think of a bargaining chip. She had time for just one more plea.

"That's fine!" she exclaimed. "I'll ask somebody else. Like the Deepwater Vandal. They say she's powerful, too."

Instantly, the water froze. "No," Liberty commanded. "Don't."

"What choice do I have?"

"Stay away from that beast."

"She's the only other sea-born I know of."

"She'll betray you," Liberty cried, and the sun blinked out. With a gasp of surprise, Cassia looked up to see a dark, spinning cloud expanding across the sky. It resembled a whirlpool, inverted.

"If that's true," she hastily added, "you can protect me by answering my question." Cassia forced her gaze downward, meeting Liberty's brown eyes. "I will find my father, with or without your help."

"Fine," the sea-born hissed through gritted teeth. "Fine. He's under the poison Sargassum. They say he won't leave the place. Not even for a day. I pray that the leviathan doesn't bite you in half."

With an abrupt twitch of Liberty's hand, a wave pounced across the island and dragged Cassia back toward the *Explorer IV*, where it sloshed her onto the deck. There, Cassia lay on her back, trying to catch her breath. Overhead, cotton-fine wisps of clouds, which had scattered across the sky when the inverted whirlpool broke apart, cast dapples of shadow on the blue ocean.

The poison Sargassum. She knew that Sargassum was a type of seaweed; it floated in the open ocean as clumps of buoyant yellow-green algae. But Cassia, who'd memorized most species of deadly plant, knew that Sargassum wasn't poisonous. What did Liberty mean?

She wiped seawater from her cheek and sighed.

Whether by chance or at Liberty's command, the ocean current drew the *Explorer IV* away from the drowned city. By sunset, no trace of any island remained on the horizon.

"Well?" Vandal asked, climbing over the rail. "How'd it go?"

"My father lives under the poison Sargassum," Cassia said. "Does that mean anything to you?"

"Indeed." Vandal crossed the deck, stooping to look at the painting in Cassia's lap. "Pretty roses. You have a gift."

"Did you really betray Liberty?"

"Nah," Vandal said, grinning. "We used to be friends. Then she tried to destroy a boat of scavengers—did it right in front of me, no shame!—so I put her in time-out."

"You what?" Cassia asked.

"Welded her in a barrel. Dropped the barrel into a deep-sea trench."

"Seriously?"

Vandal shrugged. "She clawed her way out fairly quickly. Can you believe that homicidal freak used to teach arithmetic to children?"

"You mean she was an elementary school teacher?" Cassia watched Vandal prep the sail. It stretched to catch the wind.

"In a former life."

"What made her this way?"

"A field trip," Vandal said, staring at the dark water. "Thirty children on a boat. I won't horrify you with details, but the ocean destroyed many lives that day."

"Poor babies." Cassia grasped her bag of lavender and sage. "But that's not what I meant. She's depraved. Cruel."

"She's sea-born. The change messes with our heads. Gives us compulsions that are tricky to ignore. Same way it's hard to ignore hunger when you're starving."

"Liberty thinks my father will kill me. But. He'd never. Right? There's no way . . ."

Vandal gazed into the distance. "I guess that depends on what he lost, and what remains."

She smiled sadly. "He lost . . . me."

CASSIA'S STORY

My father was a treasure hunter, so naturally, I believed that he'd died at sea. People in his line of work have to visit dangerous places, like New Mariel, diving for gold and diamonds. The treasure he recovered barely covered the ships he lost, with equipment and crew taking everything else. Thing was, Dad always promised he'd retire once he found the big prize: the tomb of the Green-haired King, an old ship filled with incredible riches. Then he'd buy me the prettiest dresses and get Mom the garden she always wanted. That was his dream.

They say Dad was a good captain. He paid well and never asked the crew to take risks he wouldn't also take. Unfortunately, I have only one memory of my father. We were visiting a tide pool, holding hands so I wouldn't slip on the sharp rocks.

Frankly, I have more early memories of missing my father. Waiting on the pier, watching the horizon for his boat, asking Mom when he'd return. See, right after I was born, Dad read a paper about ocean currents and topography, and he had an epiphany about the tomb's location. Finally knew how to pinpoint that elusive burial ship. As you can imagine, he wasted no time or expense to test his theory, and his tenacity paid off.

After my third birthday, Dad sent a message by pigeon. They'd found it! They were preparing to dive. "What does that mean?" I asked my mother, and she said, "He's coming home soon!" She actually smiled. Mom just 'bout never smiled when she discussed my father's work.

We went to the fish market a couple of days later, and as I looked at the gleaming ocean, I saw a bright yellow sailboat, which—from afar—resembled *Explorer III*, Dad's main sailboat. In a surge of misguided toddler enthusiasm, I scampered toward the water, shouting, "Dad! Dad!" Like it was possible for my squeaky voice to carry over miles of ocean.

The next two weeks are a blank. Apparently, I slipped down a seawall, hit my head, and nearly drowned. After they dragged my body onto land and made me cough up water, I still struggled to breathe. The lung damage became pneumonia, and at one point, the medicine man warned my mother that I was probably dying. In a state of despair, she sent a letter by pigeon to *Explorer III*, hundreds of miles away from land. The letter explained everything, begging my father to hurry home so he could say goodbye.

Well, I pulled through. But our family still lost one person.

For the longest time, I believed that Dad perished during a freak storm. Mom didn't want me to hate her. I could never! If anything, this tragedy was my fault.

Last year, at my coming-of-age observance, she shared the truth. Shortly after Mom sent the letter, my father transformed into the leviathan. I can only imagine that moment: He'd finally found the tomb of the Green-haired King—all those riches lost for centuries, and now he could give his family a good life, as he'd always promised—when bad news dropped from the sky. Dad thought I'd died because of him, that I'd chased him into the ocean, drowning.

That's why the transformation might be reversed. He didn't actually lose me.

But even if he's stuck in a leviathan's body, I want another memory of my father. The chance to tell him "I love you" and "I miss you." To talk about my gardening and my dreams to become an herbalist and medicine enchanter.

Is that so much to ask?

THE LEVIATHAN

As they sailed farther into the North Tethys, Cassia painted mountains and forests. Sometimes, she thought she saw ghostly, shimmering land on the horizon, but the visions were only mirages. Until one morning, floating algae—Sargassum—clotted the water. Flecks of red, blue, and gray garbage were tangled in the stringy clumps, living nets.

"He's near," Vandal said; she'd stayed on the boat past sunrise. "Now approaching—fast for a leviathan!" Sea spray clung to the branches of her head coral, which glittered, a crown of bone and liquid jewels.

"Where's he coming from?" Cassia asked, tightening the straps of her life vest. "What direction?"

"Below." Was that a trace of worry in Vandal's voice? "Get over here. Hurry!"

Cassia moved beside Vandal, standing close enough to feel a chill. The boat lurched, bobbing off-kilter. This was not the steady motion of natural waves. It was a disturbance.

"Close your eyes, Cassia," Vandal ordered. "Look away."

"What? Why?"

Vandal's arms split into tentacles, transformed into eels.

Mouths opened across her body, sharp with shark teeth. "Rule two," commanded a hundred voices, all hers. "Do as I say."

"No." She grabbed an eel arm, held it firmly, her fingers curling around the creature's neck. Its eyes rolled wildly, but she wasn't afraid. "Don't hurt him, Vandal," she pleaded.

Suddenly, a mouth rose from the ocean, surrounding the sailboat with a ring of stalactite-shaped teeth and rubbery black gums. If the leviathan closed its mouth, they'd be swallowed whole. Vandal's body writhed in a storm of changes, as if preparing to unleash all the forms within her shell, but Cassia continued to hold her back.

"Dad!" she shouted. "It's me, Cassia! I'm alive!"

For a second, the leviathan simply floated, his mouth wide, as if frozen.

"Do you remember?" she asked. "I was small the last time you saw me. We visited a tide pool full of purple urchins and little green crabs! I thought they were so pretty I wanted to take them home, but you said they'd die if we moved them. So you promised we'd visit again. We still can!"

With a low, pained rumble, the leviathan sank, his mouth retreating back into the water. Cassia released Vandal and then sprinted to the edge of the deck. There, she pressed her belly against the wet metal rail and looked directly into the ocean. The leviathan was below them, his hungry mouth still bared. Teeth and darkness were all she saw. "Dad! I missed you so much."

"Cassia," the leviathan rumbled. Then, almost questioning, "You're old?"

"It's been almost fifteen years." Her voice was hoarse from shouting, but she raised it anyway. "I survived the pneumonia. The letter was wrong."

"What?" He sank another meter, and despite the leviathan's great size, he reminded Cassia of a timid vole retreating into its burrow. "What letter?"

"The letter Mom sent." Had he forgotten? Was it even possible for a sea-born to forget their greatest heartbreak? "I was deathly sick, and you were exploring the tomb of the Green-haired King—"

He cut her off, his voice the rumble of an erupting deep-sea volcano. "I was not! The king's burial ship is still lost."

Wide-eyed, Cassia looked at Vandal, who shrugged.

"No, Dad," she shouted. "You found it. Fourteen years ago."

"That was a decoy! An oversize tin can full of rot! Where are his barrels of opal? His sculptures of jade? His golden armory and his secrets etched in stone?"

Cassia had no answer to those questions; in fact, her certainty in everything—in her plan, in her father, in herself—crumbled. "Is . . . is that why you changed, Dad? Because the tomb was worthless? Because you'd bet everything on a tall tale?" That couldn't be true. She shook her head. "No."

The *Explorer IV* rocked wildly as the leviathan twitched; with a gasp, Cassia clutched the rail for support.

"Come home," she begged her father. "Please. If you're trapped in a sea-born body, I'll find a job along the coast. Visit you on weekends. It'll be great." She'd always wanted to become a traditional herbalist, but there were alternatives. Algae farmers, marsh gardeners. Justice could help her make connections, meet a good adviser. Cassia was miserable at sea, but the coast was a liminal space, and she'd been happy there once, long ago.

"Someday." He sank another meter.

"Wait!" Desperate, Cassia reached into her pocket. "Is it treasure you want?" she cried, grasping the pouch of chains. At the first jingle of gold, her father paused.

Poised there, Cassia thought of the years without him, the grief, the guilt. The weeks at sea, the lies she'd told her mother, the risks she'd taken. And she almost understood her father's heartbreak, how crushing it felt to pour your heart into a journey that ended in disappointment.

Almost. There was one major difference in their journeys.

Slowly, Cassia exchanged the pouch of gold jewelry for the satchel of herbs. With a firm shake, she scattered its contents into the ocean. Sage and lavender dusted the water.

"I grew these," she whispered. "Aren't they precious, too? Isn't a garden better than a tomb?"

Without a word, the leviathan vanished into the depths.

VANDAL'S STORY

"What now?" Vandal asked. They'd been sailing in silence, Cassia sitting cross-legged on the bow so she didn't have to look back.

"Return to the dockyard and let Justice borrow the *Explorer* while I study in the mountains. Probably oughta tell Mom about this adventure. I told her that I planned to go sailing with friends before school. Didn't elaborate that my friend is a sea-born graffiti artist who loves the color violet."

"Good luck with that conversation," Vandal said, moving to sit beside Cassia. "Will she be mad?"

"No." Cassia envisioned her mother, kneeling in her garden, weeding and planting, her skirt smudged with dirt, her hands buried in the earth. A patient, canny, gentle woman. "She'll forgive me. Honestly, I don't deserve a mother like—"

"Hey," Vandal interrupted, softly. "That isn't true."

"What?"

"You deserve love."

The boat swayed gently, small waves sloshing against the hull.

"Thank you," Cassia said.

Together, they admired the pink-tinted clouds for a minute.

"You know, there was a time," Vandal said, "when my people lived on an island in the crescent gulf.

"We were many things. Artists, architects, teachers, healers, poets, and fighters. Some of us were even troublemakers. Others were heroes. But the world mostly knew us for our land.

"The island was rich with bright violet clay. Outsiders called us the ultraviolet people. We used our clay as sunscreen, coating our faces and arms with vibrant paste. We shaped the clay into pottery and dyed our clothes with its pigment. Even some of our buildings had the clay in their walls.

"Visitors from faraway places visited our home, wishing to trade. They crossed the gulf in fantastic ships. Some vessels were powered by the wind. Others carried a hundred rowers with long wooden oars. Then came the steam-powered ships, the submarines. The outsiders coveted our island for its color. Blue and violet dyes were difficult to manufacture. However, my people would not trade our land for anything. Homeland is a mother. Do you know what I mean? We refused to hollow her out, bleed her, sell her. What would remain of us, then? Without a home, we cannot survive.

"Several countries attempted to invade our island. But we had a powerful defender. Home was surrounded by choppy water, and vast coral reefs prevented large ships from approaching our shores. Every invasion failed. We'd protected her. Our mother. Or so we thought.

"Then the sea began to rise."

Vandal's body grew spines. Eyespots appeared down her back, up her arms. Her hands tightened on the wheel.

"It started slowly. Only elders noticed the change. The gradual thinning of our beaches, the erosion of our violet cliffs. The timid push of record high tides, one after another. Summers were hotter, hurricanes were stronger, the reef began to die, color leaching from the coral, leaving nothing but white bones. No reef meant no reef fish. No reef fish meant starvation. And all the while, our home was drowning.

"I was the last child born on that island; my parents were tasked with a sacred vigil. Together, we waited for the last sliver of ultra-violet land to vanish below the ocean. My parents told me stories of happier days. They described our cities and sang our songs. I learned about our artists, architects, teachers, healers, poets, and fighters. And most of all, our troublemakers and heroes. When I was young, I thought there must be some way to save our home and return to prosperity.

"But the more I studied, learning about the world beyond our barely there island, the less I could hope.

"There was no reversal, no cure. It was too late. And if I'm perfectly honest, we never had a chance.

"When my parents died, I buried them under the last remaining acre of violet land. They joined the ancestors. But my change didn't happen then. I still carried one hope inside me."

"What?" Cassia whispered.

"To be reunited with my family someday. To be one with our homeland. The sea swallowed my island before that could happen.

"Only then, when there was nothing left, did I stop fighting."

In her peripheral vision, Cassia saw a woman with rich brown skin and shiny black hair. But when she turned, the sea had reclaimed Vandal's body.

"The end of your story is wrong," she quietly said.

"Ha. Seriously?"

"Yeah." Cassia pointed to the flag, which was still marked by a violet handprint. "You found a new fight."

"To annoy people?"

"To make sure the world remembers. I'll share your story, Vandal."

When they shook hands, Cassia swore that Vandal's grasp was warm.

"So you aren't selling this sailboat?" the sea-born wondered out loud. "Just lending it to the fisherman?"

"Uh-huh. Someday, I'll use it to visit family and friends."

"Well, then." Vandal stood. "You'll need to learn how to sail. C'mon. Plenty of time to cover the basics."

That evening, Cassia memorized terms like "mast," "starboard," and "schooner" and practiced basic knots on a short length of rope. As she tied a figure-of-eight, Vandal climbed into the water, uncapped her can of violet paint, and changed the ship's name into a bouquet of flowers.

THE NIGHTINGALE'S LAMENT

Kerri Maniscalco

Tonight, Skye Nightingale thought as she fastened her lucky seahorse clip in her dark auburn coiffure, *Mr. William Hayden Anchor would utter three fateful words and make his cursed move.*

Skye studied her features carefully, looking for any hint of her true motive—anything at all that might cause trepidation in her mark. Her blue-green eyes glittered as if she had a naughty secret and her golden skin looked pleasantly kissed by the sun.

Without a doubt, Mr. Anchor would tell her those pretty lies and suspect nothing.

This Season, her very first out in Siren Society, several men before him had whispered those same lies before stealing a kiss—oftentimes more, if the gentleman was the villain she'd sensed he was—only to find themselves mysteriously dead within hours.

All killed in unfortunate maritime accidents. A fate that, thankfully, wasn't too strange for their island off the western archipelago of Seabright.

In true Siren fashion, Skye chose her suitors with caution, never picking someone too well connected, which would raise suspicion, even if darkness tainted his soul, marking him as prey. Skye always thought of the consequences—a binding spell that would imprison their whole family's magical nature—should she fail by alerting human authorities. Her sisters hadn't yet made their debut and she'd not do anything rash to jeopardize their coming out in Society.

Instead of being too obvious, Skye stole secret glances at sailors who came to the Treasure Box to hear her and her sisters sing, their voices and looks likened to angels, though some still in possession of their wits swore the dimples the eldest flashed were gifted from the devil himself. If her wicked grin didn't gain the attention of her marks, it was the way Skye's gowns scandalously clung to her curves that eventually lured them in.

Men had daggers and blades aplenty, but she knew a well-timed swish of her hips was a powerful weapon itself. Perhaps not for all men, but the villainous ones she had designs for were transfixed by her body and the enticing manner in which she wielded it. If their predatory gazes devoured her while she sang on stage, Skye knew they were hers for the taking.

And take she did.

It was in the marks' nature to hunt those they deemed helpless and weak, but it was in hers to kill. She was the most fearsome thing in these waters. Until her sisters made their own splashy debut, of course. Then god save the fools who tried hunting women on their island.

Skye was especially intrigued by the sailors who'd docked with the intention of offloading their goods, hurting some "whores" without a care, and swiftly returning to their own islands.

Each of her former marks were young men who weren't long for their world anyway, thanks to their trade on the often rough western seas, or the questionable company they associated with. And if one of them drowned after seemingly imbibing too many spirits? A simple tragedy.

And tragedies certainly seemed to plague the Nightingale three. Most villagers in Fisher's Bay looked upon the unlucky sisters with great sorrow, though whispers still reached her of the tragic Nightingale curse to never find true love. But she wasn't looking for love. Skye yearned for something much more satisfying.

A sharp knock at the front door indicated William was right on schedule. Skye's lips curved upward in her signature grin. It was almost time for his private serenade.

She smoothed down the front of her pale green bodice, twisting to see if the darker ribbons keeping her decent remained in place. They held beautifully. With luck, they would remain that way until William confessed his false love at the close of her song and went to unwrap his gift. Admittedly, Skye was rather looking forward to that part of the evening.

Mr. William Anchor had a sinful grin of his own. Dark, mysterious eyes and the low rumble of his voice were also quite intoxicating. She had spent more than one evening over the last week he'd courted her imagining his sun-bronzed fingers trailing across her golden skin as he whispered the kinds of things no proper lady—of good breeding or otherwise—should wish to hear. Skye's body flushed with anticipation. If she hadn't sensed the darkness in him, that predatory sixth sense that kicked in, signaling trouble, she might have dismissed him.

Wanting a mark was forbidden in Siren Society.

She turned from the mirror but was halted by her raven-haired middle sister.

Coral shot her a worried look. "You're certain he's the one?"

"Of course I am. Whyever wouldn't he be?"

Coral fingered the polished cowrie shells at her throat, her expression contemplative. "There's something about his eyes I don't trust."

"It's not his eyes I'm after, so that suits me just fine." Skye waggled her brows suggestively, which only made her sister sigh.

"What of your heart?" Coral challenged, her hands dropping to clutch at her own chest as if she were suddenly pained. "You've never been taken with anyone before. You know the rules. And the consequences of breaking them."

"I assure you my heart is not in any danger. He's a handsome mark, nothing more."

"Let this fish off the hook," Coral urged. "You'll find another one better suited."

Pearle, their youngest sister of seven and ten years, and resident eavesdropper, stepped into the small bedchamber, her golden locks falling in waves down her back as she shook her head.

"Coral is right. I don't like this one, either. Or the way you blush whenever he arrives. He looks like trouble and not the sort we usually like to dabble in. Have you seen the way the sea swells when he walks near it?"

"It does not, and even if it did, then that's all the more reason to choose him." Skye looked at each of her sisters, their matching sea-green eyes staring right back, filled with worry. She knew what they were thinking and prayed they'd not bring it up before her big night. "All I need to do is lure him to the lighthouse and sing. I doubt it will be that difficult. Unlike convincing the two of you that all will be well."

"And if he's Poseidon's—"

"He's a mark and nothing more. He's certainly not some nightmare prince sprung to life and landed here. In Fisher's Bay." Skye cast an accusing look at Coral, whose open mouth was poised for a rebuttal. "Not another word out of either of you. Trouble or not, I know what I'm doing."

"Like Mother?" Pearle asked quietly.

Skye's breath caught. Their mother hadn't been seen in more than a decade, and while some had their suspicions, there was never any evidence to prove her fate one way or another. All Skye knew was one day she'd gone after a particularly nasty mark and never returned.

And that fueled Skye to hunt as many of those predators as she could in her first Season. She was so successful she'd been featured in the Society papers each week since she'd debuted. Her sisters were wildly proud, taking turns reading from each gossip sheet until Skye's cheeks burned crimson and she wished to dive under the safety of the waves.

"Don't wait up," Skye said. "I have a feeling if all goes as planned, it will be a gloriously late night."

Before her sisters could dampen her spirits, Skye hurried down the narrow stairs and opened the door, offering a bright smile to the man standing in the shadows.

"Miss Nightingale." William flashed that grin that made heat pool low in her belly. One thing her sisters had gotten right: He was trouble. "You're as enchanting as ever tonight. Dare I say that dress combined with your voice would make even the sirens of old lore jealous?"

"You flatter me, Mr. Anchor. Apologies for keeping you waiting." Her heart thumped madly in her chest, as it was wont to do whenever the tall, muscular sailor was near. She was almost certain that was the only reason for her speeding pulse, and not his all too accurate remark. "Would you care to take a walk?"

"So proper this evening," he teased, offering his arm like a perfect gentleman. Something Skye knew he wasn't as he'd already kissed her like a well-seasoned rake, his body pressed against hers until she felt the power of his attraction and, immediately upon parting, had to take a dip in the icy ocean simply to cool the lingering heat from his touch.

That had been a first. Usually when a mark made a move, her skin crawled like graveyard worms as she allowed him to paw at her until she was certain enough of his intentions to attack. Skye never permitted things to get too far; she only waited until they roughly hiked up her skirts and pushed for something she was not willing to give. Then she'd sing their souls away with a grin upon her lips, watching the life bleed out of their hateful eyes.

William hadn't been like that. He'd kissed her senseless, then walked her home, ensuring she made it safely inside. He hadn't known she rushed out to the sea once she was certain he was gone. Hadn't known she'd spent hours trying to erase him from her thoughts. She was the huntress but at times felt their roles were reversed. Which was why this needed to end tonight.

It was only a matter of time before the darkness she sensed in him emerged.

As they walked down the dirt path toward the sea, she subtly ran her gaze over him, noting that—unless he was far wealthier than a modest sailor and had a valet—he'd taken time to shave and press his shirt and trousers. His leather boots gleamed in the moonlight as if he'd freshly polished them before arriving on her doorstep, looking like sinful promise incarnate.

He had designs for her, all right. A whisper of suspicion wrapped itself around her, but Skye promptly shrugged it away. There were old stories that cautioned sirens away from a supposed wayward prince who stole more than hearts himself. The very legend her sisters had tried to frighten her with tonight.

"I noticed a lighthouse down the road," he said casually, drawing her attention back to his chiseled features and full lips. It was a face fit for a prince. Or a pirate straight out of a romance novel. "I'd love to see it up close. If you're game?"

If Skye was surprised he wanted to visit the very site she planned on taking him to this evening, she didn't let it show. "I think that's a grand idea. Have you heard any of the ghost stories while in town?"

"Only the one where a woman moans from dusk 'til dawn." He smiled much too sinfully for Skye to have mistaken his flirtation for an innocent slip of the tongue.

Her skin flushed pleasantly, though he hadn't said anything untrue. Old stories *did* tell the tale of the Wailing Widow, a story of a woman who cried out for one entire night, though the main consensus was she was wailing from grief. Not the naughty reason William implied.

The unabashed rogue.

"You sound as if you believe that story is real, Mr. Anchor."

"Oh, I simply *hope* there's a bit of truth hidden in there." He watched her intently. "What do you believe, Miss Nightingale? Do you think we'll hear a woman moan this evening?"

Skye's lips twitched at the blatant double entendre. Lord, he was skilled at being so deliciously bad. It was a right shame it was his soul and not his . . . heart she was after. Each evening he'd grown bolder, more daring with what he'd said, as if testing her mettle. Skye liked him entirely too much, and perhaps that did make him dangerous.

She offered him a coy look. "As you said. One can only *hope*, Mr. Anchor. It would certainly make an interesting story."

The new smile he gave her was carved from pure wickedness. "Perhaps it's time to rewrite the tale."

They strolled the rest of the way in companionable silence, pausing once they reached the base of the massive blue-and-white-striped lighthouse, its proud light flashing high above. A beacon of safety for some. For others it was simply a warning.

William left her to wrench open the door, sticking his head inside to call up. "Hullo?"

"Old Mr. Baxter is likely sleeping in the outhouse," Skye offered, stepping past him and making for the winding stairs. She grinned over her shoulder. "He's rather fond of his drink and always passes out while tending to nature's call."

William shot her a look of amusement and followed her up the stairs without further comment. She felt the heat of his gaze on her as they traveled in silence, and *perhaps* she swayed her hips a bit more than necessary as they ascended to the top of the observation room.

Some men complained that women ought to mind their bodies and clothes, to not draw attention, that if they were too appealing, they silently asked for unwanted advances. That *they* were the ones to blame.

Skye, however, believed women could waltz through the village without a stitch of clothing and still not be responsible for someone else's rotten actions. Looking and touching were nowhere near the same. Anyone who argued otherwise was questionable in her eyes. Bakers often carried tempting elderberry tarts on trays past her, and she managed to not snatch one even though she could.

There were plenty of good men who never took by force something they hadn't been gifted freely. Those were the men her magic left be. She could simper and undress and they'd either watch with muted interest, avert their gazes, or offer their jackets to someone in need.

Not once had her Siren instinct ever been triggered by an innocent. No matter how harmless William might appear, there was a reason her magic had chosen him. She couldn't forget it. The last mark had tried to take her right there against the wall. But William, if he was planning to strike, didn't take the bait. Curse him.

Skye moved to the window and looked out at the dark waters, admiring the silver glint of the moon. For some reason, her mother had named her for the heavens instead of the ocean, though it suited her well enough with her blue-green eyes. Similar yet different from her sisters' vibrant green. While swimming the soulless bodies out to sea, Skye often found her attention drawn to the stars at night, sparkling like diamonds for all the world to dream upon.

She pushed thoughts of her mother away and focused on the task at hand. It was time to end this charade and move on to the next mark before this Season's end. "Beautiful, isn't it?"

"That it certainly is." William slid up beside her, stealing glances she pretended not to notice. "Do you come here often at night?"

"Sometimes. When I wish to be alone with my thoughts. Or to practice a new song."

This admission had his head fully turning in her direction. "Will you sing something for me?"

Would she ever. She twisted and boldly met his stare. "Perhaps. But only if you're *very* good."

His eyes flashed with something that indicated being good was suddenly the furthest thing from his mind. A tiny thrill shot through her at the thought of what was to come. *No*, she shouldn't desire his touch, especially since it would seal his fate.

And yet . . .

"I can be extremely good when motivated. Though I find behaving badly to be more fun." William removed a coin from his pocket and flipped it in the air. "Heads, I'll be good." He tossed the coin up again, one brow arched in challenge as it fell back into his waiting hand. "Tails, I'll be wickedly bad. Are you brave enough to leave it to fate, Miss Nightingale?"

William Hayden Anchor was, of course, not his given name. But Miss Skye Nightingale, the young woman Hunter was fairly certain was a vigilante murderess, didn't know that. Nor was he convinced that "Skye Nightingale" was her birth name either. At least not all of it.

After hearing her sing one crowded night, he'd searched the birth records in Fisher's Bay and not a single Nightingale had been listed. Perhaps it wasn't so strange for a songstress to choose a

128

stage name perfect for her craft, but he had other suspicions. Especially when the man who'd been ogling her all that night vanished the next evening without a trace.

When he asked around the pub where she worked, barmaids simply shrugged and said as far as they knew, all three sisters had been born right there in the small house atop the bluff. Though no one could recall meeting their father, only Mira, the missing mother, God rest her soul.

If they proved to be the soul-stealing monsters Hunter suspected they were, the irony of the villagers' sentiments had him regularly biting back curses. Though, pretending to be a sailor as he was, that lack of decorum would hardly raise any brows.

"Well?" He gave Skye a lazy grin meant to undermine the calculation in his gaze. She watched him toss the coin up again, seeming to decide if there was trickery at play. There was, naturally, but she hadn't asked to inspect the coin. Yet. "Ladies choice. We can play a different game if you prefer something less . . . scandalous."

She turned her blue-green eyes on him, looking far too intrigued by the idea of scandal, and a bolt of awareness shot through him. Out of the corner of his eye he noticed the waves churn, a direct response to his heightened mood. It was a right shame he'd have to destroy her.

Skye was truly what mortals called a diamond of the first water. Flawless. If one overlooked the murdering part. Fortunately for him, he wasn't the mortal sort, nor was he the kind to overlook a tiny little character flaw such as murder. No matter how interesting or pretty the mark was, she was a creature to be hunted and slain and nothing more. Hunter tracked maritime myths and legends across the continent—from krakens to sirens and every scaled or fanged monster in between. As Poseidon's eldest heir, it was his duty to rid the world of the sea demons his father had mistakenly made eons before.

Skye might be a beautiful monster, but she was still a monster. The flutter in his pulse and the sudden stiffness in his trousers would simply need to remember his motto: Marks were forbidden.

He was about to suggest a new game when the murderess squared her shoulders.

"Very well, Mr. Anchor. Let's see what fate has in store for us tonight."

His heartbeat picked up speed, even knowing the ending of this particular story. He tossed the coin in the air once more for good measure, then slapped it on the back of his hand, keeping it hidden from her view. "Care to do the honors?"

"Don't mind if I do."

Skye's attention took its time traveling from his steady gaze before dropping lower to thoroughly inspect his mouth and then finally the hand he offered. Lord save him. The siren hadn't even used her power yet and he was already falling under her spell. This needed to end soon. She was by far his most dangerous mark to date. Luckily for him, her back was to the sea. He might be able to lie, but the magic that connected him to the ocean never did.

She moved until the toes of her heeled shoes were almost touching his. Up close, he could smell the clean scent of her soap mixed with a slightly floral perfume that made him suddenly envision her unbound auburn hair spilling over his pillow.

To his growing horror, Hunter's imagination didn't stop there. He pictured dipping his head between her thighs, watching her writhe beneath him while he pleasured her.

"Everything all right, Mr. Anchor? You look a bit flushed." Skye ran ungloved fingers over the back of his hand, circling closer and closer to the coin he still held hidden.

He tried to keep his expression plain, to keep his breathing steady, to not give away how badly the sea demon was affecting him.

"It's a bit warm in here."

"Indeed." Skye gently pried his hand away and smiled. "Tails. Looks like it's my lucky evening after all. I believe you promised to be very wicked." She tilted her face toward his, stepping close enough for him to kiss. "Are you still game, Mr. Anchor?"

His magic burned in warning, the first time his weapon had done so in her presence. Skye, enchanting and beguiling as she was, was a threat. It was exactly the reminder he needed. He'd already dallied too long after discovering the truth of what she was. There was no logical reason for him to prolong their encounter. It was time to set his sights on the next mark.

"I'm always game, Miss Nightingale. The real question is whether you can keep up."

She bit her lip, seeming to need a moment. He knew precisely how his words could be interpreted. Though he wasn't implying what she thought.

"I rather enjoy a good challenge," she said at last. "Should we play a round of truth or dare?"

Got you, sea demon. He didn't bother hiding his grin. "I dare you to go for a midnight swim with me."

❦

It was the second time that evening William had caught her off guard. And Skye didn't much care for the disorienting feeling. "I thought you wished to hear me sing?"

131

"I think your voice will carry over the waves in a most pleasant manner," he said. "Is the dare too wicked for your tastes, Miss Nightingale?"

"Not one bit. I'll have to disrobe . . ."

"As will I."

Unbidden, she pictured slowly divesting him of each layer of his clothing. Watching as more and more sun-bronzed skin was bared to her. From their previous kiss, she knew he possessed hard muscle and wondered if it looked the way she imagined it did, given what she'd felt. Then she allowed her thoughts to wander further, to feeling the weight of him atop her as he sunk into her warmth and slowly thrusted until she lost herself in a rhythm more tantalizing than that of the sea. Which was strictly against Siren rules. If anyone in their Society found out, she'd be ruined. And if her sisters found out . . . that was another story entirely.

"Very well. Lead the way, Mr. Anchor."

He flashed her another devilish grin and headed for the stairs.

Usually, her marks didn't care to waste time with games. They had a plan and put it into action once they knew they were alone. William still hadn't attempted to kiss her, let alone attack. And while he was suggesting they swim in the nude, there wasn't any leering on his part. No predatory stare. He simply looked like a young rogue out for harmless fun.

Yet Skye's magic was growing insistent that he posed a serious threat. Part of her wondered if she should feign a sudden headache and return home until she figured him out, but the thought of facing her sisters and their accusations kept her feet stubbornly planted where they were. Foolish, perhaps, but she could certainly handle singing away his soul if things got tricky.

"Watch your step." Once outside, she led him down a partially hidden path that curved around the bluffs. After descending to the shore, she paused to survey their surroundings. The cove was well out of view from any of the surrounding bluffs. No lights other than that of the moon shone down upon them. No wandering eyes.

Mist hung midway up the cliffs as if offering privacy for the dastardly deed about to take place. No one would spy them getting undressed or swimming out to sea. A fact she was well aware of as William wasn't the first young man she'd taken here. Nor would he be the last.

"This is beautiful, Miss Nightingale. Secluded. Have you—"

"You aren't stalling, are you, William?"

"Are we using our given names now?" he teased.

"I believe we're about to be very . . . intimately acquainted." Skye pivoted until she faced him, ensuring she had his full attention before slowly tugging the ribbons on her bodice loose.

It was time for her to regain the upper hand here. His attention was riveted to her fingers and each deft movement they made with the garment as she slipped one strap over her shoulder, then the other. Skye knew the moonlight would paint her skin an unearthly shade, would accentuate the shadows cast by her curves and invite his gaze to linger.

He needed to stop talking and confusing her heart and make his move so she could end this. She'd never gone so far for a mark before, never had to remove any of her clothes, and yet standing before him, stripping down to her underthings as he watched with hooded eyes, wasn't disturbing her in the manner it ought to. In fact, she wasn't disturbed at all.

Which was a problem.

"Are you going to join me, Mr. Anchor?"

"Ladies first, as always."

Perhaps it was the challenge burning in his eyes and the slight upturn of his lips that indicated he believed she'd call his bluff. Or maybe it was the sudden stirring of the sea—a reaction that seemed perfectly timed to her heartbeat. William Anchor had no idea whom he was dealing with.

"Very well." Skye shimmied the gown off entirely, letting it pool in the sand, then reached for the hem of her slip. A strong sense of satisfaction filled her as his gaze locked onto the movement of the silk inching up her thighs. Her heart pounded in anticipation; surely he was about to pounce now. The hungry look on his face indicated he wanted to. Desperately.

And yet, as she continued to slowly drag her hemline upward, he did nothing more than unabashedly drink her in as if she were a delicacy to be savored. Curse the insufferable rake. William was going to simply stand there, watching until she stripped entirely. Or folded the bet.

That was the glint in his eyes. He had the look of a young man who believed he'd won.

Losing wasn't in her nature. She exhaled quietly and lifted her slip up past her hips, then tugged it all the way over her head. There. She stood nude and proud as the moonlight shimmered over her skin. Skye took a step backward, relishing the way the icy sea lapped at her ankles, its coolness soothing the growing heat spreading across her body. William's attention dropped to where she stood in the water before he brought it back up to her face, his expression now serious.

"Your turn, William. Unless you forfeit the dare?"

His eyes flashed with heat and something else she couldn't quite read.

"I never lose, Skye." With little fanfare, he shucked his jacket and trousers off, then yanked open his shirt, revealing a body the gods would envy. He stood there a moment, as if sensing she needed a second to take in the sight of him and all his raw, masculine glory, before slowly prowling toward her. "You look like you want to devour me."

She certainly wanted his soul. But the way he was stalking forward, all animal grace and danger, made Skye suddenly wish for other things a little bit more. She couldn't help but slide her gaze over his proud, thick length. She wasn't the only one affected. "If you enter the water in that state, something might very well devour you. At least in part."

His laughter shouldn't sound so rich and melodious. It also shouldn't cause her pulse to speed, but it defied both expectations. "If you're so concerned about my well-being, perhaps we ought to stay on the beach. I'm certain we can come up with more interesting dares. The water's turning a bit rough anyway."

It certainly was. She tried to steady her pulse, to rein in her magic. "And what would you suggest instead?"

William's smile was sin incarnate. "Devouring, of course. I could go first, if you'd like."

Skye couldn't tell if her magic was buzzing over the sudden roaring of her pulse. If William touched her, the way his expression hinted he desired to, she was in trouble. Repulsion wouldn't be the emotion she felt. And singing his soul away would be rather difficult with her lips on his.

The wind gusted, blowing the two sides of his shirt apart. A large tattoo on his ribs caught her attention, though unless he turned his body toward her, she couldn't make out what it was.

He was almost upon her, and if he laid a hand on her skin, she'd be ruined. And so would her sisters. Before Skye could fall prey to his sultry bedroom eyes, she turned and dived into the chilly water, his sharp curse the last sound she heard before submerging herself completely.

Hunter watched the siren take to the waves like she was born to do. Her movements were graceful yet contained an edge. She was a predator in the sea, and the ease with which she moved in the deep water reminded him of that fact. It was a good thing she entered the ocean when she did. He'd almost let himself get snared by the heat in her gaze, the hunger. If he didn't know any better, Hunter would swear she truly desired him and wasn't simply trying to capture his soul.

And he'd be a right fool to let that happen, just like the rest of her victims.

Once she was far out, Skye turned to him, her wicked mouth curving into the sort of grin that made his damned length grow harder. Killing a monster shouldn't be arousing. He'd have to get his mind checked after he finished this mission.

"Are you coming, William?"

He shrugged his shirt the rest of the way off, then walked into the waves. The cool sea greeted him like a good friend, the water hugging his calves, almost playfully dragging him deeper as he walked farther in.

Thankfully Skye was too far away to notice the supernatural response. The ocean was his birthright, more so than even hers. He waded out to his waist, absorbing the charge of the sea's power as it enveloped him. Skye circled closer, her gaze locked onto his.

The moonlight made her skin glow. She almost looked like a goddess. Goose bumps prickled his skin. Two of them entered the sea, but only one would reemerge.

"Will you sing for me now, Skye?"

A strange look crossed her face, there and gone in an instant. He almost swore it looked like regret. Before he could question her—or better yet, his sanity—the siren swam up to him, closing the distance almost completely as she adopted that devil-may-care grin. "You'll have to hold me. Otherwise, I get a bit carried away when the music strikes."

Knowing what he did of her magic, it was likely the truest statement she'd ever offered him. He steeled himself and reached out, placing his hands on her hips, drawing her nearer still. Where she stood now, her upper body was no longer hidden beneath the water, but her long locks had come undone, covering her chest. Hunter had been listening closely and heard the sharp intake of her breath. It wasn't from fear, and he wondered if she'd also felt that spark.

"Like this?" he asked.

Skye's focus darted to his mouth as she bit her plump bottom lip. "Perfect."

They stood there silently, each plotting their next move. At least that's what Hunter assumed, based on the way the siren had gone quiet.

"Well?" His voice seemed to startle her from a trance. The siren blinked as if suddenly recalling where she was. What she was meant to do. "If you don't wish to sing . . ."

Her gaze sharpened. "I do."

And yet she still waited to start. Or to end him, more fittingly. For some cursed reason, Hunter wanted *her* to make the first move before he took her out. His heart thumped in anticipation, the feeling causing tingles along his body. All his senses heightened, his magical weapon burning beneath his skin. He knew she was ready to strike but for some reason she held off. So he did too.

Skye was transfixed by his mouth, like she wanted to kiss him one last time. Hunter was more than willing to oblige.

"You're impossibly intriguing." He slowly dipped his head toward hers, allowing ample time for her to pull away, to begin her death song.

Skye surprised him by angling her face up and brushing her lips against his, the kiss a whisper spoken by lovers in the night.

Perhaps it was the power of the sea, or the silvery moonlight dancing across her skin, or the way she gasped into his mouth when he dragged his hands along her sides, but Hunter finally gave in to the siren. He kissed her like his soul was in jeopardy, knowing it was true, but in that moment he stopped caring.

Skye kissed him back just as recklessly, her mouth parting to welcome his tongue, her small hands roving across his chest, down his abdomen. Needing to halt her downward exploration, he pulled her flush against him. Her warm body pressed against his arousal, and instead of being scandalized, Skye seemed to awaken. Her gaze grew impossibly hungrier as it fell to where their bodies met.

Hunter wasn't sure which one of them moved next, all he knew was the siren was now in his arms, her legs wrapped around his waist. He carried them deeper into the water, wanting to keep them hidden from view. Skye was entirely too close and not nearly close enough as she deepened their kiss. He met her hunger with his own, sliding his silken tongue against hers in a kiss that would be their undoing.

"William," she breathed as he started kissing down her neck, intent on giving her everything her body was asking him for. The sound of his false name on her lips brought him back to his senses. He drew away just as she opened her mouth and began to sing.

Had he been mortal, the song would have dragged him into the icy depths below. He would have gladly given up his soul just to hear her finish her song.

The problem for Skye was *she'd* miscalculated now. He wasn't mortal. And her song didn't affect him. Hunter watched her lose herself in the melody, admitting to himself she truly was something impressive to behold. She was so lost to her song, trying desperately to tear his soul away, she hadn't noticed the ink now glowing on his side; his magic's response to hers.

When she finished the last line and finally met his gaze, chest heaving from exertion, her brows pinched together.

"I don't . . ." Her attention shot to the glowing ink, her gold skin going as pale as the moon. "You can't be him. He's not real."

"I feel real enough, don't I?" Hunter didn't move closer, didn't blink when she slowly put distance between them, swimming farther from shore. "Say my name, Skye."

"Hunter." Her look indicated *he* was the monster. Ironic, given she'd just attempted to murder him. Skye met his gaze, seeming to come into herself. "Poseidon's miserable heir."

"It's been a true pleasure, siren. But I'm sure you know how this story ends."

Skye glared and spat his words from earlier at him. "Perhaps it's time to rewrite the tale."

She dived under the water and swam as if her life depended on it. Hunter smiled and called upon the trident glowing beneath his skin, drawing forth his family's weapon of choice until it was solid metal in his fist, and did what he was named for; he hunted.

"May the best sea monster win."

SEA WOLF IN PRINCE'S CLOTHING

Adriana Herrera

The island of Desecho is located exactly at the center of the archipelago of the Seven Suns. We are visible from every island and as I watch the court guards of Isla Mayor load our trunks onto the barge that will carry them to the island, I wonder if Desecho looks as small to outsiders as it feels to me.

"Please tell me you didn't pack that dagger in there?" my cousin Dhanyeris whispers in my ear as my luggage disappears into the hold below. I shrug, which earns me a glare. I glare back and continue to watch my mother pace around the pier.

"Are you sure you stored everything you need, Somi?" Mother asks for the third time. "This will be all you have for *your* time away."

A sick kind of satisfaction courses through me at the bitterness in that "your." An invitation to the Ofrenda—the only time that my kind, the Acayias, are allowed to come to the larger islands of the archipelago of the Seven Suns—had not arrived in our house for a very long time. Not since my sister Yemi's death. This time my mother was not asked to attend. In fact, I am the only one in my family invited to this year's offering. No one was more surprised than me. We all expected—had counted on—my cousin Dhanyeris to be this year's selection. The beauty and grace of the Acayias in her family are legendary, and each year one of them is of age, they are the chosen ones. I am not beautiful and I am not graceful, and yet when the letter from Isla Mayor arrived, there was only one name.

Mine.

If my mother only knew what our intentions were. What Dhanyeris and I planned to do now that *I* was to face the man who had destroyed my Yemi . . .

I close my eyes at the images of my sister's smiling face. Of the gap between her front teeth and the dimples on her cheeks. I force myself to remember those last days, after Yemi was brought back from Isla Mayor. Her once joyful eyes, dull like pools of dark water. Her smile replaced by a painful grimace. Her dulled, opaque tail, which once shimmered with red, yellow, and gold. A sob threatens to bubble up my throat as the memory of her limp, lifeless body brought back by one of the Sea Wolves fills my head, but I smother it down. I can't fall apart now, not until I've claimed our revenge.

"Everything I need is there," I assure my mother one more time.

Dhanyeris, who has been standing next to me, turns around

and wraps her arms tightly around me. I can almost hear my bones creaking from the grip of her skinny arms.

"Stick to the plan, prima, okay? Don't do anything impulsive," she whispers as my mother stands to the side, sending us suspicious glances.

Likely because Dhany and I have never been this close. Growing up, she was always obsessed with the Ofrenda, with fulfilling her role as a concubine for one of the princes of the kingdoms; I judged her harshly for it. I vocally opposed the way that our kind is exploited for the pleasure of the monarchy, only to be used and then discarded. Like my sister was discarded. Like Dhany's mother ultimately was. Our pain, our loss, our rage united us. We planned for this day, for this chance to avenge our loved ones. But we thought Dhany would be the one to do it.

"Me oiste, Somi," she insists, and I nod once.

"I'll do exactly what we agreed. I'll find our counterpart after the offering." My cousin tightens her hand on my shoulder and then kisses my cheek. Our plan hinges on my arriving at the meeting place at the assigned time. There I will meet the ally who will help me carry out our revenge. I am ready.

"When you plunge the knife into his heart, tell him that Yomira's daughter will dance on his grave."

"Dhanyeris, let Somi go," my mother snaps, and my cousin loosens her grip on me, but not completely. We're still close enough to talk without anyone else listening.

"The meeting place is——" she starts, but I cut her off.

"I know, I know," I tell her. "The hallway of portraits." I'm not offended at Dhany's nerves. There is a lot riding on this. It all hinges on my finding the one Sea Wolf who will help me get to my target. There are many things that could—and probably will—go wrong. One thing is certain; I may not return to Desecho. I swallow down the tears that rise to my throat at that thought. Harden myself to the mission ahead. "I will avenge them." The thought of delivering my cousin's revenge as well as mine rushes through my blood. I imagine it surging inside me, readying me for what I'm to do on this night.

Once the trunks are secure, the captain of the barge rings the bell. Acayias can't step onto water vessels of any kind; it's a law as old as the kingdoms. Our party will swim the short distance to the island ourselves, with escorts, of course. I move to the rocky ledge, my feet prickling with the need to leap into the water.

My mother holds me back. For a moment, I think she looks worried, scared. The sun in my eyes must be making me see things.

"Stay beside the chaperones, and don't drift from the school." There is a sharpness to her voice as though she suspects that once we pass the Ring, I'll take off to parts unknown. It's not as though I haven't thought about it, but Yemi's memory keeps me on course. Mother's gaze drifts to the Sea Wolves waiting on me.

"Don't disgrace yourself, Somi." What she really means is, *don't disgrace me*, but I only nod. "An Acayia needs to behave. You don't want to attract the wrong kind of attention from one of the sugar princes." Meaning that I didn't want to appear ill-disposed to my role as future broodmare for the kingdoms.

When I don't answer, my mother grips my chin hard. I can sense my cousin's eyes on me, begging me to not provoke my mother. To not ruin things. Telling me that I must get to Isla Mayor without making waves. That our plan now hinges solely on me.

"I'll behave," I mutter, looking at the Sea Wolf guard patiently waiting for me to leap into the water. Her eyes are hard, but I can see more than frustration in them. She is scared for me. My chest constricts when I remember that this might be the last time I see my mother. What I have agreed to do will alter the course of my life, and hers. Impulsively I throw my arms around her middle, and she lets out a surprised puff of air at my unusual display of emotion.

"I'll miss you, Mami," I whisper, and she runs a hand over my hair like she used to when I was little. I squeeze my eyes, forcing the tears back, and take a breath while my mother holds me. Then, without looking back, I leap into the water.

The Sea Wolves break the clear blue surface of the water in a perfect semicircle. Sharp, angular faces, their upper bodies ripple with muscles. Beneath the water, their gray tails glisten. Beautiful and hard, as if they'd been dipped in steel. It's the first time I've seen the elite guard of the kingdoms since the night one of them brought my sister back to Desecho. Some of them are our cousins and our brothers; others are offspring of Acayias belonging to other islands in the archipelago—all of them the bastards of the kingdoms. The male sirens who are fathered by the kings of the archipelago and birthed by the Acayias. They exist only to protect the kings. Taken from their mothers as infants to be trained in their task. Dhanyeris said they never speak, only escort the Acayias underwater. Like us, the Sea Wolves are bred only to serve the kings, who see them as no more than living, breathing armor.

But like my cousin, I know there is a revolution brewing among the Sea Wolves and the Acayias. The Sea Wolves are the most ruthless killers in the kingdoms, but they are bound by magic from ever harming the monarchs they are trained to protect. That is why the resistance needs the Acayias for their revolution. The Sea Wolves are the shields, but we, the ones who give life to the protectors of the kingdoms, will deliver the mortal blows to the monarchy. Tonight I intend to be the first.

❦

To reach Isla Mayor, we must swim through the Ring, the magical barrier placed there to keep the Acayias from coming to the bigger islands uninvited. As we approach the Ring, I can feel the magic holding back its currents so we can swim through. On any other day besides the Ofrenda, the Ring's conflicting currents circle my island, barring the Acayias from the rest of the archipelago.

We are not allowed to move freely in the kingdoms. Our kind is much too wicked. We *lure* men to their perdition, they say. Our beauty and our wiles so entrancing that we trick them away from their wives . . . ruin lives with our devilry. We can only ever be the concubines of the kingdoms. Caged, confined, vanished, exiled. Being born into this world should make it easier to accept it as my lot, but some days I feel as though I am my anger. That it's blended itself into my muscle, my bone, my blood. That it's the very water I breathe in. The blood in my veins. I will use all that rage to avenge my sister's death.

The swim is fast without the Ring disturbing the currents, and we arrive on the shores of Isla Mayor Oeste before noon. My tail is long and graceful, cutting across the water seamlessly, keeping pace with the Sea Wolves. The other Acayias, eight in total, look so eager to get to land. I swim past them in disgust. Some of their own mothers were murdered in the courts and still they long to be courtesans. I think of Dhany, whose mother was killed by the queen of Isla Larga. She had her throat slit out of jealousy because the king broke the rules and kept bringing her to his bed after she'd borne him a warrior for his army of bastards. Every one of the girls about to be offered to sugar princes tonight has had a loss like that. Despite the easy passage, I'm still nauseated when I reach land. Whatever the hechiceré did to remove the Ring's barrier lingered in the water. Our wobbly land legs are under us by the time we wash up to the sand, and the chaperones quickly gather us in a cluster before we start our unsteady ascent to La Casa de Las Ventanas.

The change once we leave the water is always strange. Not painful exactly, but it's awkward. Like my legs are being stretched very thin. It takes some time before they feel right to walk on. When we reach the house, I am steadier on my feet.

I've never been to the home for the Acayias on Isla Mayor before, but it's a place of legend. The house sits on a cliff halfway up Caña Mountain, where the Sugar Palace—the seat of the king of Isla Mayor Oeste—was built. From my island, I could see the house jutting out the side of the mountain, with its winding stone staircase, round and iridescent, like a pearl. Inside, everything is white, silver, and blue. Crystalline, like the reflection of the ocean was made of stone and glass.

"This is fancy," Brisa, one of the Acayias, whispers in excitement, and she sounds like she used to when we were little sirens swimming around our island together. Before we each learned about loss and pain. Before we each understood our own survival would likely be our destruction.

The place is impressive, but fancy is not what comes to mind. More like a holding cell. The place where they prepare us to be picked over like cattle by the kings and princes. I promised my mother, I promised Dhany, I would remain calm, but I can't control the fury that burns in my chest and spills out of my mouth.

"Trying to figure out whose ass you need to kiss to stay here?" I ask, my tone nasty. Brisa's mouth twists, her hand offering me a gesture of what I can do with my question. The other Acayias pretend they do not hear us. But instead of walking away, she comes closer. Her eyes blaze, but it's not anger I see. It's frustration.

"Why are you always so mad, Somi?" Brisa asks in an exasperated whisper.

"How can you want to be the concubine of the people who treat us like we are disposable?" Brisa flinches at the venom in my voice, then narrows her eyes. But before she can respond, one of the chaperones shushes us.

The hostess of the Casa walks toward us. She's dressed much more elegantly than anything I've ever seen in Desecho. Her frock is similar to the ones we use, but instead of coarse linen, hers is a silky material. Tight around her torso and loose past her navel. It is done that way so when we are in the water, our tails can move freely without constriction. The collar is about an inch wide, and right under it, I can see from her markings that she is joined to another.

When Acayias mate, a priestess etches around their necks the names of all the mothers in their mate's line. A testament to the lineage that they each have joined. It is the echo to the markings done along our spines when we reach our twelfth year. On that day the names of all the matriarchs in our line are written with ink touched by the blood of our oldest mother. Our mate's ancestry around us, and our own, holding us up.

The Acayia never forget.

I think of what I will do tonight at the Ofrenda and smile, but it slides off my face when I look out the window toward Desecho and remember my mother. I know I will never see her again.

"Welcome, sirens. I am Dismanda," the hostess says in the melodious, sweet voice our kind are known for. "You will have time to rest before the carriage arrives to take you up to the Sugar Palace." She looks at the chaperone who escorted us here from Desecho and smiles. "Thank you to Coralia for getting you here safely, but I will be taking you up to the Ofrenda tonight."

Coralia smiles too, but it doesn't quite reach her eyes. It's a slight that an elder from our island isn't considered fit to step into the Sugar Palace. But like a good, obedient Acayia, she smiles at the woman's slight. In truth, it scarcely matters who takes us up to the palace to be picked over like fruit. By the time we are instructed to go ready ourselves, the sun is already starting to dip. I wait until my roommate leaves the washroom to search for what I will need tonight. Even though Dhany warned me against it—had assured me the Sea Wolf will have a weapon for me—I've brought my own. Yemi's dagger. The blade, thin and long, which I will plunge straight into Prince Chraxon's neck. I imagine myself gripping the cold larimar hilt and pushing it in. But when I unfold the towel I'd wrapped it in, it's not there. I quickly rifle through the trunk, fruitlessly. It's gone.

Dhany warned me that the Sea Wolves would go through our things. That I should not risk having a weapon discovered. Because of my stubbornness, I've lost my sister's dagger. I wipe angry tears from my face and attempt to calm down.

"You have to stick to the plan, Acayia," I chastise my reflection in the mirror.

I sigh and reach for the map of the castle I've brought with me, the one Yemi drew for me. Finally, I pick up from my trunk the locket with my sister's likeness. When I kill Prince Chraxon, her face will be the last thing he ever sees. I run the pad of my finger over the dried sap that was poured over it to preserve it, then wipe away the hot tear slithering down my cheek with the same finger.

"You should be here," I whisper, voice clogged with sorrow and rage, remembering my sister who loved singing and could swim faster and deeper than any of the other sirens. "I will make them pay."

I look at the clock and panic when I see that I'm almost out of time. Dismanda will be calling us to the carriage soon. I make quick work of putting on the yellow dress that Dhany thought she would be wearing tonight. The color is bright, like the petals of a sunflower. The hem and the sleeves are embroidered with golden thread. Scrolls that look like rolling waves.

Dhany has instructed me that my contact will be looking for the dress. There will be so many people there, I hope he sees me. Then I turn and look in the mirror at the eye-searing yellow dress and figure he will definitely be able to find me. A nervous shiver runs through me at the thought of being alone with the Sea Wolf, then I remind myself he needs me as much as I need him. No matter how strong, he will need me to kill Prince Chraxon. I allow myself a moment of self-doubt. A few seconds of nervousness and fear as I contemplate what I have agreed to do, before I quickly stuff the locket inside my bodice and walk outside.

"The guard is here," Dismanda, who is exhaustingly chipper, says. "We are expected at the palace in a quarter of an hour. The king will not be pleased if we make him wait."

My heart kicks up into a hammering staccato as Dismanda points me to the front of the line. "I want that beautiful yellow to be one of the first things the princes see," she tells me as though she is offering me a great honor.

I nod and rush to my place. I slide a hand over the bump under my bodice where my sister's face is hidden and hope I have the courage for what I need to do.

"Tide take me," Brisa gasps with excitement as we cross the golden gate of the Sugar Palace and see it for the first time.

Unlike La Casa de Las Ventanas, the palace is not fully visible to outsiders. Protected by what I assume are a myriad of incantations and by a forest of the outrageously tall Quixot palm trees. I know why they hide. With their subjects struggling from year to year to feed themselves and their children, fighting tooth and nail to rebuild after each increasingly destructive and unpredictable cyclone season, it's obscene to live in this much opulence.

The Sugar Palace is not made of sugar as its name suggests, but it was built with the gold that sugar provides. The insatiable appetite for sweetness well beyond the archipelago makes it so the seven kings can build and maintain these gilded monstrosities. The palace is made of sandstone; it almost looks like one of the sandcastles Yemi and I would make as children in Desecho. There are glass windows everywhere and turrets sticking up so high they blend in with the clouds. I can't deny it's beautiful. Beautiful and decadent. Vulgarly excessive and unnecessary, much like its inhabitants.

"Is that Prince Ix'ciel?" another of the girls in our carriage asks, and I lift my gaze to the place where she's directing her finger.

Our carriages arrive in a procession along the circular entrance of the palace. Awaiting us is the palace guard, not the Sea Wolves, who are likely hiding behind the curtains. Dhany told me the palace guard is mostly cosmetic, another accessory in the ritual of the Ofrenda. The Sea Wolves work out of sight, only appearing if there is immediate danger. They are whom I need to look out for. They will be dressed in black and lurking in the shadows. But one of those dangerous warriors is here to help me tonight.

I just need to find him.

"Remember, don't get out until we tell you," Dismanda reminds us. "All the Acayias must touch ground at the same time, your heads bowed in reverence."

"Now!" Dismanda shouts as the doors to our carriage are flung open, revealing a ramp. Immediately we start descending in perfect unison with the others.

The king and his sons, as the hosts of this year's Ofrenda, are standing at the door of the palace. The queen of Isla Mayor Oeste brought to the light five children, but only the oldest, Prince Chraxon Ok'un—my sister's murderer—and the youngest, Ix'ciel, have survived.

Like all men of the courts, the prince who ended my sister's life is hauntingly slender, almost skeletal. A parasitic, wormlike body bred to feed on the labor of others. A man whose hands are never soiled with the blood he orders to be spilled. His brother, on the other hand . . . is not what I expect. A head taller than every other man standing in the courtyard, Prince Ix'ciel looks like a killer.

"That's definitely Prince Ix'ciel," Brisa murmurs. I narrow my eyes at how breathless she sounds. But she doesn't notice, her gaze locked on the prince. I know he'd been brought to the light a year before I was born, but he looks like one who has lived many lifetimes in his eighteen years.

Ix'ciel's eyes are an unusual yellow that makes them appear like embers. Brown skin the color of mamey and a mouth that is much too lush and pink for a face so hard. His size and demeanor give him an air of menace. A wolf within a flock of sheep. He is dressed finely, as a prince of the court would, but on him it almost looks like a distraction from whatever weapons he's carrying under that regalia.

"I wonder if the rumors are true that the queen lay with one of the warriors of Isla Mayor Oeste because she feared her children kept dying due to the king's weak blood." Brisa's whisper echoes my own thoughts.

"He looks like a Sea Wolf."

"Brisa," Dismanda whispers, her voice full of reproach. "Are you trying to get in trouble?"

Brisa widens her eyes, seeming to realize the gravity of what she'd done. Speaking poorly of the royal family is a punishable offense. That is one way to mitigate dissent: silence anyone who dared imply that the royal family didn't live up to the perfect beacon of morality they claimed to be.

Without another word, we fan out in front of the king, our heads bowed, knees bent.

"Straighten, my sons would like to see your faces," the king commands, and we all obey immediately.

We stay like that for a long moment while the king and Prince Chraxon take stock of our party, while Ix'ciel observes the proceedings with disinterest from a few feet behind. Only two or three of us will get chosen, the rest sent back to Desecho. Dhany would have had the royals fighting over her beauty, but Dhany isn't here. I am.

I keep my eyes downcast but lift them slightly when Chraxon calls out the color of Brisa's dress. She looks scared as she walks toward him, shudders when his hands touch her face. The king calls for Estrella, who is tall and strong, with hair the color of the sunset. She holds her head high, but I can see her chin tremble with disgust as he pulls her closer. My stomach turns, and suddenly a wave of revulsion and fear almost makes me double over. What if I don't find him? What if I am not chosen? What if I am and I'm forced to face the king or one of his sons without a weapon to defend myself?

All at once the daunting realization of just how flimsy this plan is pummels me. Everything hinges on my being noticed and chosen and all I know is how to disappear. It will take a miracle for this to work. If I am not selected, I will be sent back to the Casa de Las Ventanas. I will not get a chance to reach my meeting point in the hall of portraits. I won't ever have my private audience with Prince Chraxon. As I struggle to center myself, a prickle of alertness makes me look up and I find myself staring right into Prince Ix'ciel's leonine eyes. "You in the yellow dress." I don't react; it's as if my feet are stuck to the ground. A shove to my shoulder snaps me out of my trance and I remember I'm wearing the yellow dress.

"Go," Dismanda urges. "Hurry." She pushes me so hard I stumble.

Prince Ix'ciel coaxes me forward so that I am standing only inches away from him. My heartbeat is a violent thud in my chest, so hard, so fast that I feel it between my temples, in my legs, in my belly.

"What is your name, Acayia?" His voice is deep and steady. He is so tall that I have to lift my head back all the way to look at his face. He is too handsome, and the swoop in my belly, the prickling in my skin is not disgust at all. I hate him for it.

"I am Somi, Daughter of Desecho." For a second, he seems surprised at my name; his brows furrow and he looks behind me at the Acayias who are left.

Prince Chraxon notices our exchange and turns his attention to his brother and me, his gaze bouncing between us. "You know very well not to select any until I've had my pick." His nasal voice grates my nerves.

"I thought you were finished," Ix'ciel growls.

The frail prince turns to me, his vacant eyes suddenly curious. "You seem familiar; has one of your kin been to an Ofrenda before?" His clammy fingers grip my arm and I wonder if he'd even remember my sister if I were to say her name.

A rumbling sound escapes from Ix'ciel. Chraxon lets go of me, but his eyes narrow into slits as he lifts his own head to glare at his younger brother. The animosity between the two men rolls off them in waves. There is no love lost between these brothers.

"I will have this one too," the older prince says, his hand flicking toward me. Then his mouth lifts into a sinister grin. "You can bring her to me yourself, since you seemed so taken with her."

I feel faint with relief at being selected. Now all I need to do is slip away from the group long enough to reach the meeting point.

"Well done," Dismanda praises those of us who were selected as the royals head inside. "You lucky few will be escorted to see the princes."

Dismanda gives us ten minutes to refresh ourselves before we are to meet our handlers. We are taken to a changing room inside the palace right above the hallway where I am to meet my accomplice. I am itching to go searching for him, but I make myself wait five minutes.

"I need some fresh air," I whisper to Estella, who is too busy reapplying makeup to look at me, and slip away.

I quietly make my way down the stairs, praying that I don't encounter anyone. I have the map clutched in my hand, but I've pored over it for so many months that I don't need it. I turn right, looking for the corridor holding the portraits of all the sugar monarchs. I force myself not to run as I spot the double doors I've been looking for. I just need to slip inside and my ally will be waiting. Just as I reach them, the right door opens and Prince Ix'ciel steps in front of me.

I clap a hand over my mouth to keep in the scream threatening to explode out of me. For an instant I indulge in a fantasy where I leap at him and scratch his eyes out. It helps, but not enough to make me sound anything but furious when I open my mouth. "What are you doing here?" I ask, jaw tight as I send him my most hateful look.

"It's my palace," he scoffs, and my already ramrod straight back stiffens further. "And I should be asking you why you're here."

His body is blocking the doorway completely, his wide shoulders almost brushing the wooden frame. After five failed pregnancies, the queen had given up on more children, but in her fiftieth year she brought Prince Ix'ciel to the light. Unlike his brother, who has always been frail and of ill health, Ix'ciel is the pride of Isla Mayor Oeste, strong like an ox with the face of an angel.

"You look nervous," he tells me as he looks down at the floor—or not at the floor. At the hem of my dress. When he lifts his gaze, I see something that had not been there before. Surprise and something else I can't quite pinpoint. "I was not expecting you," he tells me.

The prince is my contact? It can't be. I was supposed to meet with one of the Sea Wolves, with one of the prince's personal guard. This must be a trap. He's been made aware of our plan somehow and his guards are coming for me. I hear them, their heavy boots coming down the hall at a purposeful clip.

Run, Somi, I tell myself and try to get away, but Ix'ciel grabs me by the arms as the sounds of the guard get louder and louder. My heart is beating painfully in my chest as his strong arms lift me up from the ground, except instead of throwing me to his guards, he tugs me inside the room with him.

"Please. Follow my lead or all of this is over," he whispers in my ear as he sets me down against a wall. But my legs are unsteady, cold tremors zigzagging up and down them as I struggle to remain upright.

"Let me go," I cry in frustration. His hands are like vises. I can't move at all. But I have my feet, and I use one to stomp one of his, hard.

"I'm here to help you," Ix'ciel groans in frustration, his large body looming over me. His palms are pressed to the wall somewhere over my head and I realize he's trying to cover me from whoever is coming. My entire range of vision is him and I'm shivering again. I'm surrounded by a cloud of coconut oil and lemongrass. I feel faint and tell myself it's probably because his body is blocking the water from my line of sight. An Acayia must always be in view of the water.

"Liar, you're trying to debilitate me," I seethe. I hate him for being bigger, stronger, for having the power to destroy me with just a word. I hate him because no one so evil should be this beautiful.

"If I were, you would already be detained," he whispers, and I bite my tongue.

"Who's there?" a voice calls from just outside the door, and he sucks in a nervous breath.

I can see the panic in Ix'ciel's eyes; he doesn't want these guards to discover us any more than I do. And as he said, if he wanted to turn me in to the guards, he'd have already done so.

"They must be rounding up the Acayias for the private audience," I whisper, and he clamps a hand over my mouth.

"Stay quiet," he hisses against my ear, and my legs feel liquid again. Like I've just come out of the ocean. "If they suspect you, this is all over." I want to bite the hand keeping me quiet, but I know he's right. I can't go in to see Chraxon without a weapon. The weapon that Ix'ciel is here to give me. If they take me away now, everything will be ruined. Just then the guards burst into the room. I panic and grab the sides of his head, push myself up, whisper a breathy "sorry," and crash my mouth to his.

Thunder crackles around me.

My dry lips graze his and I can smell the sweetness of the mango he must have eaten earlier. I can almost taste his surprise, also something darker, electric. Nothing about this moment should be like that first plunge into cool, soothing water after hours in the hot sun. The guards' shouts are only a feet away from us, but Ix'ciel does not push me away. His big hand cradles my cheek as he parts my lips with his. Our breaths mingle and I tentatively tip my face, craving the connection.

It's my first kiss.

My first kiss is with the brother of my sister's killer. Nothing about this moment should taste like a bite of ripe fruit exploding on my tongue. Nothing about this night is supposed to offer desires and purpose beyond avenging my sister. The brother of my sister's killer is my accomplice. He pulls back from the kiss and makes sure to cover me from view of the guards.

"Get out of here," he roars at the men. "Can't you see I'm busy?" The indignation in his bark has the men retreating in a flurry of apologies while I lean against the wall, trying desperately to calm the beating of my heart.

"Well," I say with feigned cheer. "This was highly unpleasant, let's never do it again," I lie as I smooth the front of my dress in an effort to regain my composure once we are alone again. "The knife." I thrust my hand out. "They will be looking for me to be taken to your brother." The tremor in my voice hurts the delivery.

"You sound a little breathless, siren." He seems utterly unaffected by the kiss, which infuriates me. I bare my teeth at him, and he laughs in my face.

"Give me my weapon," I demand through gritted teeth. The gloating smile fades and his expression grows serious.

"You must follow my lead," he informs me as he pulls out something from under his jacket. A flash of light blue catches my eye and I gasp.

"My dagger." I am close to crying as he hands it to me.

"You can't be reckless like that again," he tells me, and shame courses through me. "And I will help you. I loved your sister." He grins at my look of surprise and points to the blade. "I recognized this. She always had it with her. She was also the only one who ever showed me kindness in this palace."

"Yes." I nod, mollified by his words. There was so much bad about Yemi's time in this place I'd forgotten the few crumbs of joy she experienced. She'd talked about Ix'ciel. Of how his brother mistreated him. I see in the flash of regret behind his eyes that he is telling the truth. I want to ask him what he remembers of my sister. I want to tell him she cared for him too. But instead focus on lifting my skirt so I can strap the knife to the harness on the inside of my thigh. When I finally glance up, Ix'ciel quickly turns his attention elsewhere, his face blushing.

"Are you ready?" There are moments one can never quite prepare for, even if it's what you've told yourself again and again will be the answer to everything. But my life and my revenge are in Ix'ciel's hands. I nod again and he quietly leads me out of the room.

The moment we step outside we almost crash into Dismanda, who looks extremely unhappy with me.

"I was showing the Acayia my family's portrait," he informs her in a haughty tone.

"Of course, Your Highness," the siren rushes to answer, her eyes downcast.

"My brother has requested I personally bring her to him." Dismanda doesn't challenge the dismissal, sending only a cursory glance to Ix'ciel's hand, which is on my shoulder.

"This way, Somi." A frisson of something I can't quite identify runs up my spine when he says my name. He speaks so close to my ear that I can feel his breath on my neck.

I follow him through the hall, the sounds of our footsteps echoing in the empty corridor. We arrive at a turret and make our way up the stairs.

"These are my brother's private rooms," he says ominously,

before leading me inside. It's a circular room with ceilings so high I can barely make out the frescoes. Prince Chraxon is lying on a nest of pillows with a few older Acayias by his side. None of them looks like they want to be there. The rest of his court must be waiting for him in the main hall, because there are only a few guards here and one adviser who is kneeling by the prince listening to what he is saying. Brisa and Estrella are shakily standing to the side. Yemi told me what happens in these "private audiences" and though I know it won't get to that, I feel sick with dread.

Ix'ciel's hand tightens on my lower back like he can sense my apprehension. "He won't get to touch you. But if you can't do it . . ." I shake my head.

"No, I promised I would do this." I am trembling with fury.

"And you will," he assures me. I don't have a single reason to believe him, but somehow, I do.

"Brother," Ix'ciel calls sharply, directing his gaze to the older prince. Impossibly, he looks even more sallow and ashen than earlier.

"Ix'ciel, I thought you'd put up a fight over me taking your pet." Chraxon's voice makes my skin crawl.

"Nonsense, brother. It is your party, after all." I'm a little impressed with how Ix'ciel manages to sound so rude, while technically saying the right words.

"Come here, siren," Chraxon says, and the way he looks at me makes me want to run. "I know who you resemble now." He smiles at me, and it turns my stomach. I don't want to move. I want to turn around and jump back into the water, swim away. But I have my blade. I can avenge my sister. My aunt. Every Acayia who had been used and discarded by these kingdoms.

I am scared.

"Look out the window," Ix'ciel tells me when I feel my legs start to weaken. His large hand is like a brand between my shoulder blades. I look to the water and feel my strength coming back.

Everyone's eyes are on me. All this attention on one Acayia. The princes sparring over some little siren will be the gossip of the court. Then I remember that what will happen—what I will do—in the next minute will be the only thing the seven kingdoms will speak of for a very long time. It will change the future of the archipelago.

"So you're the sister of that useless siren I was given," Chraxon says placidly. I want to lunge at him, but Ix'ciel's arm holds me back.

Keep your head. I hear my cousin's words as if she were here. I've thought about killing this prince every day since my sister died; I cannot allow my temper to ruin my only chance. "Come here, siren," Chraxon coaxes, his gaze dripping over me like thick, greasy sludge. Everywhere it lands, my skin crawls.

I shuffle forward and stop right at the edge of the ring of sand, the grittiness of it touching the tips of my bare toes. I can feel Ix'ciel's hot gaze on me. Although some sirens can sense the vibrations in a room, I never have. But even so, the space feels like a rope being pulled so tightly it's about to snap.

"Closer," Chraxon demands, his fingers summoning me. I hesitate at the request, but Ix'ciel pushes me forward, and I almost stumble. What if this is part of his plan? What if he's setting me up?

"I said come *closer*, siren," Chraxon roars, his voice wheezy.

I step toward him, my movements sinuous, but Chraxon pulls me roughly and I land on his lap. I immediately look up at Ix'ciel and warn him off. I can do this. *Let me do this*, I plead with my eyes.

"Your sister didn't have enough meat on her bones, that's why she didn't last." His breath is foul like rotten fish and I fight the gag at the stench. I close my eyes for just a second and I see my sister's face that last day.

I reach down and draw my blade, but Chraxon grabs my wrist hard and the knife crashes to the floor. I hear a commotion and see that two guards are now restraining Ix'ciel.

I've failed.

This was my chance and I've failed.

"Call on the water," Ix'ciel cries, but I am frozen. I don't know what to do. Sirens have been forbidden from conjuring the water for centuries. Doing so is punishable by death. Acayias were banned from the bigger islands because we had enough power to drown a city without a drop of water falling on the ground. It is powerful magic and not all of us have the strength in us. I have tried before and the water has never responded to me.

"I don't know if I can," I tell him, and he shakes his head in frustration.

"I know you can," Ix'ciel tells me, his eyes fierce as he fights off his brother's thugs. Beads of sweat run down my brow, the cords in my neck straining with the effort it takes to conjure the ocean up to this tower.

"What are you doing?" Brisa screams.

"I am bringing the waters." Two guards grab for me roughly, but Ix'ciel's broken free and rips me from their clutches.

"Chraxon and his father have taken so much from us," I yell to the Acayias. "We can end this," I plead, signaling to Ix'ciel, who is restraining the guards. I put my hands out and my sisters do the same.

And the waters come. We don't have to hold on for very long.

The gasping begins almost immediately, bulging eyes, and men scratching their necks as invisible water clogs their airways. The guards fight to breathe, and Chraxon claws at his throat. Three Sea Wolves climb over the window, like shadows of death, and descend on the prince and his men. It is as swift as it is deadly. They make their bloody way to the room, slaughtering the prince's cronies as they silently gasp for air. But the eldest prince is still alive, trembling with fear as I approach him. Ix'ciel is restraining him.

"I am your brother," he cries pathetically, but Ix'ciel only sneers.

"You are nothing to me." He then turns to look at me, then at Yemi's knife on the floor.

I grab it and move to strike.

"More guards will come soon. Finish it. I cannot," Ix'ciel urges me, and I stumble at his confession.

"I can't," I sob. I can't do it. I can't avenge my sister even when I am handed her killer on a silver platter. A tear rolls down my face, and I feel Ix'ciel's strong hand wrap around my smaller one.

"We'll do it together." His hand grips mine and we plunge the knife in together. I have to swallow the sick that rushes up my throat as Chraxon falls dead at my feet.

For a breathless moment I collapse into Ix'ciel's arms, tears pouring out of me for the first time since my sister died.

Then I remember where I am, that the guards must be on their way. That they will find all these bodies and we'll be executed. Because just as silently as they'd come, the Sea Wolves have gone.

"Go!" Ix'ciel shouts to Brisa. She hesitates, only for a moment, and leaps out the window and into the sea.

He stands between me and the window and I realize I've made

no plans beyond this. I didn't think I'd survive. I can't go back to Desecho, not after I've killed the crown prince. I can't stay here.

"My brother was just a warning," Ix'ciel tells me. "The revolution is coming. The revolution is waiting for us." He runs to one of the large windows above the ocean and extends his hand to me. I take it.

I let go of him for a moment and kneel to pull my sister's knife from Chraxon's chest. I wipe his blood on my dress and strap it to my thigh. I reach for Ix'ciel.

"I'm ready."

NOR'EASTER

Katherine Locke

The Great Nor'easter of 1962
Monday, March 5, 1962
Lem

There's a space between the shore and the deep ocean, where ships sit on the floor of the ocean, visible above the waterline at low tide, and entirely mine at high tide. The water's warm here, not the cold of the ocean, nor the heat of the shore where the waves break and the humans splash. We mers call this space the inbetween, and other mers try not to spend much time here—there's a risk of being seen, a risk of being hunted, a risk of being hurt, a risk of being stranded. Our myths say that once this was where we flourished, where we could come and go from land and sea at will. But as humans spread, so did their hunting, their fear, their dominance of the seas. And like the whales the humans still hunt, we went to deeper, colder, darker waters for safety.

I slip into the concrete ship off the shoreline, dragging my hands across its rough interior. It'd sunk here decades earlier and the humans had left it. It's hard to drag a concrete ship off the floor of the ocean, it turns out. Juno, Tobi, and I had turned it into our space. Our parents never came this close to shore, so used to the deeper ocean. It was just us younger mers.

Mama calls me rebellious, but I know she doesn't mean it. She just doesn't know what to do with me. *Rebellious* would mean leaving, and I know I'm not leaving, even if I want to. I've seen what leaving her pod did to her. I don't want to feel that way. She can't lose me—not after losing Papa. I'm staying here, even if it's risky. Even if it's not always safe. It has to be safer than elsewhere.

I keep telling myself that anyways.

Every year, being here feels more and more like being beached. Trapped with a name that isn't mine, in a body that feels foreign, that surprises me with what it does and does not do against my own will. Like trying to get into a sea I cannot reach, stuck in a place that's too hot, too sandy, too exposed.

I'm not leaving, though. Where would I go? Everyone knows this is the safest place for us mers. We've been chased from everywhere else.

Juno shows up first, Tobi right on her fins. Juno's been my best friend since we were too small to swim by ourselves, and Tobi joined us a few years ago. When I'm with them, I don't feel beached. I don't always feel like myself, but maybe I don't know myself enough to know that yet.

Juno pushes hair off her face, her gills bright pink down the sides of her neck. If she kept her hair short like other mers, it wouldn't get tangled across her face or irritate her gills, but she likes it long. It's almost to her tail now.

"There's a storm coming," Juno tells me. "A big one."

"She's been going on about this the whole way around the Point," Tobi complains.

Juno's sensitive to the water's changes, but she's not always right. In fact, she's rarely right. She gets it right about 30 percent of the time. Still, 30 percent is better than I'd get if I attempted to guess the weather, so I try to listen to her. Tobi's less patient than me.

"Like a hurricane?" I ask.

Juno scrubs her face in frustration. "I *know* you're going to say hurricanes don't come this early in spring."

She's right. That is what I was going to say.

"The water's not warm enough," I say to try and support my argument.

"I *know*." Juno is annoyed. Tobi must have been shutting her down the whole way around the Point.

Tobi rolls her eyes at me. Her hair sticks up in tufts all over her head. If Juno cares too much about her hair, Tobi cares too little. They're opposites. And yet, they don't seem to find their endless bickering exhausting. I do. Sometimes.

Juno draws on the rough hull of the ship. "There's two tides."

"We know," Tobi says dryly.

"Tobi," I warn.

Juno draws with a shaking finger, a circle to the left, and then to the right, overlapping. "There are two storms, coming on the different tides. This is where they're going to collide."

I frown. "When?"

Juno shakes her head, which pulls her hair across her face and gills again. "Tomorrow. Day after tomorrow. Soon."

She talks like this when she gets anxious. In short, choppy sentences like waves ahead of a storm.

"It's a new moon tomorrow," I say quietly.

We all know the moon phases like the back of our hands.

This makes even Tobi pause. New moons, like full moons, make for stronger tides, more intense tides. The water comes faster on a new moon.

Juno's head bobs.

Tobi swears and then says, "Juno, we were supposed to have fun today. This is aggressively not fun."

I'd almost forgotten that tomorrow's my birthday, the first day I'm allowed to leave our pod and find a new one if I wanted. I'm the oldest of the three of us. I think they're both watching me to see what I'm going to do.

But I keep seeing Juno's fingers circling to the left, then the right, and the way her hands shook. A shiver goes down my spine. Something feels off. I don't think Juno's wrong about this one.

"Come on," Tobi says. "Let's go harass some dolphins."

She swims out and Juno and I are left in the ship.

"I know I'm right, Lem," Juno says softly. It sounds like a question, though.

I bump my tail against hers. "I believe you."

But still, we follow Tobi.

Tuesday, March 6, 1962
Cape May, New Jersey
Lidia

The rain starts in the morning. It isn't like rain in March is unusual. We don't think much of it. We're used to it now. We've lived in Cape May for the last two years, part of a wave of immigrants who moved here to work the Jersey Shore when people came for the summer. Only we stay year-round, like the nuns at the Point, and like the fishermen over on the Bay.

There are not many Poles down here, but we try to pretend we don't care, that we're American now and we can fit into American society. That isn't true—Mama doesn't speak English very well, and so she relies on Papa, Helena, and me to translate for her. The boys understand Polish but don't speak it. They were all born here in the United States. The boys are American. Papa's English is perfect, with almost no accent now. It's Mama, Helena, and me stuck in the inbetween, pulled between Poland and America, between the two languages, the two customs, the two traditions. And these days, it feels like Helena's leaving for America too.

My younger brothers Julian, Marek, and Antoni are running around in the backyard while Helena and I help Mama in the kitchen. We plan on having the Indyks over for dinner, and even though we can't afford it, Mama likes to pretend we can, so we will have roast chicken, roasted potatoes, cabbage, roasted vegetables, and more.

"I won't have anyone saying that Piotr Miodek cannot put food on the table for his family," Mama says.

Papa always could put food on the table. But this dinner feels extravagant.

"We'll start the paczki just before supper," Mama tells us.

"I can't," says Helena, staring intently down into the gravy she is stirring.

I stiffen next to her but say nothing.

"What do you mean, you *can't?*" Mama demands.

"I told Gregory that I'd see him this afternoon." Helena glances sideways at me and I hold her gaze. Her eyes beg me to speak in her defense, but I cannot. This is where it feels like she's forgotten the way we were raised. I haven't. Not yet, anyways.

"Gregory Smith? You are still seeing this boy? No. I will not have it," Mama says, slapping the table with her flour-covered hands. "You will be with your family for dinner. Your father's home for dinner tonight!"

Helena's mouth tightens, even with the bribe of a rare dinner with our father. The only person more stubborn than Mama is Helena. I bite my lip, knowing what's coming. I just hope Helena doesn't use her ultimate insult to Mama, when she says, *this is America, not Poland*. It cuts Mama right to the bone.

"I'll be home for dinner, but Lidia will need to help you with the paczki," Helena says calmly, steadily.

I'm surprised by her tone, surprised enough to see my cue, and take it. "I'd be happy to, Mama."

In truth, I hate making paczki, and Helena knows it, but this is the role of the middle sister. Peacekeeper.

Mama just grunts, like she knows she lost the fight, and mumbles to herself. Helena throws me a quick smile, and I try to return it. She goes back to stirring, and I go back to chopping the vegetables, listening to the rain batter at the windows.

Tuesday, March 6, 1962
Lem

The dolphins are nowhere to be found.

"Boring," Tobi declares.

But I wonder if they've gone to sea, past the storms. Dolphins and whales, they always seem to know things the way that Juno knows things, but they don't share the information with us mers. We have a tenuous relationship with dolphins and whales. I like whales better—they're naturally good-natured. Dolphins. Dolphins are dicks. That's why we like to harass them. It usually comes back to bite us in the tails, though.

We're by the Point, where the sea meets the bay, and I can see the humans walking down the road that leads from the lighthouse northward. I wonder where they go. We can go deeper into the sea, below the storm, or out to sea, past the storm. Where do the humans go? Does the land go farther than I can see? How would they get away from the water?

"What about the humans?" I ask.

"What do you mean, what about the humans?" Tobi asks.

"We can't talk to the humans," Juno says in a quick, tight voice. "It's against the rules."

So is her long hair; and my name, which is different from the name I was given at birth; and the way I like to be addressed; and Tobi's obstinance. There are a lot of rules we ignore, just to get by.

"But where will they go?" I ask.

"We don't even know there's a storm coming," Tobi points out.

Juno sighs. "It's coming. I know it is. I'm not wrong, Tobi."

"We can go deep into the ocean or way out to sea," I argue. "Where do they go?"

"It's not our problem," Tobi reminds me. "They like to spear us and eat us."

"Tobi," Juno admonishes her.

They're delicate around me, when it comes to this. Since Papa's death.

But still—he wasn't speared here. These humans hadn't been the ones to spear him.

I don't know why I go so close to shore when that's exactly what got my papa killed, but he was killed up north, and these humans have always seemed oblivious. They barely notice the sharks, much less us.

We live here peacefully by not drawing attention to ourselves. We live here peacefully because we stay below the radar, playing by the unspoken rules that we don't exist and humans ignore us, the way we ignore them.

"They're not made for the sea," Juno says.

"But we are," Tobi says. "And we have to protect the pod."

I don't want to draw attention to the pod. I don't want to get into trouble. I don't want to get killed. But it doesn't seem right, when we know something is going to happen, to keep that news to ourselves.

Yet when Juno tugs at my fingers, I let her draw me away from the shore and the oblivious humans walking into the spring winds.

Tuesday, March 6, 1962
Lidia

Before I went to bed, after the Indyks left, after the last paczki was eaten and everyone's fingers and faces were covered in powdered sugar, Papa kissed my cheek and squeezed my hand. "I'm going back to the hotel."

I paused, gripping his hand. "But the storm, Papa."

He gave me a wan smile. He worked so hard at the hotel. He had started there as a bellman, carrying people's bags, and now he managed the hotel. It was the quiet season, but they still had guests to care for, even over the winter.

"Someone must care for people during the storm, maleńka,"

he said. "These guests—they do not know how temperamental the ocean can be."

I kissed the top of his head. "Be safe. Close the shutters on the windows."

"Of course," he said with a smile. "Help your mother with the boys."

I gave him an eye roll over my shoulder, but with a smile, so he knew I didn't mean it, unlike Helena, who hadn't come home from Gregory's house for dinner. "I'm always helping Mama with the boys."

"I know," he said.

Outside, the winds began to howl.

Wednesday, March 7, 1962
Lem

Mama is teaching one of the little ones how to crack open mollusks. They're trying to use their head instead of the rock. She's laughing, and my heart aches. I haven't seen her laugh and smile at me in a long time. When she looks at me, all I see is the worry in her face.

When I slide up behind the baby, I wrap seaweed around my hands and tickle their belly, surprising them, and they shriek with laughter. Mama smiles affectionately when I pull them backward into the water and we wrestle beneath the waves.

We finally surface and Mama says, "That's enough now."

She sends the merling off to play with the others. She's still watching them disappear into the fading sun when she says, "Something's worrying you."

I am a bad liar. I gave up trying to lie to her face a long time ago.

"Juno thinks there's going to be a bad storm," I say quietly.

Mama frowns. "It's spring. Hurricanes don't come in the spring."

"A big storm that isn't a hurricane," I clarify. "Maybe you should move the merlings farther into the marshes. Just to be safe."

She looks alarmed. "Closer to shore?"

It goes against everything in her bones, everything she's lived through, everything our ancestors have lived through. I know this. I know that every scale and scar and fin and gill and bone and inch of flesh on her trembles at the thought of shore as safety.

"Just think about it," I suggest again, even though I know there's not a lot of time. Maybe, when it's time, she'll remember my words.

"You think too much of shore," she says quietly. "It worries me."

Sometimes I wish she'd worry less and love me more.

There's no point in explaining that I don't think about shore too much, that I just like the warmer inbetween waters that she avoids.

She's almost moved away from me when I ask her, "Do you think, if it's a really big storm, somehow we should warn the humans?"

I know the moment it leaves my mouth that I should have let it be. It's a sore spot for her.

She doesn't like to think that I'll make the same mistakes she did.

"It's spring. The storm will not be so bad," she says. "You're overreacting."

She says that a lot. That mers of my age are dramatic. That

we're overreacting. That in her day—and that's when I tune her out. The tides are changing.

I wish she could see that.

Wednesday, March 7, 1962
Lidia

We can't go to church for Ash Wednesday. We can't leave our house.

"This is a storm," Mama says softly as she and I stand in the kitchen, washing the last of the dishes from Fat Tuesday. The way she says it, I know she means, it's a *big* storm.

"I didn't know it was supposed to be this bad," I admit. "The radio didn't say anything."

I listen to the radio and read the paper, both in English, and share relevant news with Mama. I don't share all that I know. She doesn't like to hear about war.

"It'll pass," Mama assures me. "You know these storms. One day max. At least your father's safe at the hotel and Gregory's mother called me to say Helena could stay."

I can hear the disappointment in Mama's voice, but I know she's grateful too. She hadn't heard from Helena until this morning, and she'd managed to keep her worry and anger in check when talking to Gregory Smith's mama. I couldn't tell if she was madder that Helena had disobeyed her, or that Gregory isn't Catholic. He is Presbyterian. Mrs. Smith might as well have said he was born on the moon as far as my mother was concerned.

"The boys should work on their piano," Mama murmurs.

I take the hint. "I'll call Antoni down."

She gives me a wan smile, one that betrays her worry. "Thank you."

Antoni plays piano just fine. Nothing special—Julian is the most talented of the boys, but he has no heart for it—and it is easy enough to correct him without paying much attention.

Mama hadn't wanted to move to the shore. Her parents were miners back in Poland. She wanted to move somewhere like Pittsburgh, West Virginia, somewhere with cold and coal, like she was used to. Papa was born in Warsaw, and he'd been a mathematics student before the war. When he came here, he was just another war refugee—he couldn't get a job teaching and no university would accept him. This was the only job he could find. Mama does the laundry and cleans houses for the summer folk down here.

I've never seen her go into the water. Not once. None of us knows how to swim. Everyone else down here learns how to swim, if only for safety's sake, but Mama won't let us. She is terrified of the ocean, of the water.

And as I sit there and correct Antoni's fingers on the keys, tell him to slow down and do it again, I keep my attention on her, watching her as she stands at the kitchen window, gazing out over the water that begins to crawl in little waves into our backyard.

Wednesday, March 7, 1962
Lem

Juno doesn't gloat when she's right.
There is no victory in being right.
The waves rise and rise.

Eight, ten, fifteen feet.

And then they double in size. Thirty.

Forty-foot waves.

We can't dive deep enough. Mers hold on to their merlings and each other, creating chains of mers getting tossed around in the surf. I can see Tobi with her parents and her siblings, and Juno with her sister, everyone knotting together the best we can. I hold on to my youngest sibling, duck my head into my mama's shoulder like I'm young again, too young to swim off by myself, young enough to be shark bait.

It feels like the sea is fighting us, fighting us like we're the enemy, like we're not made from the sea itself.

Something hard scrapes against me, bumps into me again and again as the waves batter at us. I twist, seeing a piece of painted wood in the water. It's just a piece, the length of my hand. We see things from the humans all the time in the water and don't think much of it.

But then the water around us begins to fill with debris. Human debris. Radios and dresses, shoes, a car tire, a picnic basket, the sign from a shop, empty bottles, and full crates.

Juno's words float up to the surface of my mind. *They're not made for the sea.*

We don't cross paths with the humans. Not when we can avoid it. Same way we feel about the sharks off the coast. Like the humans, they come for warmer waters. And like the humans, they aren't exactly friendly.

But it irks me. The letting them sit there to be swept out into the ocean. The waiting for the inevitability of death. I've heard stories from when my parents were merlings, of a time when the ocean was full of explosions and bodies. One of the first stories my father told me when I came of age was about the first time he saw a drowned human. And I remember the look on his face.

Most mer had done nothing. It was a human war, not a mer one. We'd enough trouble of our own, they'd said. Not our war. Not our dead.

But Mama had told me another story.

She came from a northern pod, up where the waters were frozen year-round, where the people hunted whales and seals and sometimes mer, where the days were long or short and very little in-between.

She told me of a story where an explosion took a boat and broke it in half. Of human children in the water. And she'd saved one, because she looked like my mother's little sister who'd been lost to an orca when she was a small merling.

Mama had been in trouble with the pod. She'd been punished. Banished. Sent south to warmer waters that scalded her scales. She'd been alone until she found our pod who'd taken her in, though she had different customs, though she had different names for seaweed and whale. Words she refused to give up, traditions she passed down to me and my siblings.

It's why she's afraid I'll lose my pod. Because she lost hers. And it crushed her, I think.

A thunderous crash rolls through the ocean. Not a wave, but something different. I know what it is.

Wednesday March 7, 1962
Lidia

Antoni, Julian, and Marek huddle between Mama and me in our parents' bed. Rain puddles on the windowsills and on the floors, and there's a bucket at the foot of the bed where the roof is leaking. We barely fit in this bed together, but we're holding on to each other like this bed will be our salvation.

The wind howls, drowning out the sound of my mother's prayers, and the boys whimper, Antoni holding my braid in his fist. It hurts, but I can't bear to tell him to let go, especially since I'm holding on to him like the wind might snatch him from my arms. Last autumn, we'd seen a single hurricane, Hurricane Esther, and she'd been nothing like this. This storm's relentless. There's been no lull, just a constant pounding on the house from all directions.

The wind takes a shutter off the house with a bang and Marek screams into Mama, setting off the other two boys.

Mama strokes Marek's hair and whispers in Polish, a tongue some of us are already forgetting, "Have you heard the story of the three princes?"

They quiet, listening to her tell the familiar story. I can only think that she's run out of prayers.

Wednesday, March 7, 1962
Lem

I thought that the humans would be in the ocean. That isn't exactly true.

It's more like the ocean came to them.

I've seen storms up and down the shore my whole life, and I've never seen anything like this. Not one. The waves are relentless. They come so fast I'm exhausted just rounding the Point. The beach is eroded all the way through South Cape May. The water beats sand into our faces, cutting our arms and cheeks. Debris pummels us—roofing tiles and boards from the sides of houses and the boardwalk, plastic lawn chairs and umbrellas.

When I swam away from Mama and grabbed Juno and Tobi, they'd come with me without question. I guess that's the thing about best friends. They'll be there when you need them, without questions.

The thing that we understand, because we live in it, that humans do not understand, is that the ocean takes what it wants, when it wants. And there is nothing anyone can do about it. Humans think they are exempt from this, that they can somehow thwart water just by standing on the land.

First the ocean takes the places where the humans play.

Then the ocean takes the places where they walk.

And then the ocean takes the places where they live.

No one's above the water.

A sign floats by. HOTEL.

It's winter, though. There couldn't be many guests at the hotel. In the summer, it'd be full, but they evacuated the town during storms in the summer.

We swim past.

Wednesday, March 7, 1962
Lidia

The water reaches the back steps by 9 A.M. The kitchen by ten.

"It's the tide," says Mr. Indyk when he and Mrs. Indyk arrive at our doors, soaked to their chests. They live on the first floor of the house around the corner. There are three apartments in that house, and we all know that the families above them don't like immigrants.

"Of course," Mama says. "Come in."

The three boys, Mama, the Indyks, and I sit upstairs. The three bedrooms are small—they aren't designed for three adults, one near-adult, and three rowdy boys under the age of eleven. And by now, Mama's soothing stories and prayers and the sanctuary of huddling under a quilt have lost their allure.

"I want TV," whines Antoni.

"There's no TV," mutters Julian.

"Antoni, why don't you practice the piano?" I ask, finishing a drawing of piano keys on a piece of paper.

"I don't *want* to practice piano!" shouts Antoni. "I want to watch TV."

"There's not any TV—" I begin.

Mama grabs his arm and shakes it.

I yelp. "Mama!"

Mama hisses right into Antoni's face. "The TV is underwater. If you go downstairs, you will be under the water too! Do you want that?"

We all fall silent. I stare at Mama, at her grip on Antoni's arm, at Antoni's scrunched-up, flushed, tear-puckered face. The Indyks look anywhere else. Julian and Marek stare at the ground, shock written on their faces. Mama doesn't lose her temper—not like this.

"Mama," I whisper again.

She lets go of Antoni. Her hands shake.

The wind screams at the house, and the whole structure shakes violently. It feels as if it is swaying. Mama begins to pray again, and Antoni clings to me. I wrap my arms around him and close my eyes, wondering if I should pray too but not finding the words. What did God have to do with a storm?

"It wasn't supposed to be a hurricane," cries Mrs. Indyk.

I do not tell her that this is not a hurricane.

Hurricanes do not come and stay for days.

Hurricanes roll up the coast, a storm on a road trip.

I lift my face from Antoni's hair and look out at the blackened sky.

This storm is not ceasing. It will never end.

Mr. Indyk goes to the front window, overlooking the ocean. He peers up and down, like he can see anything outside.

"There are cars," he announces. "Floating down the street."

Then his shoulders still.

"Jan," says Mrs. Indyk. "What is it?"

"Nothing," Mr. Indyk says in the tone that adults use when they mean something is very wrong but they won't say it in front of the children.

"Jan," says Mama, stopping mid-rosary. "What is it?"

Just before he speaks, I know what he is going to say.

"The hotel," he says softly. "The hotel is in the ocean."

Mama. She screams.

Me, I push Antoni into Mrs. Indyk's arms, and I run down the stairs.

I run into the water.

Wednesday, March 7, 1962
Lem

The farther we follow the water, the harder it gets to swim. The water rises slowly as it goes in, and it's begun to withdraw for low tide. We can't risk being beached, not this far in, especially among the people and the debris.

I don't know why we're here.

But leaving the humans to die, just because once they'd hunted us, that doesn't sit right in my stomach.

Mama was exiled from her pod for saving a human.

I could be too. I don't want to be. Juno and Tobi wouldn't come with me. I don't think they'd leave their families for me. And I'd get that. I love my mama and my younger siblings.

But I think of an ocean full of bodies, like my parents remember.

And I don't think that we should see an ocean like that again. Not if we can help it.

Juno tugs my hand, pulling me to the surface. She and Tobi have clearly had a conversation I missed.

Tobi shouts, her gills at the line of her throat flaring red with inflammation. "We can't go farther. It's too dangerous."

I don't care. "Tobi. Please." I turn to Juno, reaching out to take her hand and squeezing it hard. "Juno."

She hates to be the tiebreaker and I can see it in her face.

Just then, maybe fifteen feet away from us, a girl—a human girl, about our age—staggers out of a home, right into water that is as high as her chin. She flounders, arms flailing in every direction, and those legs. So many limbs. But not enough limbs to save her.

She falls into the water, right next to fish and ducks.

She never even gets a chance to scream.

Wednesday, March 7, 1962
Lidia

I'm underwater, and seawater fills my mouth, choking me. I open my mouth to scream, but it's just water, and water, and more water. When my arms flail, they hit debris. My dress catches around my ankles and I kick furiously. But something's pulling me underwater, my foot's caught.

Then thin fingers and strong hands come under my arms and I'm hauled bodily out of the water back onto the land.

I gag and retch seawater all over my rescuer. I gasp for air, chest heaving, and push my hair out of my face. Papa. I have to get to Papa.

What I see stops me in my tracks. Three—people. Beings. They have human but slender faces, and wide, glassy eyes. Their necks are ribbed, flaring red and pink, like a fish gasping for air on shore. Their torsos are bare, and below their torsos—

Fins. Their bodies melt into scales and then finish like fish tails.

I'm staring; I know I am.

"You can't swim," snarls the one with short-cropped hair closest to me, maybe my rescuer. "What are you thinking?"

"Papa," I whimper.

Their faces, already quite sickly pale, blanch.

"Where's your papa?" asks another with long jet-black hair that pools around her like machine oil in the water.

"The hotel," I whisper, staring past them at the destruction. "I am dreaming. I have drowned. Haven't I?"

Behind me, I hear someone scream. Mama's climbing into the water, screaming for me. My mama, in the ocean. For me.

"Mama," I cry. "Stay inside."

"Where's your father?" asks the demanding fish-person in the front, the one who'd saved me.

"The hotel," I say, desperate. If this is a fever dream, I've had worse. If I've drowned, perhaps I'll see Papa again.

"Stay inside," says my rescuer. "Stay. Inside. We'll bring him back to you."

I believe them. I don't know why. But I do.

I stagger through chest-deep water back to the stairs, pulling myself up by the railing that's starting to pull away from the wall. Through the kitchen window, I can see those—I don't know what they are. Half fish, half people. Something out of a fairy tale, or a little painted ceramic sold along the boardwalk.

I pause on the stairs, watching as the three of them dive into the water, their fish tails flipping above the sandy, wreckage-filled water briefly. And then they're gone.

Gone, I think to myself, desperation filling my chest. *Gone like Papa.* But I can't think that way.

At the top of the stairs, it's Julian who pulls me into the room. I flop onto the floor in my soaked dress, breathing hard, while my mother falls to the ground beside me.

"I can't lose you too," she sobs into my wet hair.

"They're going to save him," I whisper.

She doesn't hear me, but it doesn't matter. They promised. They promised they'd bring Papa back to me. To us.

Wednesday, March 7, 1962
Lem

The hotel is not quite in the ocean—but it isn't far from it. It's drifted three blocks, onto Beach Avenue—if Beach Avenue hadn't fallen into the sea. There are no more bicycles, no more umbrella vendors, no more vendors, no more little shops selling their wares that would be left too close to the sea's edge so when high tide came, it'd take those little tchotchkes into the sea.

Juno swims in the lead, her knowledge of water and waves and tide guiding us through the wreckage toward the hotel. The water is higher, rougher, now. The waves seem to come one after another, colliding on top of each other like they are in a rush to connect to the bay, to wipe Cape May right off the map.

"The storm's getting worse," I call to Juno.

She doesn't stop swimming. "I know. It's the third high tide of the storm."

❦

The hotel teeters on its side, its foundation swept out from beneath it from the storm. I heave myself onto the porch.

"Hello!" I yell. I hear nothing in return. Not one human voice. Just the wind and the waves.

"Lem," says Juno softly. "I don't hear—"

"He's got to be here," I say, desperate. I heard the human girl. She spoke in one language to her mother, another to us. She is in-between too. And I know the feeling of being willing to drown to save someone. That's why I'm here.

"You can't take something back from the sea," says Juno.

"He's not dead!" I yell in frustration. I roll over, sitting up and pushing myself to the edge of the porch. The water surges up and down the porch, but my fingers dig into the wood and I do not let it move me.

"He's not *your* father!" Juno cries out.

The storm slows, quiets, and it's just the three of us hanging onto a half-collapsed, sea-eaten human structure.

Juno looks pale and rattled. "Lem. I'm sorry."

But she's right.

Before I can answer, a voice comes from inside the hotel. "Yes? Hello? Please help us!"

"Did you hear that?" I ask Juno and Tobi.

Wide-eyed, they nod. We flip ourselves back into the water and swim around the building, holding on to the cedar siding and gripping the windowsills, trying to see into the half-collapsed structure.

"Hello? Hello?" we call in unison, our voices bouncing off the sounds around us.

"Yes! We're here," a man shouts back. "Please help! Someone's injured!"

We find them in the rear of the hotel, clinging to a door half torn off its hinges. A man with sandy-colored hair and kind, but desperate, eyes, and an older woman, with a deep cut on her forehead, and a leg wrapped in rags. She doesn't look like she's fully conscious.

"Thank you," gasps the man. "Where is your boat—"

He freezes, seeing us.

I grimace. "Sir—"

He doesn't move.

I can't speak.

Suddenly Juno is there behind me, her hand squeezing my hand. "Your daughter sent us. We can get you home safe."

The man wipes his brow, adjusting his grip on the woman. "My daughter?"

"Lives in a house over there," I say, pulling words to my tongue again, pointing in the general direction. "Blond. Doesn't know how to swim."

The man inhales deeply. "Yes." He stares at our fins, at our tails, at our bodies. I want to crawl under a rock, sink into the sea, and never surface.

Then he half drags, half carries the woman closer to me, handing her off. I wrap my arms around her, and she screams and struggles but the man says, "Evelyn, please. Please. Just let them help you."

The woman just sobs.

The man looks at us and says, "I'm Piotr. This is Evelyn."

"Lem," I say.

"Juno," says Juno, reaching for his hand.

"Tobi," says Tobi, taking his other hand.

"Thank you," Piotr says again. "Thank you."

Thursday, March 8, 1962
Lidia

The power goes out, sometime after Papa and Evelyn make it back to the house. By midnight, we don't have any fresh water. No heat. We're cold, and wet, and the water rises overnight and through the midmorning up to the top of the stairs. We have nowhere else to go.

But then it begins to recede.

Slowly.

One hour at a time.

One stair at a time.

By the afternoon, we can make it into the kitchen. Everything is ruined. The walls, the carpet, the furniture. All the food we had in the house. Everything is gone. The Indyks go home. They've lost everything too. The boys can't stand it in the house anymore, so I take them on a walk.

We're the highest point in Cape May now. Six hours ago, we couldn't leave the second floor of our house, and now, the water is everywhere but our street. The damage is immense. Houses with no foundations. Streets just gone. The hotel is out at sea. The Convention Hall teeters on the edge of the pier. The sand drifts in waves, cut by the sea and the wind, nearly up to Washington Street.

I look everywhere for the mermaids, but I see no sign of them. Surely there'd be mermaids beached somewhere, washed up by the storm. But it's like they don't exist at all, like they never existed.

Papa had just given me a knowing look when he came home with the hotel's receptionist, Evelyn, with a wounded leg. He told Mama that someone with a boat had rescued him, but I could tell—it'd been the fish people.

Helena hasn't come home yet, but a neighbor came around this morning to tell us that the Smiths lost power and their phone was down, but Helena was safe. Mama seemed relieved after that, like she could actually rest and sleep. She only let us go out once she knew Helena was safe.

"What are we going to do?" asks Julian, looking around the town. He sounds grown up all of a sudden, like he's twelve and not ten. Antoni and Marek kick storm trash down the street, laughing. Resilient.

"I don't know," I say truthfully. The hotel is gone. I don't know if we can clean up the town enough for guests this summer. I put my hand on his shoulder. "We'll figure it out."

He gives me a doubtful look, but he nods. He's still young enough to trust me when I try to make him feel better with half-truths.

"What really happened?" he asks suddenly.

"With the storm?" I ask, confused.

"No. You went outside, and you came back soaked, and an hour later, Dad came home. What really happened?"

"He was saved," I tell him. "Some brave people who could get through the storm."

He gives me another one of those looks.

A half-truth is not a lie.

Friday, March 9, 1962
Lem

Three days. Five high tides. Spring equinox, and two tidal systems. A perfect storm. That's what Juno calls it. A perfect storm.

When I swam back to my family, my mama kissed my cheeks once, twice, three times, four times, as if convincing herself I was real.

"Mama," I whispered. "I'm sorry."

"Brave," she called me. And then she said, for the first time using the name that I chose, and not the name she gave me when I was born, "Brave, brave, Lem."

On Friday, the ocean feels like herself again. The waves roll up on the shore in a steady, relaxed manner. The ocean water is clear, without the murk of sand and debris.

Juno, Tobi, and I go out to the concrete ship. We dive and explore, even though we know every inch of the ship. I think we just want to know that this, at least, hasn't changed. This, at least, hasn't been changed. Because everything else has been.

The shape of the shoreline. The feel of the Bay. Where we live has a deep scar cut through it, and it doesn't feel like anything is going to be the same again.

Finally, we're there too long. I can feel the awkwardness about to build.

"Come on," I say. "Let's go find some dolphins to harass."

"Boneheads of the sea,"Tobi says cheerfully.

"Pretty sure that's us," says Juno.

We swim away from the wreckage of the ship and the shore. It'll still be there when we come back, along with all the things we haven't said. But that's for another day. Another tide. We've made it through the storm.

Together.

❦

The Great Nor'easter of 1962 was a real storm that devastated the Eastern Seaboard of the United States, destroying thousands of homes and lives. The effects of the storm can still be seen on the coastline today in what's there—and what is not.

THE FIRST AND LAST KISS

Julie Murphy

"**D**o you think it hurts?" I asked. "To always have legs?"

On the last full moon of our Wander Year, I lay on the beach alongside my twin brother, the water lapping over our fins as we watched the moon travel across the sky. I'd walked on land before. We both had. Twenty-three times to be exact, and tonight would be our twenty-fourth.

Titus squinted up at the stars sparkling through the velvet curtain of night. "I don't really spend a lot of time thinking about lesser beings or those who choose to live like them. I'll simply be glad when this is all over."

There was something there, under his voice and directed at me, that I couldn't quite decipher—disgust, perhaps—but that was always the case between me and Titus. Our whole lives, everyone constantly told us how lucky we were to have each other and what a special bond we shared. As twins, we should have been perfectly in tune with each other.

But Titus was always a mystery to me. There was the Titus the world saw—the one who could charm and set everyone at ease, just like our father and king. Then there was the version of him that lurked beneath the surface. Everything he said had a double meaning, and very few caught on to that duality.

The moment I realized I could never fully trust or know my own twin, my cynicism spread like a disease and soon went from an inkling to a certainty. We were still so young. Five or six, maybe. Our governess lost her favorite hairpin, and when I found it, Titus said we should leave it or she might think we stole it. Then, just hours later, he returned the pin and reaped all the reward of something we were both starved for: affection.

Our father always said we were different sides of the same coin. My fascination with the human world was balanced by Titus's disgust. His white-blond hair, which he kept swirled back into a serious bun, was the opposite of my dark black-blue mane that swept behind me like the kind of seaweed that could kill a man.

Titus didn't like me; he tolerated me. Or maybe he hated me. I sometimes thought our father did. It was my birth that killed our mother, his one true love, after all. I was the surprise twin that sent our birth from difficult to dangerous.

We were opponents before siblings.

"Do you feel that?" Titus asked, his voice more vulnerable than usual. He hated this part when our bodies existed on a frequency that wasn't quite human and not quite merperson.

Thrill coursed through my veins, but my brain didn't have the ability to untangle my thoughts into a response for him, because the tip of my fin had begun to tingle. I forced my gaze to the sky as heat rolled up my body with such great force that it ached. Twice a month, for the last year, I'd relished this change.

Wander was a yearlong tradition. Every month had two Wander Tides, when all young merpeople between the ages of seventeen and eighteen would experience a transition from fins to legs—but only for the night. Just a handful of hours to experience life as a human for twenty-four nights.

The Wander was meant to guide us in truly appreciating our way of life and to understand our neighbors, and sometimes enemies, on land. It wasn't so simple or safe either. Every night away from the water was a risk. If you didn't make it back by sunrise on any of those twenty-four nights, you could never return to life below the surface and every memory of your life would blur until it didn't exist at all. Some missed their return by accident and others were fully aware of the choice they'd made. On the rare occasion when a merperson chose not to return, their decision became a blemish on their family's honor. But nevertheless, each merperson had a choice—consequences and all.

Tonight was our eighteenth birthday and our last Wander Tide. It was my one last chance to choose a different life. After that final tide, my fate would be sealed. But because I was a princess and second in line to the throne, my choice was a formality. I *had* to return home. My fate was sealed the moment I entered this world.

But I couldn't help but wonder. I couldn't help but imagine what my life on land might look like.

Titus hated how far I strayed from the beach on our Wanderings, but over the course of twenty-three nights, I'd found myself drifting further and further away from Titus and the watery depths we called home.

As I looked down to see my fin transform into legs, Titus reached for my hand, his grip strong and almost threatening.

"Happy Birthday, Ulla," he said without a hint of cheer in his voice.

On my first Wander night, I spent a lot of time wobbling through the sand. Most of that first time was spent trying to trust my legs to carry me. But the glow of the boardwalk motivated me to overcome my fear.

I'd watched the boardwalk from afar for so long, with its glowing Ferris wheel and constant stream of people, their laughter rolling over the waves. I was so fascinated to know what drew in crowds night after night. It reminded me of the times when I'd seen something shimmering on the ocean floor. It would glint and wink as the sun danced over the current above, and I would chase after it—sometimes for hours—only to find out that it was nothing more than a discarded piece of trash from the shore.

I didn't have to imagine the lights and the sounds any longer, though.

Now I knew them by heart. The smell of the warm nuts and sickly sweet cotton candy. The bright lights glimmering into a blur. And the cacophony of laughter and thrill-seeking screams. I wondered if the memory of it would sting when, after tonight, the best I could do was float beneath it and eavesdrop from below.

I left Titus on the beach, perched on the same bench where he'd spent nearly every night on land, waiting like a pouting child for the sun to rise. He transformed involuntarily like we all did and refused to go inland and explore.

But I had plans much bigger than sitting and waiting for the sun to meet the horizon.

I stepped onto the boardwalk, noticing my clothing, which always seemed to adjust based on my body's needs. Tonight, there was a chill in the air as the warm months were coming to a close. The black cotton of the dress hugged my ample hips and round belly, and my feet were clad in black boots that made me want to furiously stomp my feet. Much better than the flip-flops I'd had on the last few times. And the word *flip-flops*? What silly human had decided on that word?

None of it *felt* real, though. My fingers slipped through the fabric like mist and then crushed against the nautilus around my neck. Titus and I had been given gifts on our first birthday. His: the trident, and mine: the nautilus. Each gift came with power and responsibility, both of which neither of us had fully explored. According to my father, though, the nautilus represented the voice of the people. When I listened carefully, I could hear the whispers and songs of our people. Since the nautilus was small and discreet, I'd brought it with me on land, but Titus's trident would cause too many questions, so he always left it under the surface, which only added to his disgust for our time here.

Not only was he without his precious trident, but we also looked human. Like Titus and the rest of our kind, my skin's purplish shimmering undertone had faded into a bluish pale. I looked human enough to pass. By moonlight at least. And my normally sharp teeth appeared dull . . . and safe.

Meandering down the boardwalk, I tried to soak up every noise and smell that I knew I'd miss. That first night, my senses had been so overwhelmed. It felt like someone had reached into my head through my ears and squeezed my brain. It was something

I never could have prepared myself for. I'd never realized how quiet it was below the surface, but this noise . . . I had to wonder, how was it ever quiet enough for humans to find their own thoughts?

Now, though, as I pushed deeper into the throng of humans, I forced myself to feel every little sound, smell, and sight.

I searched the crowd for Poppy, the nerves in my stomach turning into a jumbled frenzy. She'd said she'd be here, waiting for me. Where was she?

As I drew closer to the Ferris wheel, I found a line of people wrapped around the base.

The pit of my stomach lurched as one by one, they filed into tiny carriages that took them from the bottom of the wheel to the top and back again. Being that high up in the sky was unnatural.

I heard a familiar laugh.

And then I saw *her*, and my heart lit up like a carnival game.

Over the years, I'd watched Poppy for as long as I could remember. The shores of my family's territory were full of bright lights and mechanical rides and a perpetual rotating crowd of humans. But unlike most humans who found their way to the beach during the warm months, Poppy came back almost every day. This place was her home. Every week a new flock of people would appear, and within a few days, the only trace of them would be the debris they left behind. Bottles, cans, and the occasional discarded children's sand toy.

Poppy was constant. Even when the water was much too cold for her. As a child, I found it fascinating to observe any human who looked to be the same age as me, but Poppy especially. As she grew up, so did I. Sometimes, watching her felt like looking through a mirror at a different version of myself.

She'd called herself a "townie" when we first met, and said she'd never gone farther than her bike could take her. She felt stuck. Like me. She lived with her mother and she'd once told me that their life together felt like two strangers who'd been thrown into the same place at the same time.

Titus and I never knew our mother. All we knew were the pieces of her our father chose to share. It was never the full picture, and it wasn't like what I'd observed of Poppy and her mother.

From afar, just beyond the sandbars, close enough to watch while still a safe distance from the beach, I could see that Poppy loved her mother even though she shouldn't. Poppy would race into the water with a shriek, the waves splashing against her thighs. She'd call to her mother, begging her to look for just a moment.

"Over here!" she'd say before diving under a wave. "Mom! Look!"

But Poppy's mother was always a bit too far away in more ways than one. Whether she was nose-deep in a book, sipping on a glass bottle filled with amber liquid, or tethered to a man whose gaze was already drifting to his next pursuit, she was never fully there.

That never stopped Poppy from calling to her mother over and over again until one day she was old enough to go to the beach by herself.

"That human girl is going to drown," Titus had once said. "Father says the young humans are too brave and too dumb for their own good."

And I quite liked how reckless that sounded. Whether it was true or not, it was enough to make me want to be there to catch her if the waves ever became too violent.

Over the years, I'd seen her come to this beach in tears and in joy and at times in desperation. One night not long ago, I spotted her standing in the waves, fully clothed as the moon soaked her fragile shoulders. It took every bit of self-control not to circle her like a shark.

And then we met. I'd had every intention of searching for her on my first Wander Tide, but she beat me to it. I sat in the sand, still trying to understand the mechanics of walking, when she plopped down only a few feet away. My heart thundered in my chest. For so long, she'd felt as distant as a story. But she was here. She was real.

Her eyes were watery when she turned to me and said, "Does it count as being broken up with when you were planning on breaking up with them first?"

"Sounds like a draw to me," I said, something in my belly tickling.

Her long auburn hair slid over her shoulder as she nodded. "What are you doing here?" she asked. "Only sad people go to the beach at night when it's cold out."

"I'm not sad," I told her. "Yet. That could change at any moment."

She turned to me with a snort, and we talked for a little while longer before she took me to the boardwalk and demanded we order hot chocolate, which remained my favorite human delicacy.

The thought that tonight was the last time I'd see her up close made me ill. I wanted this night to last forever.

She wore frayed shorts and a lavender shirt cropped just above her belly button. Her light auburn curls were a halo around her head.

And then she saw me.

"Ulla!" she called as she waved her arms over her head.

I shuffled through the line of grumbling people to meet her.

"You came," she said as she hugged me, her arms wrapped around my waist in a way that made my throat go dry.

"I said I would," I told her, feeling a little stung that she expected anything less. It wasn't like she could just call or text me, though, and there was really no good way to explain why I was here so randomly and for only a night at a time.

"It was getting late. I thought I was being stood up." She looped her arm through mine and we slithered through the line.

Before I knew it, Poppy was pulling me toward her friends. "Ulla, you remember Izzy and Veronica, right?"

"Izzy," the tall one said, and then pointed to the shorter girl curled into her side. "Veronica."

They both smiled over their shoulders before leaning into each other and whispering softly. I knew them both from previous Wandering nights and they always reintroduced themselves as though we'd never met. It was a power move I recognized from the courts at home. Still, I didn't mind either of them, though I hated to share Poppy with them, tonight of all nights.

"I'll wait over by that bench while you go for your ride," I told Poppy, pointing to a cluster of picnic tables with young people covering every surface as they passed cigarettes and slushies back and forth.

"Oh." The word fell like a single raindrop.

The man at the front of the line pointed Poppy and her friends toward the open metal door, the carriage swinging and creaking on its hinges.

Titus was right. Humans were too brave and too dumb.

"I don't like heights," I explained. "But I'll be close by."

I stepped toward a small opening in the fence hemming the

line in place. I'd barely be able to squeeze my hips through, but it was better than riding this death wheel.

"I won't be long," she said as she began to slide in beside Izzy and Veronica.

"Sorry," the man told Poppy. "Only two people at a time."

"Oh," she said. "I'll . . . uh, just wait here."

"Or you could ride solo, Poppy," Veronica offered. "Unless you're afraid."

Izzy frowned, her brow pinching together, before her gaze found me. "What about you?" she asked as she pointed to me. "Can't you ride with her?"

Poppy turned to me sheepishly. "Pleeeeeease. I've been their third wheel for the last three months."

The man operating the ride looked to me. "Well, what's it going to be?"

I looked up. Bile began to rise in my throat. I'd watched this Ferris wheel my whole life and never during my last twenty-three Wandering nights had I found the courage to go for a ride myself.

But this was it. This was my last chance.

And it was with Poppy.

"I'll—I'll ride with you," I said, the words out of my mouth too quickly.

"Yes!" Poppy howled.

The man grunted with a shrug and stepped aside for the two of us.

Following behind Poppy, I did my best not to look up. I settled into the seat beside her, my hip pressed against hers. The space was narrower than I expected, but she didn't seem to mind the proximity. The man lowered the bar over our laps and hit a red button, sending us up. My heart ricocheted in my chest.

Ahead of us, Izzy turned and waved, making their seat swing chaotically.

The air on land already felt thinner than it did below the surface, but as we began to move, it felt even thinner and I couldn't inhale and exhale fast enough. I thought being up here with Poppy would be fine, but I couldn't untangle my thoughts enough to think about anything other than my body hitting the boardwalk with a splat.

"Are you okay?" Poppy asked.

I quickly nodded *yes* and then shook my head. *No*, I was not okay.

She turned to me. "I'm so sorry. I shouldn't have let you come up here. I didn't realize you were so scared of heights. I thought it was just like . . . I don't know . . . a quirk. Like, I'm scared of butterflies, but not in a way that makes me panicky . . . Actually, I don't know that for sure. I've never been in a swarm of butterflies."

"You're scared of butterflies?" I asked breathlessly.

"Like you have room to talk," she said as she leaned over. "We're, like, five feet off the ground right now. Maybe six. If we jumped, you'd probably land on your feet."

"You have too much faith in my balance," I told her.

The wheel began to move slowly, much too slowly.

I squeezed my eyes shut, hoping that might somehow trick my mind.

I'd spent so much of my life skimming the lowest surfaces of this world, and yet the thought of floating above it was too much. All I could think of was falling so hard I would never wake up. Surely that wouldn't happen. Surely humans wouldn't willingly get on this giant metal wheel if they often plummeted to their deaths. But if a mermaid died during their Wandering, they were truly dead. There was no magic strong enough to escape it. Under the surface, our life expectancy was triple that of a human's and our bodies were much more durable in the salt water. But on land, we were as delicate as humans. Titus despised feeling so powerless, and I found it thrilling in a way. Except for this exact moment, when all I could think about was falling to my death.

"Okay, now. You're okay," Poppy said. Slowly, her fingers slid over my knuckles as I gripped the bar on our laps. "God, I really am so sorry. We can sneak into the arboretum and you can lock me in the butterfly exhibit next time I see you."

I'd been waiting for her to hold my hand since we met during my first night on land, and I hated that it had only just now happened to ease my fears. My pounding heart began to slow enough that I no longer felt blood rushing in my ears. "You certainly apologize a lot," I finally said.

"Excuse me?"

"Just now." I held my eyes shut still. "And before, with your friends. And then two weeks ago when the ice cream scoop fell off your cone. You apologized to the sidewalk."

Her hand began to pull away and I clapped down with my other hand so she couldn't move. "It's helping," I said.

"The first apology was for MY SHITTY FRIENDS!" she yelled the last part up at them. "And the second was for my shitty mouth. And the sidewalk apology was more for the people who would have to walk through my shitty ice cream."

"Shitty?" I asked. Father had gone to great lengths to make sure we were well versed in the human behavior and language native to our coastlines. *You can't defend yourself from what you don't know.* But *shitty* was new to me. "What's so *shitty* about your friends and your mouth?"

She laughed quietly. "My friends are shitty because they fell in love and now I'm just their spare tire."

"Spare tire?" I asked.

"Their third wheel," she supplied.

I nodded. Even though I couldn't make exact sense of the phrase, I thought I understood the meaning.

"And my mouth is shitty because I never think before I speak."

Finally, my breathing slowed long enough for me to open my eyes. We swung in the wind, and I shuddered, my hand tightening on Poppy's before forcing myself to let her go.

"Strong grip," she said as she shook the circulation back into her fingers.

"Now it's my turn to say sorry."

"Let's call it even," she offered. "So you've really never been on a Ferris wheel?" she asked. "Maybe some secret Ferris wheel trauma I don't know about?"

I shook my head.

"A tall building? A mountain? A ledge?"

"This feels . . . different," I said, half lying.

There were plenty of mountains and ledges hidden under the surface of the ocean, some so impossibly huge that humans would be terrified to know they even existed. But that was the magic of the sea and perhaps why my kind had survived for so long: Humans only believed in what they could see. To them, the waters were a bigger mystery than they could ever fathom, and if they only knew, they might realize how insignificant they truly were. And Father always said that humankind feared nothing more than insignificance.

"Well," Poppy said as she stared out into the thick, dark waters, "it's an honor to watch you face your fears, Ulla. If you asked me,

I'd say you weren't scared of anything. But I like this. I like knowing something can crack your shell."

"My shell?" I asked, my fingers instinctively running over the nautilus around my neck. "What shell?"

"Oh, come on. Mysterious Ulla who appears randomly out of nowhere!"

"It's not random. I told you . . . my parents are divorced. We come to see our father when he has time for us. And I'm here tonight, aren't I? Just like I said I would be."

"You won't even give me your phone number," she said with a pout. "If Izzy and Veronica hadn't seen you too, I might wonder if you were even real."

The wheel stopped, and Poppy must have seen the panic in my eyes because she quickly dropped her frown and said, "Don't worry. We're not stuck." She peered over the edge. "Just loading more passengers. We are at the very top, though. If you're going to look, now's the time."

I shook my head. "Just being up here is enough."

"Oh, come on. You're really going to put yourself through all of this and not take in the view?" She held her hand out for me to take. "We'll do it together."

I inhaled deeply through my nose and took her hand. A calming warmth spread from the tips of my fingers at the touch of her skin. Our shoulders had brushed. Our fingers had grazed. And we'd even shared brief hugs, but being near her was always intoxicating. And holding her hand made my rib cage feel like it might splinter.

"Okay," she said. "Let's do this."

For a moment, I'd forgotten where I was and why my pulse

had been racing to begin with. All I could think of was our hands intertwined.

I peered over the edge onto the dock and there was something familiar about watching all these people from a distance as they milled about in their own little universes. The bright lights from the games were a blur, like a setting sun on a calm sea.

On the other side were my familiar waters. How many times had I found myself under this exact dock despite my father's warnings of it being much too close?

Just then a gust of wind swung our carriage forward and I let out a yelp.

Poppy pulled me to her and held me in her arms, a wild laugh ripping through her chest. The wheel began to descend, and I let out a sigh as the ground grew closer.

She sat back with a grin and said, "At least we didn't get stuck this time."

"You've been stuck on one of these?" I ask, my eyes bulging.

She snorted. "This thing gets stuck a couple times a week. At least."

The moment we touched down to the loading platform and the man running the ride lifted our lap bar, I stumbled off the ride as quickly as I could.

All around us, food stands and games were closing up for the night, rolling down metal grates and tying down thick tarps.

"Where are you two headed?" Poppy asked her friends.

Izzy turned to Veronica as she bit down on her lower lip.

"Somewhere dark?" Veronica asked her. "Somewhere quiet?"

Izzy nodded eagerly before turning to Poppy. "What about you two?"

Poppy turned to me, swaying on her feet. "Wherever the night takes us?"

"Lead the way," I confirmed.

"We could go back to my place," Poppy said. "My mom probably isn't home."

"Okay," I agreed as Veronica and Izzy drifted ahead of us.

"Are you here with your awful brother?" Poppy asked.

"Sadly," I said with a laugh.

"Does he always scowl that hard? Didn't anyone ever tell him his face could get stuck like that?"

"That sounds very scientific," I told her as our shoulders brushed.

"Where exactly does your dad live again? Is he renting one of those beachside cottages? They're the only rentals on my side of the island that aren't apartments," she said. "They're just down the street from me."

I nodded. My very flimsy plan since we first met was to let her fill in the details and just follow along.

"What exactly does your dad do again?" she asked.

"Uh, I guess . . . sort of like a manager."

"Wow," she said. "You're a steel trap, huh? How have I known you for almost a year and I could count on one hand how many things I know about you?"

I wanted to know everything about her, but that would never happen if I didn't give a little, and if tonight was really my last night, what did I have to lose? "My dad is . . . in the family business. My brother and I are supposed to take over, but I guess I'm not really interested."

We turned off the dock onto a dark stretch of boardwalk that ran along the beach where Titus and I had been just an hour ago.

"Ulla!" an approaching voice called. Even without his fins, I recognized his silhouette.

"Maybe he just has resting scowl face," Poppy said with a giggle.

I laughed, but it came out uneasy. "Stay here," I said as I gently pushed her under a small pool of light shining onto the walkway from one of the many beautiful houses lining the boardwalk. "Don't move." I'd never trusted Titus with anything I loved in sight.

"Okay . . . ?" she said uncertainly, which was fair, but there was this pulsating need inside me that had to have her in my line of sight, as if I could somehow protect her here on land when I was completely out of my element.

"Let's go," Titus said once he was within a few feet of me.

"What? Go where?" I whispered.

"Home. I'm over this. What's the point of waiting out these last few hours?"

"But we have until sunrise."

"Nothing says we need to actually stay until then. This whole Wander thing is ridiculous, honestly, and as soon as I take Father's throne, it'll be the first thing I abolish."

My chest burned with the kind of ferocity that scared me. The kind of ferocity that could tempt me not only to not follow him home right now but also to challenge him. I couldn't imagine a world where my people didn't have this chance to decide for themselves. To choose a life at sea or on land. And how arrogant of him to even assume he'd have the power to do such a thing.

"I'm not going," I told him, feeling suddenly small. "I'm not throwing away this chance."

"This chance for what? To live as one of them for just a few more hours? Hasn't it been enough this last year? What more is there to see of this pitiful existence?" He peered past me to Poppy, whose fingers hovered over her phone as she bit down on her lower lip. "I knew you'd go searching for her."

"She has nothing to do with this," I told him in an even voice. Titus had a long history of taking everything I cared about. Toys . . . friends . . .

"Maybe you can be her little pet," he said. "Or maybe you think she's worth never coming back and forgetting your entire life for."

"I'll be back by sunrise," I told him, even if the words felt more untrue than ever.

"Fine," he said. "I'll see you at sunrise." He shoved past me, and his gaze followed Poppy.

"I can't believe that's your brother. You two seem so different." She stepped out of the little spotlight where I left her. "He looks like drama."

"My twin," I told her.

Her eyes widened. "You're an onion! Endless layers."

I grinned. I'd tried an onion one night at a produce stand. It was incredibly potent and I'd later found out they weren't meant to be bitten into.

"The Fabio hair is great, though," she said.

"Fabio?" I asked as I watched Titus disappear into the darkness.

"Yeah, he was on all those old romance-novel covers back in the day. My grandma has hundreds of those paperbacks."

I watched as she kicked a rock down the boardwalk.

"Actually, I still have her whole collection," she said. "If you still want to come back, maybe borrow one . . . or something. I promise I'm not trying to murder you or anything."

"Is that how most hunters lure their prey?" I asked. "With romance books?" I'd always been fascinated by all the people reading on the beaches of our shore. We had our own forms of story-telling, of course, but books were one of those human possessions that never survived in the ocean long enough for us to properly inspect and appreciate.

She laughed in a haughty sort of way. "No, I'm pretty sure murderers don't use romance novels to trap their victims, though it would certainly work on me. And my grandma."

"I've never read a romance novel," I told her as I followed her off the boardwalk and right down the center of a completely empty street. I'd thought about lots of things in the years leading up to my Wandering Year, but I'd never imagined what the world looked like beyond the boardwalk. Seeing it the first time was a little disappointing. The ground was so hard and all the buildings—some were uniform and others looked like little nests. Signs in the windows. Trinkets in the yards. But now, on my last night, I felt the same sort of fondness I felt for goblin sharks or monkfish. They were ugly, but in a way that charmed me.

"You should borrow one of my books," Poppy said. "It's not a trip to the beach if you don't have a book to read."

"I don't know when I'd be able to return it."

"Grandma always said never lend anything you expect to get back."

"Well . . . I guess I'd like that very much, then."

I followed Poppy for a little longer until the salty ocean air was faint enough to be a memory. The building she led me into was crumbling with chipped paint and windows blurred with years of grime. She led me up a few flights of stairs until we stopped in front of a door labeled #432.

"My apartment," she said. "If my mom's home, she's passed out on the couch, so we'll have to be quiet walking to my room."

I nodded, and she unlocked the door.

Inside was a collection of stacks. Boxes, books, magazines, clothing, cups . . . I'd never been in a human's home, but Poppy's made me feel confined and stifled. The air was musty and the television cast a glow on her sleeping mother, who I immediately recognized. From far away, she'd always looked so beautiful and effervescent, but sprawled out on her couch, all I saw was smudged makeup and a tray full of used cigarettes.

Poppy took me by the hand when she noticed me looking, perhaps a little too closely. At the end of the hall, we walked into her room and she sealed the door behind us like a vault.

Poppy's small bed was perfectly made, and the collection of books she'd promised me was organized by color rather than by subject or alphabetic order—which was a chaotic little detail I couldn't help but treasure.

She kicked off her shoes and invited me to sit down next to her on the ground. The room was so small there was no way around our bodies touching in some sort of way with every move we made.

"Sorry," she said. "I still can't believe the landlord counts this as a bedroom."

"It's nice," I told her, even though I only meant it about her room specifically, and mostly because she was in it.

I watched as she rifled through stacks of books to curate a pile for me. I couldn't decide how to break it to her that it wasn't possible for me to take any of these with me.

"You don't have to go back to your dad's if you don't want to. You can stay the night here," she said after a while. "No offense, but your brother sort of seemed like an asshole."

Asshole was a word I *did* know. "That's a good way to describe him."

"Why was he so upset?" she asked.

"It's our birthday," I explained. "And I think he had a different idea of how he expected tonight to go."

She slid a stack of well-loved paperback novels toward me. "It's your birthday and you didn't tell me? It's like you keep totally pointless secrets for no reason. Well, consider these books my gift to you!"

I examined the pile. Lots of bare-chested men and even one about merpeople. The cover showed two lovers who were much glossier and lovelier than anything I'd ever seen below the surface. That's not to say my people weren't beautiful. We were, but in a vicious sort of way that was meant to lure in our prey . . . much like I'd done over the last few months with Poppy. And it didn't even require my using books as bait. I grinned to myself.

"I know they look silly," she said. "But I love them. Romance novels promise a happily ever after, no matter what. I love the formula of them and how I'm still surprised in so many ways. It turns out there are endless ways to tell the same story. Besides, no one shits on Jason Bourne or James Bond for doing the same thing over and over again."

"Not silly," I told her, avoiding the fact that I had no idea who those men were. "Thank you."

"Did you think about what I said . . . about staying here tonight?"

"How long do you suppose it is until sunrise?" She had no idea what I was truly asking. How much longer did we have left?

She looked at her phone. "Maybe four or five hours. I can sleep on the floor. You can sleep on the bed. Or we can just squeeze onto the bed together."

"I think I'd prefer to squeeze in with you," I told her.

"The bed it is!" She stood and changed her clothes, so I trained my gaze to the floor, but at my core, I'd always been rotten, so I stole a glance or two at her spine and the curve of her breast.

"Do you want to borrow anything?" she asked. "Something to sleep in?"

"Uh . . . I'm fine in this."

She threw me an oversize T-shirt anyway. I watched myself in her dusty mirror as I moved to peel off my dress, expecting my fingers to slip through the fabric, but instead it moved with me.

I watched my reflection in the small mirror on the back of her door, marveling at the wonder of my own human body even if it was just an illusion. I tugged on the borrowed clothes. Even though I was round in all the places she was concave, it fit.

She lay down with her back pressed into the wall and held the blanket open for me to crawl in beside her.

"Everything okay?" Poppy asked through a yawn.

"Yes," I said as I lay down beside her with a smile, our heads sharing one single pillow.

I turned to my side and made no effort to hide how closely I watched her as she wove in and out of sleep while we talked about the kinds of things that were easier to say in the dark.

She told me about her mother and how Poppy was certain she was never meant to be a mother, but she loved her nonetheless. It was the kind of love that hurt. The kind of love that felt like it was suffocating you the more you let it in.

I told her about my mother and how I didn't know her very

well. Even though the truth was that I didn't know her at all. I told her about my brother and my father—as best I could at least.

Poppy was turning eighteen soon and she'd been saving for a van to travel the country.

"We'd make good travel partners, I think," she said through a yawn and fluttering eyes. "If I could ever get you to tell me all your secrets. Or at least your phone number. That'd be a good start."

I looped a strand of hair behind her ear. "Go to sleep," I told her. "My secrets will still be there in the morning."

She nuzzled her forehead close to mine, and my heart began to stutter in my chest. "Not without a kiss," she told me.

A kiss! And who was I to deprive her?

I'd dreamed of kissing. Of being so close to someone that the only way to draw them closer was to press their lips against yours. And above all, I'd dreamed of kissing this girl. My Poppy. My brain lit up like the lights on the boardwalk as she leaned in closer.

Poppy's soft lips brushed mine, and maybe it was too much too fast, but I'd never forgive myself if I missed this opportunity. So I slid my tongue against hers as her hands gripped my hips, pulling me closer to her in a surprisingly urgent way.

"I've waited a long time for this," she said in a breathy voice.

"I guess you've been taking notes from all those love stories." My lips grinned against hers as I pulled back just enough to leave a trail of kisses along her jaw and down her soft neck that begged to be bitten.

Poppy let out a quiet moan that slipped into a yawn. "If I fall asleep, will you promise to pick up where you left off when I wake up?"

"Yes," I said without thinking twice. "Yes. I promise."

And I meant it.

I'd thought about what it might mean to choose this life. But it had never felt real. Not once. Lying here with Poppy, though, I could imagine an entire life. And that was always my trouble. I could easily see the future, but never my place in it.

Until now.

If waking Poppy up in the morning with a kiss meant leaving my life behind—one that was so fraught to begin with—I'd happily never breathe in the scent of salt water again.

Poppy kissed my nose and turned so that her back was pressed against my chest. She pulled my arm around her waist, and I immediately tightened my grip on her.

"Good night," I whispered.

I thought I would be satisfied to just meet Poppy. And then once I'd met her, I had to *know* her. Now she'd been my first hand to hold. My first lips to kiss. But all these firsts just made me want seconds.

It wasn't enough to have memories of her.

I had to have *her*.

I stayed awake all night, preparing to say goodbye to my life below the surface. How could I ever dream of returning to the sea when Poppy was right here with me? The thought of letting go of my family and our way of life felt impossible. But suddenly the end of my story that I'd known so well for so long was disintegrating like a book drifting to the seafloor. Excitement fueled by uncertainty ballooned in my chest as I lay there with Poppy breathing softly at my side, her cheek resting on my shoulder.

When the sky began to leak with light, I untangled myself from her and slipped my boots back on, taking a moment to wiggle my toes once more. I pulled the dress over my T-shirt so I didn't have to part with her scent even if we'd be reunited soon.

I owed Titus a goodbye—or maybe I owed it to myself. At least he could tell Father and the rest.

Poppy's mother was still asleep when I left, along with the rest of this little seaside town I'd soon call home.

As I turned the corner off Poppy's street and onto the boardwalk, Titus was nowhere to be found. In the distance, I saw a splash, but otherwise, the morning sea was calm. Surely, even if he'd already returned to the water, Titus would come back ashore for me.

I sat down in the sand far enough away that the water wouldn't touch me. I didn't want the ocean or her magic to have any confusion when it came to my decision.

As I leaned back on my elbows, I wondered how my memories might slip away. Would it be gradual or all at once? Would something about this beach always feel vaguely familiar? And how would my brain fabricate a past rich enough for me to believe?

"Ulla!" a voice cried, cutting through my endless uncertainties. "Ulla!"

I jumped to my feet and spun around.

"Ulla!" This time it was a panicked shriek. One I knew.

"Poppy?" I called, terror rippling through my chest. "Poppy! Where are you?"

"Ulla!" she screamed again, and this time I knew exactly where it was coming from.

In the distance something splashed again. But how could she possibly be out there when I'd left her in her bed just moments ago?

Titus. He must have taken her.

"Let her go!" I shouted at the sea. At my brother. Hot tears spilled down my cheeks. "Give her back to me!"

A devious chuckle rolled across an incoming wave.

"Ulla!" she screamed again, her voice cracking, and that time it broke me.

The sun hadn't pushed over the horizon yet. Maybe there was time. I could get her and make it back to shore in time.

I walked straight into the water, and it took my body a moment to adjust to the motion as the waves grew taller and angrier, slapping me in the knees and then the chest, nearly pulling me under.

But my legs remembered that they were never legs at all as I dived headfirst under a wave and began to swim. Her muffled screams drew me farther and farther until finally I surfaced just past the sandbar.

I shielded my eyes as I squinted into the sun.

The sun. Oh god. It had crested the horizon.

"Poppy!" I screamed from the pit of my stomach.

"Ulla?" a soft voice called. "What are you doing out there?"

"Poppy?" I could see her then, so far away and on the beach. "But I thought . . ."

Just ahead of me, Titus surfaced, his lower body underwater while he leaned against the sandbar. "Handy little toy," he said before dropping my nautilus shell in the sand.

I reached for the cord around my neck where I wore the shell day after day, but of course it was gone. He'd taken it, perhaps when I was distracted by Poppy on the boardwalk.

"It mimicked her voice beautifully, don't you think? I wonder what else it can do that you've been hiding from me."

Fire seared inside me as I dived for him. I afforded myself a brief glance down. My human clothes had deteriorated and all that was left was my iridescent black fin. My skin had returned to its soft purple undertone.

It was too late.

Before I could surface, Titus was there, waiting for me, his hair billowing in the water and his deep turquoise fin glittering in a patch of sunlight.

In a show of furious power, he pushed his trident through the water and stopped me, suspending me and every living thing near us in place. "She will have no memory of you or the nights you shared. You must know that this is for your own good."

"I decide," I said through gritted teeth. My breathing was shallow and moving enough to even speak was a task. "I decide what is good for me. You stole that choice from me. You stole *her* from me!"

"You're not just any merperson, Ulla. Neither of us are. As much as I hate to admit you might be important, I need you. How am I to rule if my own sister were to reject our way of life?"

"I don't know," I spat. "Your throne isn't my problem."

"Yes, it is. It has been since the moment you were born. And you and your stubborn will have been its biggest threat." He freed me from the grip of his trident, my body crumbling against the current. "Gather yourself. Father is waiting for us." Then he disappeared into the depths below.

My body began to sink, the weight of my sadness pulling me down.

Before I drifted even farther, two eels curled around my arms and carried me up to the sandbar to retrieve my nautilus shell—my gift and my downfall.

"Don't forget me," I quietly sobbed as the realization of what had just happened ripped through my chest. I'd never walk the boardwalk again. I'd never find Poppy waiting for me. She'd never tease me about keeping secrets. I'd never read her romance novels or sneak into her room. Every single one of our firsts would be our lasts.

In the distance, Poppy was there on the beach. She'd already begun to trudge up the sand to the boardwalk. I nearly called for her, but there was no doubt or uncertainty in her step.

Whatever memory she had of me was already gone.

Ugly sobs tore through my lungs, and hot tears cascaded down my face as I lay back in the sand, the water washing over my fin, claiming me.

One day, after the sadness passed, I would destroy Titus for what he'd done. I would carve the joy from his world until he was nothing but a rotting fish carcass. I promised this to myself, and I would never, ever break another promise again. Eventually, I let the waves pull me away farther and farther from the beach and the sandbar.

The sea held my tears, but it would never be wide enough or deep enough for my rage.

THE MERROW

⚓

Zoraida Córdova and
Natalie C. Parker

JOSIE

Ever since I was little, I've loved going to my mother's work. Though if anyone asked, I'd deny it. It's bad enough my friends at my old school lovingly referred to me as "Josie Aguilera, Fish Girl." No one wants to be called Fish Girl, no matter how many times they tried to convince me it was a "superhero" name. You don't see Fish Girl fighting beside Aquaman and Namor in comics, do you? Anyway, it's the only thing from my old life I don't miss.

My new life revolves around the Sea Life Kansas City Aquarium, which opened a new extension to its facilities last year. As I file out of the yellow cheese bus, I squint at the harsh glare coming from the sleek structure better suited for New York City than the Missouri riverbank. This building, this job is the reason my mother uprooted us for a two-year contract in the middle of nowhere.

Technically, *technically*, everywhere is in the middle of somewhere. Since I lost the family vote on relocating, I've done everything I can to protest our extended stay. I even dyed my black hair the pale turquoise of sea glass, nearly poisoning myself from the amount of bleach it had taken, but my mother's face in the morning had been worth it. Doctor Beatriz Aguilera did not usually react. She was of the parenting school of thought that believed giving kids attention meant losing the war. It was a sort of "take the high road" mentality that I did not always believe in. And if I was going to miss my old friends and old city and old school, then everyone would feel it. So when my mom pursed her lips and her left eye twitched at the sight of my new hair, it felt like winning a small battle.

I asked her for a ride, but she made me take the bus. It felt like her own silent retaliation for my new sea-blue hair. I tell myself it doesn't matter, because I love spending the day in the aquarium. It beats sitting alone at school because, hey, guess what? Being the new girl sucks hairy monkey butts. Being surrounded by kids who've known one another since preschool doesn't help. But field trips give me the opportunity to wander on my own. That is, until Mr. Lee assigned us each a buddy, and I was the odd girl out.

"I guess you're my buddy," Mr. Lee says, and grins at me.

"I guess," I mutter, wishing I could bury my head in my vintage jean jacket like a turtle.

"Come on, Mergirl," our science teacher teases me as we file in through the security checkpoint.

I suppose "Mergirl" is better than "Fish Girl."

Beth, a very peppy intern who has come to dinner a few times, is already waiting for us inside. Her tight brown curls are pulled back into a cute, puffy ponytail, and her navy blue polo has a silver stitched mermaid tail above the breast pocket.

"Hi, everyone. Hi, Josie!" Beth cries out. Everyone turns to me at the same time, squinting like they've never seen me before. Sounds about right. "Your mom is so excited that you're here, and so you're going to get the VIP treatment at our state-of-the-art aquarium theater."

Some of my classmates perk up when she spells out V-I-P. Others don't look up from their phones.

I smile at Beth awkwardly and follow the intern deeper into the cool, temperature-controlled aquarium. The aquatic entrance tunnel is filled with shimmering fish in a rainbow of colors darting this way and that. My classmates point at the massive hammerhead drifting right above us, its row of sharp teeth a threat despite its captivity.

But that isn't the main attraction, or the reason my family relocated to Kansas City. No—that is all because of the merrow.

As Beth lets us into the first two rows of the enclosed theater, I pick the seat right at the edge and hold my breath as the lights dim. The enormous wall-to-wall tank is illuminated from within. There isn't much inside, some greenery and a cluster of stone slats. The music is ominous, like the roll of thunder, and a haunting melody that reminds me of movies about ships going down in the middle of a sea storm. Beth gives the same speech my mother does at the parties and dinners she's thrown at our new house.

"Morgan, the merrow of the deep, was found by Irish fisherman John McCool." Someone snickers at the name, but Beth presses on. "He called her a merrow—after the Irish legends of creatures we call by dozens of names all over the world. From the Ottawan stories of Mennana to the Ukrainian rusalkas, Mami Wata from the African diaspora to the Lorelei of German legends to the green scaly beasties from Japan. Even the nagini of South Asian myths."

"Myth no longer," I whisper the words at the same time as Beth. Words my mother wrote herself.

"Morgan," Beth continues, "is a sentient aquatic mammal. There is so much we don't know, but as the only female of her species currently in existence, we aim to find out. Kansas City built this facility to house the creature and be her official home. In three days she leaves for a little tour around the country so all may witness the truly most remarkable find of this century. Now, for your special viewing."

I've waited weeks for this moment. For the way the light shimmers, as if there is sun filtering angel beams into the tank. I see the eyes first, black pools flecked by silver irises. The merrow swims out from her stone dwelling in long, sweeping arcs. Her tail is gray, like a shark's. Scars mark the narrow base where her fins flare out in black and silver tendrils. Her webbed hands end in claws. There is not a single strand of hair on her head, but a row of ridged spikes. She stops for a moment and looks at the spectators through the glass.

Everyone, every single person in the room, is silent as Morgan, the merrow of the deep, watches with curious eyes. I can see where she could be called "humanoid." She has a face, almost human. But she isn't human the way I am. The merrow's mouth is too wide, her small nose tapers into slits. Gills flutter at her neck, and I can see the muscle of her lean frame. A tightness forms in my chest. She is so beautiful. Everything about her is beautiful. Not just beautiful. Ethereal. Mythical. Magical. And, as a man dives into the tank with a bag of bloody fish, deadly.

THE MERROW

A clicking sound shoots through the water. *Tick-tack. Tick-tack.* I move away from the edges of the pool as Bach, my so-called "trainer," enters the tank in a sleek blue wet suit. The scent of blood enters with him. Not his, unfortunately. It comes from the squirming net of fish cinched at his side. Treats for a job well done.

Beyond the glass pane is yet another nightmarish smear of gawking expressions stacked in rows from the ground floor to the ceiling. The third and final one today. Below them, striding back and forth in front of the tank, is a young girl who speaks to them through a microphone. Her voice is muffled behind the glass, but I can hear all the things she's telling them about me. My kind.

Tick-tack.

I swirl in a slow circle while the girl speaks.

"Most of what we know about merrows comes from the stories of sailors, but with Morgan, here, we have the opportunity to combine those anecdotes with scientific observation. For example," the girl says as she holds up a finger. She always does this at this point in her presentation. Her role is as scripted as mine, though I doubt the consequences are the same for her if she misses a step. "We know from stories that merrows communicate vocally within their social groupings. However, for the three hundred and forty-two days that Morgan has been with us, she has yet to utter a single sound."

I tune out. All I need to pay attention to is the clicker in Bach's hand.

Tick-tack.

I hang in the center of the tank so that everyone has a good view of the beast. I don't always do this. Sometimes, I lurk far in the back, coiled against the bottom so that I am little more than an inky blur. I make the audiences squirm and squint and suffer to see what they've paid so much to see. But when I do that, my rations are reduced or withheld entirely, and today I am hungry.

Tick-tack.

Bach releases one of the live fish and I give chase, flashing my teeth for the audience and showing off my speed. I dart from one side of the tank to the other, adding unnecessary flourish to my pursuit, arching my back as I coil more tightly around the frightened fish. Then, I make sure I am only inches from the glass when I snatch the creature between my sharp teeth.

Blood puffs in the water and I dig the guts out with one sharp claw before I take my prize in three bites.

When the show ends, my belly is full. It is the only part of me that feels anything. I know I used to feel other things. Hope. Love. Loss. Even fear. But I have no use for those things anymore. It is only full and empty in an endless cycle. Full. Empty. Full. Empty. Empty. Empty.

Bach leaves the tank. The audience filters out. And soon all that remains are the children who come to test their cruelty against the glass. They pound their fists and smack their open palms, waiting to see if I am the ferocious creature they've been promised. The booms and pops drive deep into my chest, reverberating painfully in my bones. But I do not react.

I learned five cities ago that the reaction is what they want. The reaction confirms what they most want to believe: that I am not like them. That I am a deserving target of their worst impulses.

When I don't give them what they desire, they leave, and I am finally alone.

Except, I'm not.

She has been so still so long, that it's not until she glides down from the stands that I notice her at all. She approaches the glass slowly, with a look that's not quite cautious. She is small, short and petite, with hair the pale turquoise of sea glass. Her eyes are dark and her skin is sandy brown. But the most surprising thing about her is that she's crying.

I drift toward her. Drawn in by the quiet beauty of her. By the empathy that shivers in her tears.

She places a hand on the glass. It is a gesture so tender that it stirs something violent in me and I bare my teeth.

But she is not afraid of me. Or perhaps she is, and that is why she doesn't run away. Instead, she leans closer and says, "I'm sorry."

And then she is gone.

🐚

JOSIE

"Can I come with you?" I ask my mother.

Her brow pinches, then she looks pleasantly surprised. "Of course. You know I've been wanting you to be happy here and spending time together—"

"Okay, take it easy," I mutter. "There's just nothing to do here and Dad's at an away game."

"*Okay,*" she mimics my surly inflection but makes it playful. "But you're shadowing Beth. It's time for the merrow's weekly checkup."

I can't quite pinpoint why that phrase bothers me, but I get in the car and stare out the window at the foreign city while Mom tells me about the team diving into the Irish Sea in an effort to find more merrows to study.

Sometimes I think my mother sees me as one of her classes full of students and interns. She just talks at me, rattling off facts. Maybe it's the only way she knows how to talk to me. Maybe she's trying to fill the space because I don't know how to talk to her either.

We go through security, and in the back way to Morgan's tank. They bring her out, strapped down like she's going on a roller coaster ride. *No,* I realize. *Like she's a prisoner.* Because they can't take her too far, they lay her out right there.

"Did she rip her shirt again?" Mom asks.

Beth nods. "Free the nipple!"

I snort but Mom doesn't find it funny. "You wouldn't put a shirt on a shark. This is silly."

"You tell that to the Parents Against Monsters," Beth says. "Doesn't take much to get them worked up. What about a chain mail shirt? Very old-timey."

I roll my eyes and watch as they take Morgan's temperature. They measure her, shine a light in her eyes. They wear special gloves and pry her mouth open. I wonder if the liquid running down the side of her face is a tear or just leftover water. That feeling returns, as if someone is squeezing me from the inside. I have the overwhelming urge to cry, too. But I blink fast and turn away.

When it's over, and Morgan is lowered back into the tank, I feel helpless and angry. She shouldn't be treated that way. No one should.

"Dr. Aguilera," calls someone who rushes in. "It's the team. They might have news."

In a moment, I'm forgotten. Even Beth follows my mother like a good little guppy. I am positive I'm not supposed to be back here on my own, but the promise of the exploration team in Ireland is too tempting.

Morgan swims up, breaking the surface. She blinks expressive eyes in my direction. From up here I can see the row of spikes down her scalp might be cartilage. Silver flecks, like distant stars, mark her head, even down to the tops of her fanned-out ears.

"I'm sorry," I tell her. "I know you can't talk, but I just wanted to say I'm sorry. If my doctor gave me a checkup like that, I'd choke him with his stethoscope. Well, not really, but I'd imagine it at least. Come to think of it, every year my pediatrician gets weirder and weirder. Like growing up makes me some newly discovered species that hasn't been classified yet. I didn't mean 'weird' in a bad way. God, why am I so bad at this."

Morgan's ears twitch, like little wings. I wonder if maybe, just maybe, she can understand me. She's been alone here for so long. I know what that feels like. I know what it's like to be stuck somewhere.

"I bet you miss home, huh?" I get comfortable and dig into my jean jacket for my box of gummy worms. "Can you eat gummies? Let me check the ingredients. I mean, if you're humanoid, Mom says your stomach processes food just like us. Though you have two sets of lungs, which leads them to think you're a deep, *deep* sea creature. Don't tell my mom." I realize she couldn't if she tried. "You know what I mean."

I toss the gummy worm into the clear water. She catches it and holds it up, sniffing, inspecting, and then eating. At first, she makes a disgusted face. Then she nods and swallows.

"They're sour, but it goes away after a second. Literally, this is the only thing I can't live without." After a moment, Morgan turns her head to the side. I look over my shoulder, like I'm doing something wrong and am about to be caught. "Another?"

She holds out her palm. The skin there is moon pale, with crease lines running across her mounts and phalanges. She swims closer and this time I lean forward. She understands me. She's *communicating with me*. My belly swoops when I think I might fall, but I'm not scared. I place the gummy worm there, letting my fingers touch hers, smooth and soft.

"I'm Josie," I say. "It's nice to meet you."

THE MERROW

Josie. Of all the people who have gathered at my tank to stare and study, to poke or prod or command. Not one has offered me their name. She is the first.

She continues to speak, but I don't hear her words. My mind, or perhaps it is more than my mind, has stopped on this simple act of—it is something more than respect. Recognition would be closer to the truth. By offering me nothing more than a chewy worm and her name, she has given me something I didn't realize I longed for.

Somehow, when this girl who is no older than me looks at me, she doesn't see Morgan the Merrow. She doesn't see the wonder that has rocked the modern world down to its core. She sees *me*.

"Oh! Oh no, I'm so sorry. What did I say? I didn't mean to make you cry."

I raise one hand to my eyes and discover that she's right. My cheeks are warm with fresh tears, my eyes burning and full. I hadn't realized.

"Are you okay?" Josie leans forward, her liquid brown eyes widening. Her shoulders cross the red line that marks the boundary between safety and danger. Between the human world and mine. Her hair drifts toward the water, close enough that I could grab it and drag her down.

Part of me wants to. Part of me wants to grab this unexpected dagger of a girl and never let go. I have wanted to destroy something for so long—the doctors who take my blood and measure my teeth, the trainers like Bach who force me to perform for sustenance—that my instinct is to destroy her, too.

It would make me the merrow they tell me I am.

"I mean, of course you're not okay. I'm sorry. That was a stupid question." She flicks her hair behind her shoulder and offers me another sour worm. I swallow it. "I hate it when my mom asks me that. It's not like she wants to hear the truth." She catches herself again and adds, "You could tell me the truth, though. If you wanted."

I stare at her and it takes me a moment to understand why. Why looking at this girl has cracked the shield I worked so hard to build between myself and the humans. It is because she looks at me as though I might answer her. Where the doctors and scientists and trainers have looked at me as something less than them, as something they can and should have access to, Josie looks at me as an equal.

She swallows hard and presses her lips together. The inside of her bottom lip is stained blue and I wonder if it would taste sour or sweet.

"Is your name even Morgan?" she asks.

The question is so basic, yet so intimate, and in that instant, I decide to trust her. Just a little.

I swim toward her, place my hands between hers where they still rest on the red line. She tenses but doesn't pull away. I'm glad. If she did, I wouldn't have the courage to do what I do next.

Rising up so that my face is sheltered between her arms, protected from anyone who might see us, I say my name. The sound is sibilant and sharp like the rest of our language, and it always sounds a little bit wrong when spoken above water. Dull and flat.

Josie blinks rapidly and I can see the way her muscles flinch and dance with the effort of staying put, with the effort of convincing herself she's not afraid of me. "That's your name? It's really pretty." She gasps and stutters, "D-does it mean something? In your language?"

I nod and lift my eyes to the ceiling. "Sun," I say. My throat feels tight after so many days of silence. Like I am forcing water through stone with each word.

"I don't think I can say it," she admits.

"Call me Sun, then."

She smiles. "I knew you could understand me. Nice to meet you, Sun."

"Josie," I say, letting the name gust and hiss from my mouth.

Her smile fades suddenly, replaced by a gentle frown of confusion. "Why don't you say anything?" she asks. "To them. They think you don't understand us, that you can't talk. Why don't you show them how wrong they are? Tell them to let you go? They treat you like an animal."

I gesture to the paintings scrawled across the walls of the

room. The ones that show creatures like me, but not. The ones they pulled from their books of myths and legends.

"They treat me like a curiosity. Like a dream given flesh. They have never stopped to ask permission, only given orders," I say. "I won't give them more."

Josie's eyes water, but this time she doesn't cry. She swallows hard, nodding. "I won't say I know what that feels like, but I do know how much it sucks when no one asks what you want."

The sound of a door slamming echoes through the room and Josie startles, alarmed. She turns toward the sound, searching for any sign that we've been caught. Finding none, she releases a long breath and returns her gaze to mine. A hard determination has sharpened her pretty features.

"What if I help you?" she asks.

"Help me what?"

"Escape," Josie says. "What if I can help you escape?"

I let myself drift away, putting physical distance between myself and the inevitable hurt that will come with such an empty hope. I shake my head.

"You don't want to?" she asks.

"If you mean it, come back tomorrow," I say, and then I slip beneath the surface and into the dark.

❦

JOSIE

I didn't—couldn't—return to Sun like I'd promised.

"You've been awful quiet since we got home," Mom tells me

during dinner. Dad coaches at UMKC and when he's gone, when it's just me and Mom, things are always quieter. But Mom won't drop it. "Is this because I wouldn't let you cut school to come with me to work?"

I push the white rice around my plate and shrug. Anxiety tightens my chest as I think about Sun in her tank, waiting for me. I said I would be there, and all of a sudden Mom decides to pay attention to my school activities. "Tomorrow's not a school day, can I come then?"

Mom looks up, her smile crooked with surprise. "Since it won't require me aiding and abetting a truant, of course." She takes a bite of the sautéed salmon and watches me with that probing-mom vision. "Why are you so interested?"

My salmon's a little pinker in the center and I can't help but think about when Sun was fed. How they sometimes throw hunks of meat at her as if she were another killer whale or seal. Losing my appetite for the main course, I grab another sweet, fried plantain.

"You're the one who kept asking if I wanted to be one of your interns," I remind her.

Mom beams. "I knew you'd come around. You've always loved your little made-up monsters. Though, they're not so made up anymore, are they?"

I roll my eyes. "Please do not start on how cryptozoology is now a recognized science."

Mom nearly chokes on her wine. "It is. As dangerous as they are, I like to think the revelation of those vampires was the change the world needed. It's been decades, and we thought they were the only monsters out there. But now we have the merrow, and pretty soon, it looks like we might have our sights on more."

That draws my attention. "Really?"

"The team in Ireland seems to think they've found what could have been a nest." Mom has left her wine and food alone. Sometimes I think her work is the only thing that has her full attention. That makes her happy. "And to think, we assumed it was the last of its kind. With others, we could determine mating habits, migration patterns. The possibilities will be endless."

"You're going to need a bigger tank," I say, and she definitely does not notice the sarcasm in my voice.

"Oh, we've prepared," Mom says. "The facility is fully capable. But I don't want to get ahead of myself. First, we need to examine the merrow and make sure it's stable enough for the tracker."

I sit up at that final word. "Tracker?"

I think about Sun. How terribly lonely and scared she was. But not with me. *Come back tomorrow,* she said. My hands tremble with nerves. I want to see her. I want to *free* her. What if I *can't* get to her? What if she's the one who brings trouble for her kind? What if I've just made a terrible promise I won't be able to keep?

Mom smiles at me. Guilt makes my stomach rumble at the thought. I'm her daughter. How could she ever suspect I am thinking of doing something that would hurt, maybe even destroy, her career?

"Why can't you just let her go?" I let my fork go and it clatters on the table. "She's not—she's not a science experiment."

"Darling, this is a once-in-a-lifetime opportunity. The merrow is one of a kind, too. How many generations have speculated about the things they could not understand? How many have dreamed of this very type of discovery? We are only scratching the surface of what we know of our planet."

I scoff. "Keep telling yourself that."

She's pissed, but it quickly morphs into worry. "I know you

were in the tank with the merrow the other day. Those stories, Josie. They come from somewhere. She's haunting and so other-worldly beautiful. Like any creature from the sea. But she's not a person. She *can't* communicate. We've tried."

Clearly not hard enough, I think.

What if I told her Sun had spoken to me? Would it help? I weigh the thought in my mind while my mother stares. But I stay quiet.

"Perhaps you shouldn't come tomorrow."

"No!" I sit back and grab my soda can. I tap a rhythm on the sides. "It's just a lot, I mean. Mermaids are real, Mom. It's a lot to handle."

"I know, baby." She rests her hand on my forearm and squeezes. "And things will get better here. You're a . . . a . . . *fish out of water*."

"Dad's usually the dork."

"There can be two dorks in a couple." She sighs, checking her phone again. "Okay, bright and early. But you are not to be left alone with the merrow. If you're not with me, you're with Beth. I just think about what those vampires did to all those people and I——"

"That was the eighties," I mutter. "And those people were hunters."

"Joselina . . ."

I make a zipper motion across my lips.

Then, I lie and say, "I'll be good. I promise."

❀

SUN

The entire day is a torment.

More so than usual. Bach shows up early with his clicker and the whistle, which means he doesn't plan on getting in the tank with me just yet. He begins issuing commands—*tick-tack, tick-tack*—and I obey each one.

"Gotta get you warmed up for the show. Keep you fit," Bach says. "You have an image to maintain. It's bad enough you don't have any hair. C'mon. Up now, let's see that tail catch some air."

He blows his whistle in the triple beat that means he wants me to leap out of the water. To arc and dive in a way that is foreign to me. I was taught from a very young age that we do not show ourselves to the surface. We do not dwell near ships, we do not stalk the shore, and we certainly do not show ourselves for no reason at all. It was the first lesson my mothers taught me.

I should have learned it better.

I grit my teeth and jump, doing my best to curve my tail so that it satisfies his human notion of what a mermaid should do and be.

Bach continues mercilessly. Issuing commands one after the other until my muscles burn and my jaw aches from clenching it so hard. He doesn't feed me and that only fuels my anger.

When the shows begin, I am furious, executing his macabre ballet with dangerous precision. The crowds blur before me, their cries of delight and terror bleeding together as I tear apart the fish Bach drops into the tank for me.

They only see the deadly dance Bach has choreographed for them. They see what the girl on the microphone tells them to see. A dangerous monster they removed from the world. A predator. A threat. A perversion.

Until now, I have never cared so much. Because until now, none of them has bothered to care about me.

I resent it already. Josie and her fathomless eyes. Her pale turquoise hair.

My third mother once told me that our hearts are opaque as the blackest trenches, that we keep them hidden from others because we are good at hiding. But once we let a glimmer of light permeate that darkness, we are drawn to it again and again. Our hearts yearn for the light inside others. And once we've been lured, it is almost impossible to free ourselves again.

This is why I have three mothers. Relationships web between us like the branches of fan coral. Why I cannot stop hoping that Josie will return to me today, no matter how I try.

By the end of the day, I am exhausted. Bach is beaming, but not at me. At the others who come up to him and pat him on the back.

"You've really done something special here!" says one.

"I've never seen such a tight performance from it!" says another.

"You are a true maestro," says a third. "A credit to your name."

Bach's smile is a monstrous thing. It is predatory. Threatening. Perverse.

I slip into the deepest part of my waters and wait for them to leave. For the day to end. For Josie to arrive.

But it doesn't happen.

The shows end, but the day does not. Bach issues one final command—*tick-tack, tick, tick-tack*—and I fight the urge to bare my teeth. He wants me to swim through the portal and into their medical pool, where they will jab me with needles, take my blood, or worse. It doesn't usually happen so soon after an exam, but if I resist, they will drop the nets.

I do as I'm told, swim into the shallow pool where the doctor waits with her team. She never meets my eyes, but I recognize her now in a way I didn't before. Her dark eyes and brown skin, the slope of her nose and the curl of her lips. They are Josie's, and it is with horror that I realize the doctor who has overseen so much of my torment is Josie's mother.

The orderlies snatch me up, bind my arms, and before I even see what is happening, a sharp pain pierces my tail fin.

I thrash against it and I'm surprised when they release me back into the water. That is when I see what they've done: A metal ring has been stamped through my tail.

"There," the doctor says. "We'll never lose her now."

The satisfaction in her face is enough to convince me that whatever this thing is, I don't want it. I reach down, hook my claw into the still tender flesh of my tail, and I rip the ring out.

Blood puffs in the water. Sharp and visceral.

The doctor clenches her jaw. She fixes me with a hard look. For once, she meets my eyes.

She is the first to look away.

JOSIE

I made good on my promise to stay away from Sun. I've been allowed to visit every other exhibit. I watched a manatee swim lazily and thought about the legends that drunk sailors might have confused them for women with fins. For mermaids. My mom says that some of these animals could never adapt once they're back in the wild, but isn't that better than being cooped up? Better than having strangers stare at you day in and day out.

I want to free Sun, but does that make me a bad person for not being able to free the others?

As the day winds down, I slip into the merrow's exhibit. I pass by a tour group looking up in the great room at a giant skeleton of a whale suspended across the ceiling. I count the bones of its fins but there are too many. I can't help but wonder, if Sun had to live out her days in captivity, would they display her bones this way, too?

I keep going, eyeing aquarium employees in navy polos. Maybe it's because I feel like I'm doing something wrong, but I have the sensation that all eyes are on me. Hello, paranoid? I squeeze my hands at my sides to stop them from trembling and slip in the door as Beth leads a group out. I hurry across the carpeted floor and press my palms on the cold glass of the tank. "I'm here."

My heart squeezes with anxiety when I don't see her at first. Her silver-gray skin camouflages so well against the slats of rock on the ground that I don't see her until she swims upward in a full circle. I notice the rip in her tail, the wound jagged and raw. I press my hand on my belly. The tracker Mom mentioned . . .

"You ripped it out," I say. "That looks painful."

Sun swims to me, lining up her webbed claws against my palms. I count her five fingers and think of the whale bones strung to the ceiling. That won't happen to Sun. I won't let it. Something like hope fills me once again.

Until I hear the pressurized hiss of the door behind me and see Sun swim backward and away.

Afraid.

"I had a feeling you'd make your way back here," Mom says. She raises her brow like she's waiting for an explanation.

I catch her reflection in the glass approaching before I turn to face her. "I was looking for you."

"Don't lie to my face, Joselina."

Full name equals big trouble. Innocently, I ask, "What happened to her tail?"

Mom stands beside me, shoving her hands into her blazer

pockets. She holds her head high, watching the merrow keep a distance. "She ripped out the tracker. No matter. She'll lead us to that pod. We're going to inject a tracker instead, though we hoped it wouldn't come to that. She doesn't seem to feel pain."

I notice the plume of blood in the water from where the gash in Sun's tail still bleeds. I shake my head. "That's not true."

"How would you know that?"

"Because it's common sense!" I shout, then lower my voice. I still can't shake the anger out. "She's flesh and blood."

Mom turns to me, her usual composed demeanor cracking. "So are sharks. Sharks are beautiful creatures. But they're still animals. We study them. We learn everything we can. We preserve them. All for the advancement of the world, of knowledge. And yet, I wouldn't stick my hand inside a shark's mouth and expect it not to bite."

I make fists in the air out of frustration. "You're such—you're such a *liar*."

"You need to check your tone with me, Josie."

"Fine! But don't pretend that this is all about scientific advancement," I say. I think of the woman who spent weekends with me at the aquarium in Coney Island taking care of the small turtles. How she asked me to be gentle with the starfish. How we wrote letters to the mayor protesting the treatment of the seals, even though her boss put her on probation. When I look at my mom, I don't even recognize her. I don't recognize the moment she changed. "You care more about being the first. The *one*. You don't even want to see that she's not a thing. She's my age. She's *someone*." I shake my head. "Forget it. You're just—I don't even know anymore. But you're not my mother. Not the mom I know."

"Is that what you really think?" Mom asks, her eyes unwavering.

241

I shrug. "Does it matter?"

We're quiet for a long moment, listening to the sounds of the aquarium. Until finally, she says, "Visit's over. Go wait for me in the car."

I do as I'm told.

SUN

The room feels silent in Josie's absence. She takes all the air with her, leaving her mother gasping for breath. They were talking about me, but that was the kind of fight that has been brewing for years.

It reminds me of a fight I had with Second Mother. About stealing away to the surface more than was necessary. She was always calling me back from the edge of some ravine, reining me in, and so I rebelled even harder. Just like Josie.

This mother is not my mother, but I vibrate with the same anger I saw in Josie's expression. The anger that only comes from being held too tightly. From being held captive against my will. It blurs my vision for a second and when I blink again, the doctor is standing at the edge of the pool, her eyes locked on me. But she isn't looking through me as she usually does, with clinical detachment and wonder. She looks *at* me.

I push the crown of my head through the surface of the water and meet her eyes.

"What did you do to her?" she asks, peering at me with unbridled hostility.

I do not answer, but I am surprised to discover that for the first time since my capture, I want to. I want to speak to her and show her how wrong she is about everything. About me and about Josie.

The doctor snorts and presses one hand to her cheek, shaking her head. "What am I doing? No, I will not get pulled into this nonsense. The only thing you understand is a clicker and bucket of chum."

I sneer. I can't help myself. I snap my tongue and flash my teeth viciously. Instead of cowering in fear, she pauses, her shallow gaze turning deep with curiosity.

"Morgan," she says, after a long pause. "Is my daughter telling me the truth? Do you understand me?"

I consider sinking beneath the surface once more. Leaving the doctor to her ignorant suppositions, burying myself in the knowledge that I will soon be released and unable to return to my family. My captivity will simply change shape, with no possibility of escape. It would be easier. Smarter, perhaps. But if I can do nothing else, I can at least show the doctor that she is wrong to mistrust her daughter.

When I open my mouth to sing, sorrow cracks inside me like a shell. This, more than anything, feels like loss. The song is what connects me to all the others and I may never see them again. It is so sharp a feeling that I nearly choke on it. Instead, I lean into it, conjuring an image of First Mother as she drew me into her arms. It is a simple image. I could give her so much more, but this is painful enough.

This, more than sound, is how we communicate. Our language is a part of our hearts. We speak in the spaces between song and thought. We speak in memories and in dreams. In the face of my captors, I remained silent because to speak to them was to give them too much of myself. But things have changed. I have changed, and it is time to use my voice.

The doctor's eyes unfocus as the song fills her mind with my thoughts, my emotions, and then her eyes fill with tears.

Her mouth opens as if to say something, then it closes again and she walks away.

JOSIE

On the way home, we don't speak. We don't speak when Mom parks her car beside Dad's truck. She orders dinner and leaves me a plate on the table, but she closes the door to her office and doesn't come out until she goes to her bedroom to sleep. We are at a standstill. But what I'm going to do is going to shatter all of it.

In my heart, I know that I'm right. I know that the merrow—Sun—needs my help. I lie in bed thinking about her. Those silver eyes, the sweep of her tail. She is all sharp angles and claws, but she didn't hurt me. She could have. She could have pulled me into the tank and watched me drown, as the stories say.

I check for the time on my phone: 11:58 P.M. Dad likes to say that the worst things happen after midnight. Robberies, murders, accidents. But what about all the bad things that happen in the light of day? What about the things people do when others are watching and just look away?

When the clock strikes midnight, I get up. I pull on my sweat-pants and carry my boots in my hands. This house is so new, nothing creaks. I pick up the fob for Dad's truck, and before I know it, I'm out the door and driving to the aquarium.

Funny how ten minutes on a dark road can feel like an eternity. How something that should be muscle memory, like breathing, is a struggle with every stop sign. I thank my car-obsessed father for insisting I learn how to drive, even though I hated it in the city. Here, it is the only way I can get my friend to freedom.

I use the key cards I swiped from my mother's purse and let

myself into the aquarium's garage, backing up into the cargo bay. Never, ever, ever before, have I moved so swiftly or with so much precision. Sun's life is at stake. My mother's livelihood is at stake. And yet, my future feels murky. When I step out of the truck, everything will change. For better or worse.

I touch the rosary my father keeps hanging from the rearview mirror. I do not know who to ask for strength—but I need it now.

I get out of the truck and unlatch the back to lay the truck bed flat. There's a black tarp, which Dad keeps for rainy days, that I can cover Sun with. When that's in place, I let myself into the building from the cargo entrance with one of my stolen keycards. I wait, listening for security, but it is just me and thousands of fish.

Still, I keep to the shadows and head to the medical pool, where they keep the animals that are going to undergo procedures. When I open the door, Sun thrashes in the shallow, pale green water. She bares her sharp teeth. Then she sees it's me and I see the way her chest expands. She lets go of a cry, a song.

"You are here," she says.

"I'm here," I say. I want to go to her. To see what it would feel like to be held by her. But I stop myself. "We have to hurry."

Sun points to a door. "That is where they keep the pod that carries me."

I cross the room and swipe my mother's card. There's a red light, like I'm blocked. I try again. I try the second key card and nothing happens. An error sound, red and wrong, beeps with every swipe. I stop. Shake my head. "No, no, no. I've never seen my mother use more than these keys."

I get on my knees and look at the mechanism. That's when I notice. It's a biometric scanner. I stare at my palms. As much as

I am my mother's daughter, I don't have her fingerprints. I turn to Sun. I feel gut-punched. Breathless. Somehow, I manage to say, "I'm sorry. I—"

When the door slams open, I know it's over. It's over.

So over.

My mother stands there. She's in her pajamas, too. Her eyes are puffy and red. I've never seen my mother crying before and that does something to me that I don't have words for. My whole mouth goes dry, my body flashing hot with anxiety.

"Mom. How did you—"

"I went to your room, and you weren't there." She slowly crosses toward me. "I couldn't stop thinking about what you said to me."

Shame burns at my eyes. "I'm sorry."

"You were right," Mom continues. "You were right about me."

Sun thrashes again, like she's trying to protect *me*. But I'm not scared of my mom in this moment. Not when she places a hand on my face and cradles it.

"Never doubt that you are my life," she says. "You will always come first, Josie."

My mother goes to the door and presses her palm there. Her signature. In the morning, when the staff find the tank is empty, and people watch the footage, read the logs, there will be no doubt of what we have done.

SUN

The trip to the river is short. Josie positions herself awkwardly in the truck so that she can have one hand on the pod as though she wants to comfort me. It works, and I'm grateful.

Her mother knows exactly where to take me and backs the truck down a slope of concrete that makes moving the pod into the water easy. Then she opens the hatch and I slip into the river.

"I, ah, well, I suppose it's not quite enough to say I'm sorry," Josie's mother says, clasping her hands tightly before her. "I'm not sure what else to say though, except, I'm sorry." She grimaces and adds, "I'll give you two a minute, but we can't stay here for long."

Josie waits until she's gone and then strides down the ramp and into the water until she's up to her chest. Her turquoise hair drifts on the surface of the black water. Like this, she looks more like a mermaid than I ever have. At least, she looks like a mermaid from human stories.

"I guess you don't have a cell phone," Josie jokes. "Is there any way we might see each other again?"

I reach for her hand. Her skin is soft and warm, both the same and very different from my own. She threads her fingers through mine.

"We believe that once two hearts have found each other in the darkness, they will never be lost to one another."

Josie blinks rapidly, then clears her throat and offers me a pained smile. "Are you saying you like me?"

"Girls!" Josie's mom calls.

"Just a minute!" Josie fires back.

I smile. Then I raise her hand to my lips and press a kiss to her knuckles. "We will find each other again, Josie."

"I hope so," she whispers.

I release her hand and she retreats until the water only reaches her knees. Behind her, the pale bluffs stretch up toward the winking lights of the city. I can see the smooth arcing windows of the aquarium that has been my latest prison. The place where humans viewed me through the prism of their mythology. I still hate it, but it is also the place where I found a friend. An ally.

If there is one Josie in the world, then perhaps we are not so different as I thought.

"Goodbye, Josie," I say. "And thank you."

Josie's smile is radiant. "Safe travels, Sun," she says.

Then I let the current tug me away, into the snaking ribbon of water that promises to take me home.

SHARK WEEK

Maggie Tokuda-Hall

Everyone is simply the product of their parents' choices, and in this single regard I am perfectly normal.

Jeffrey Chang's father is the mayor of our small town, having glad-handed and lied for years. And so it is little surprise that Jeffrey Chang is kind of a slimeball. Alphabet Matapang's parents are both badasses, her mother the doctor at the abortion clinic, and her father a travel writer. And so the fact that Alphabet Matapang is extremely cool is, if not a given, not a shock.

This is also why Alphabet Matapang is probably throwing a party this weekend. Alphabet's parents leave town often, and usually when they do, she throws a party. Not like havoc and keg stands parties, but parties all the same. I am invited to these events the way everyone else is, which is to say I know I'm welcome so long as I don't act like a jerk once I get there. But I rarely go, and I certainly won't be going this weekend.

I am aware that my absence is not likely notable or even noticed. But I cannot make myself go to a party while I'm PMSing, even if it is an opportunity to hang out with Alphabet Matapang.

I know I'm PMSing because there are pimples on my chin and everything makes me want to cry. And while PMSing is perfectly normal, the days that follow, for me, are not.

I mentioned that we are all just products of our parents' choices. The thing is, my parents' choices have been somewhat . . . exotic. They met while my father was a merchant marine, and my mother was a mermaid.

With a tail.

Under the sea.

You get the idea.

She made a deal with the Sea Witch to make her a human so that she could be with my father, which is very romantic, but that wish was not granted for free.

The cost? Her daughter would be cursed, once a month.

This is not Eve's curse, a curse that I share with all uterus-havers. This is one that is specific to the magic of the sea, to my mother's choice, to the world she left behind.

Each month, during my period, a shark's mouth is erected between my lips, distorting my words, rendering them hard where they should be soft, pointed where they should be round. If I were to toss my head back in a moment of great hilarity, there would be no hiding the teeth that grow in moments and fall out in piles on the bathroom sink a few days later. Rows and rows of jagged teeth, perfect for rending and ripping and terrible for everything else.

They are my monthly nightmare, one that I have labored to

keep a deadly secret. The only people who know about my teeth are my parents, and it is with great annoyance that I tell you my parents couldn't give a damn.

"Once a month," Mother says. "You know what I worried about every day under the sea? Getting eaten by a shark." What life as a mermaid could have been like, I'll only know from my mother's stories, which are few. Talking about her home makes her sad, and Father often admonishes me for my curiosity. But she is always willing to discuss her hatred of sharks.

"They're cold and they're brutal. They can't be trusted," she says. What she does not say is that she fears that I become all these things while in the curse's thrall. She does not say this aloud, but I can see it in her face, can see the way she turns away from me during Shark Week, lets her eyes slide from me like I'm invisible.

"I love you," she says. "But you're dangerous. You can't be reckless."

This is a line of reasoning that has led us to countless calamitous quarrels, and yet she persists with it. I suppose I ought to respect her perseverance but, alas, I do not. Mother says this is a symptom of my other curse, which is to be a teenager. For his part, as soon as the teeth are mentioned, Father tends to abscond to the darkest corners of our house, suddenly immersed in some arcane and all-encompassing task. So I can hardly count on him to be in my corner in these monthly bouts with Mother.

Anyway, this is all to say that it's a bad time to be PMSing, when Alphabet Matapang invites me to come kick it at her house for the weekend while her parents are away.

"Like, at the party?" I ask. I am chuffed to be invited directly.

"I was thinking I'd skip the party this weekend," she says. "It'd just be you and me."

I blink back my shock. Just Alphabet Matapang and me? Certainly, there has been a mistake. Alphabet Matapang can step directly on my neck. Alphabet Matapang's face makes good shapes, especially when she's eating, especially especially when she's eating something unwieldy, a burger, an apple. Alphabet Matapang escorts people into the clinic her mother runs when protesters are being terrible. One time Alphabet Matapang lit Blake Vo's backpack on fire after he called Diane Sakesegawa a slut.

Meanwhile, I am the kid who sits in the library at lunch, hidden behind a book so that the library staff can't see that I'm cramming a sandwich in my face, and no one else can see that I am eating alone. When I am invited places, I assume it's because someone's parents insisted I be invited, unless it's a group project, and then I have to assume it's because I'm smart and others are hoping I might carry the load. I am aware that it is not only the curse that makes me odd. I have always felt more at ease with the parents of my peers than my peers.

Not like Alphabet Matapang, who not only gets on with most people easily and well, but is liked by everyone except Blake Vo. This is because Alphabet Matapang is a nice and good person. And yes, you're right, I have a huge crush on her, which is hardly unique, because Alphabet Matapang is the subject of numerous ardent crushes in our school.

And she has just invited me, Echo Chee, to her house. Just, in the time before fourth period starts, while everyone else is pulling their book from their backpacks, mingling at their desks, waiting for Mr. Tulithimutte. As if this is no big deal.

It is worth clarifying: This is a momentous occasion.

But. A momentous occasion that will pass me by. Imagine, being at Alphabet Matapang's house and sprouting shark's teeth.

Imagine trying to explain that, imagine telling her, well yeah, Mom was a mermaid, and heh, here we are! Welp, see you in physics on Tuesday!

Simply the potential for such unceasing humiliation is a dizzying proposition, a waking nightmare. Why don't I just fart directly into her mouth and be done with it?

And besides. Mother would never let me go, lest I be a danger to Alphabet. As if I would ever hurt her.

"I can't," I say. "I-I have my brother's . . . recital. Karate."

"Karate recital?" She quirks what could almost be a smile, but is really the shape her face makes when she wants you to know that she knows you're lying. And though her face is winsome in any shape, it would be disingenuous to say that this particular one is among my favorites. She gives a nonchalant shrug. "Okay, dude. I mean, you can just say no."

I open my mouth to make some kind of reply, but before I can further bury myself in humiliation, Mr. Tulithimutte calls for everyone to sit down. And anyway, the damage is done.

I don't even have a brother.

It is with the paint still drying on this banner day of disappointment that Mother and I have one of our worst quarrels yet. The physical blocking is not entirely clear in my memory, the fury has obscured it. But we are yelling at each other, cutting words. And I have my hand on the front doorknob when I hear myself shout:

"Because you're a selfish bitch who traded my happiness for your own!"

Mother is beautiful, I have long known this. I am perhaps more aware of her beauty because I do not share it, having inherited my father's strong jaw and thick neck. But she is not beautiful in that moment, her face contorted with emotions I don't understand or recognize, and for a split second, less than that, I have the wild thought that she's going to hit me. She doesn't, of course, and besides, she stands a room's length away from me and makes no effort to cross that distance to slap me or hug me or touch me in any way.

"Don't talk to your mom like that," says Father. He can always be trusted to break the ensuing silences created by my and Mother's moments of greater verbal cruelty. When he says it now, it's more a sigh than a command.

There's something in the resigned way he says it this time, like he knows he's fighting a pyrrhic battle, like he's just going through burdensome choreography to appease my uncontrollable pubescent emotions. This only makes me more angry, angry at the way they both treat me like such a problem. It's their completely thoughtless pursuit of their own romance that has precluded the opportunity for my own.

How do they not see what they have robbed me of?

The night and her chill have blown in along with the fog from the sea. As I fume down the street I wrap my arms around me, half for warmth, half to guard myself from my own seething resentment. It feels as though every window I pass is full of eyes that bear witness to my humiliation, watching with cold detachment, curious at the spectacle of my failure to be a normal person who doesn't hate their parents for a deal they made with a sea witch. A teen who does things like go out with friends because they have friends, and not shark teeth. If they don't laugh at me, it is only because I appear too banal to be funny.

Bad vibes only.

My phone has been buzzing fruitlessly for most of my walk, and I assume it's my parents hoping I'll discover their many angry missives and return home at once. But when I stop at the park and sit on the damp bench, there are also messages from Alphabet.

Hey dude
I'm sorry about earlier
I can tell I made you uncomfortable and I'm so sorry

The blue glow of my phone burns my eyes, and above, the stars recede, irrelevant.

you're sorry?
like, I know you don't have a brother

Throw my body into the sea, let me drown in my mother's home. Anything to escape this moment, the exact pinprick of time when Alphabet realizes I'm a complete lunatic.

I'm so weird lol
you're really not

Little gray dots, little gray dots, little gray dots, the only thing that has ever mattered in the history of time are the little gray dots.

I'd just feel super shitty if like
I was pressuring you into anything?
like since my parents aren't home
and I didn't want to throw a party bc you never come lol
I just thought having you over now would be more chill than
when like, Douglas and Blessica Matapang are lurking around

but now I also see how that's coming on kinda strong, you
know?
so, I guess what I really mean is I'm sorry, I think you're really
cool and smart and pretty and I'd like to kick it with you in
a way that is chill to you. Like, we could go to an ice cream
shop, and have friends come too, or go rollerskating, do
people rollerskate? I don't know I didn't really plan the date
part but you get the idea.

A date.

With Alphabet Matapang.

Maybe it's my anger that moves my hand. Maybe I just don't want
to have to walk back to my house and withstand more emotional
jousting with Mother, and bear the brunt of Father's fathering.

But I think it's simply that Alphabet is a magnet, and I will forever lean toward her.

I'm free right now

Little gray dots.

You sure?

hella sure.

I really didn't mean to pressure you
lol ok

Alphabet picks me up in her car, a beat-up Toyota Camry,
champagne finish faded. She has an air freshener in the shape of a
tree hanging from her rearview mirror, and grit comes off on my

hand as I open the door. Ripped seat covers, a ChapStick rolling around on the floor. A cassette player with a port plugged in. Her hand resting on the stick shift. I have not once in my life witnessed a car as cool as this one.

Gone is the bravado of the girl who texted that she was free right now. I am a fool, my mouth hanging open like, durrr, as I behold Alphabet, the Alphabet Matapang, who smiles at the open door. Her face is a perfect shape the way a circle is perfect, incapable of being re-created by human hand.

She is smiling at me.

"Wanna get burgers?"

I smile back, and I can tell from the shape of Alphabet's face that this is the response she was hoping for, and I am so relieved that for once I am able to provide a normal, pleasing interaction. Like I'm already someone else entirely, someone better, someone cool. Someone who's going on a date with Alphabet Matapang.

"Yeah. That sounds perfect."

Later, with the taste of ketchup still in my mouth, we are sitting on the couch in Alphabet's family's living room. I've been here before, for the occasional party or study group, but it feels completely different this time. As though it had been torn down to the foundation and rebuilt with walls that watch, windows that see.

At least Alphabet is fully at ease. She leans back into the couch with the remote to the TV in one hand, her hair—her perfect hair, some dyed purple, some dyed green—wound around her fingers in the other. I try not to stare, but her black nail polish is chipped and perfect, and I am hypnotized by the way her fingers brush through her hair and against the skin of her neck. She is the reason sonnets exist, and it's a pity I have no sense of meter.

It occurs to me that neither of us is paying attention to what is on the TV. The air crackles around us, tiny invisible stars exploding. And it's in this preponderance of eruptions that it also occurs to me that Alphabet will not kiss me.

Not for lack of desire. I think I'm past that particular point of self-detrimental anxiety. She clearly would like to. I can see that from the way her body leans toward mine, the way she looks at me and then looks away, cheeks pink and perfect. But likely because I have given such a wide array of mixed signals over the last day. And however obvious they may seem to me, to her my motives are inscrutable.

Still. It's with my heart pounding blood through my ears that I finally ask: "Can I kiss you?"

I have kissed before. I have done much more than kissing. But never with Alphabet Matapang. Never with the world going soft and invisible all around me. I have never wanted my eyes open and closed at the same time so badly. I want to see her face in the shapes it makes while we kiss. I want to close my eyes against anything other than the softness of her lips, the brush of her fingers on my neck, on my arms, on my face, in my hair. I am dizzy with her, drunk off the short gasp of her breath when I kiss her ear, and I am lost lost lost.

I am so inside myself that, somehow, I do not notice what is happening inside myself. I do not feel the clench. Do not notice the ache. All I can sense is Alphabet and the flood her touch brings forth. That I assume she brings forth. That I assume erroneously is my expansive desire. That is, in fact, not that at all.

There is a quick intake of breath. Alphabet pulls away.

Everything moves slowly, inexorably. A drop of blood on her lip. Her hand goes to the blood. She examines it on her finger, a shock of red on her brown skin. Her eyes move up from her finger to my mouth. My mouth. I open it to speak, and as my lips pull back, pull over my teeth, pull back too far, I know that the worst has happened. I clamp my mouth shut and the motion is jarring, spinning everything back into the regular speed, spinning us into this horrible new reality we share in which Alphabet has seen my teeth, my too many teeth. And I have cut her perfect lip and not even realized it. The snap of my jaws startles her, and I see her flinch.

"Oh," says Alphabet.

It's counterintuitive for a single syllable to bear so much weight, and yet that "oh" does it. Dismay, disappointment, disgust. And worst, somehow, worry. There is more blood now.

She looks directly at my mouth. "Shit."

Nothing can fix this. And so it is without any pretense of dignity that I run straight out of Alphabet's house.

The night is even colder now. The fog obscures the stars. Alphabet's home is not that far from mine—not an easy walk, but a doable one. I take it at a run. I try to lose myself and the memory of what just happened in the drum of my heart, the metronome of my ragged breath, the slap of my shoes on the sidewalk. I know I cannot run away from this, not really, but that does not tamp down my wild desire to run. It seems the only thing to do.

That is, until I reach the beach.

The waves lap in their hush and their roar and I feel myself pulled into them, the freezing cold around my ankles and then around my knees. As a little girl, I'd flop around in the surf, pretending I was my mother. As I got older, I realized I would never be her. Never be something magical, or mysterious, or romantic. As I stand here, I feel the grief of this truth hit me again, and again, with every fresh and ceaseless wave.

Some great romance isn't coming to save me.

I walk home, and with each step, my shoes squelch beneath my numb toes.

When I push open the front door, hoping against all reason that the downstairs of our home will be empty and dark and quiet, Mother is sitting on the couch waiting for me. I slough off my pants and drape them across the banister along with my socks to dry. I'm stalling, of course, not wanting the lecture and the grounding and the anger that are imminently coming my way. A cursory glance at the wall clock—a seashell with little pink hands, I hate it, a gift from Father to Mother in the vain hope of embracing her heritage—tells me it's past 11:30 P.M. So I'm out past curfew to boot.

Good, great, grand.

Wordlessly, I sit down in the armchair across from the couch, resigned to the trouble I know I am in and must sit through before I can go to my room and bury myself beneath a tangle of sheets and quilts and blankets until morning—and maybe until I'm dead.

Here lies Echo Chee, Mediocre Student, Bad Shark-Mouthed Kisser.

I have not yet looked at Mother's face. I dread the fury she has been bottling up to release upon my return. And so it is with some surprise that, when she starts to speak, her voice is soft and kind. Like it was when she would place a Band-Aid across my knee if I fell off my bike, or when she rubs my neck during one of my headaches.

"I'm glad you're home," she says. She means it.

I meet her gaze. She gives me a small, sad smile.

"Where did you go?" she asks. It's not a baited question, and I can see that she's just curious. I tell her what happened.

"It's not fair," she says. "You should have had a perfect first kiss. I'm sorry I took that from you."

"Ma," I say. "Not my firsht kish. Dat ship shailed in . . . fifth grade? Not. Perfect."

"With who?" she demands. Her voice is more like a friend's than a mother's.

"Luka Tong. At reshess. Told me he'd do my homework."

"Luka? The one with the spaghetti breath?" Mom asks. I nod. "Did he do your homework, at least?"

"No."

"That little jerk," she says, and then we're both laughing.

It's not that funny really, but for some reason both of us are laughing so hard it makes Mother's eyes stream and my side ache. Maybe it's because we're both relieved not to have to fight right now. Maybe it's because there is something about this terrible, no good, very bad night that has put us back on the same team. Maybe it's just that we're mother and daughter, and we love each other even if for moments at a time we hate each other, too. Maybe.

I find that I do not give a damn what the reason is, I'm just glad that something heavy, something loud feels like it has passed. Maybe not forever, but certainly in this moment.

Mother presses her fingers into her eyes, trying in vain to stop the tears, her square, perfect teeth peeking between her hands. She is so lovely when she laughs. Her amusement renders her precious, a glass figurine of a woman. She is delicate in a way I will never be. I feel my lips close around my many teeth, feel the scrape of them.

"Am I grounded?" I ask.

"No," Mother says. "But the next time you storm out of here, at least shoot us a text so we know where you are. I think that's fair to ask."

These terms are so reasonable that all I can do is shrug. I do not say that she can trust me to do this. I'm grateful that she already does.

"So she saw the teeth." This a question and not a question, the way her apology is an apology but also not something that can fix anything. I nod. "And you didn't . . . want to bite her?"

"What? No!"

Mom smiles dolefully. "I had to ask." Her eyes drift to my teeth. "There was no way to know. How the curse would affect you. Sex and hunger. They're so much alike sometimes." I shift uncomfortably. "I should have given you more credit."

This is such a wild understatement that I can do nothing but look at my feet. The memory of the night is still cloying, stuck in my throat even through the laughter. A shadow of resentment passes through me, and I have the sudden and profound need to be alone. Likely sensing this, Mother stands and makes for the stairs. She puts a hand on my shoulder and gives it a quick squeeze.

"You should get to fall in love and be reckless," she says. "I guess I mean, I should let you do that. That's what being young is all about."

I awake in the morning to cramps, and great thick clots of blood in the toilet bowl, and a slew of posts across every possible platform from Alphabet's house. A party, just as everyone expected. I see her in a few of the pictures, her mouth pulled into her perfect smile. The cut on her lip is there, and not there at all, as if it doesn't matter. Somehow, this feels worse than the moment she saw my teeth.

My parents do their best to studiously mind their own business, and without much discussion or preamble inform me that they're taking off for the day. They make no mention of where, and besides I don't care. It gives me more space to wallow and scroll. When there's a knock at the door, I ignore it, even when it's followed by the doorbell ringing. But I nearly jump out of my skin when there's a gentle tap at the window just behind my head.

I whip around, and a face is there.

Alphabet Matapang.

"Hey," she says, voice warm, lips curled around the word. "Can we talk?"

My heart is drumming a song of fight or flight, so I stuff my hands into my jeans pockets to stop them shaking. I go to the front door and clumsily lead her inside.

I cannot bring myself to speak, to flash my freak teeth at her. But Alphabet does not wait for me. As soon as her ass hits the sofa, her voice races ahead.

"I just want to say, I'm so sorry about last night." She pulls her lips into a thin line that I cannot read. "I feel so bad that I made you feel so embarrassed? Like, it's not a big deal."

At this, I cannot help myself. I laugh. Not a big round laugh, but a snorting huff of a laugh that is unbecoming and unattractive and also unstoppable. But Alphabet doesn't laugh.

"Seriously. I just wish I'd known. But then, like, I get it, why would you tell me? I hadn't earned that trust. So. I'm gonna try and earn it now, okay?"

I have not even the faintest idea what she could mean by this.

"So what, is this like a spell? A curse?"

"Yeah. Mom. Ushed to be a mermaid. Dish ish duh cosht."

Alphabet nods. "Yeah, that scans. I mean, a mermaid, though? That's dope."

When I do not respond, she smiles. "Trust me, it could be worse. At least mermaids are, like, sexy."

I am momentarily derailed by the word *sexy* coming out of Alphabet's mouth.

"So like. You're not the only one with a family curse." She takes a deep, steadying breath and then stands. She lifts her shirt so that I can see the gentle roll of her tummy over her pants.

But then, her entire torso separates from her legs. And I do not have time to consider what this means before great tattered wings explode from her back. She hovers there, her top half floating just above her bottom half, her wings beating softly in our living room.

"My mom's a manananggal," she says. "Which, is just, like, a gross Filipino monster? So. This is me."

My jaw hangs open at this spectacle. I have never heard of a manananggal before, and I do not know what to make of the one who floats above me.

"And like, as if this shit isn't bad enough? During my period I crave blood. But not, like, any blood. Fetus blood. So. I mean, don't get me wrong, I one hundred percent believe in the right to choose, but that's not the only reason I volunteer at the clinic." Her face flushes. She lets her wings slow a little, and her torso meets her legs once more, and in the blink of an eye, her flesh is whole, and the wings are gone. "Like I said. Teeth may feel uncomfortable or whatever, but at least you don't have any terrible, creepy cravings. It could be worse."

I blink at her, still in shock.

Her eyes smile beneath her eyelashes. "I haven't shown anyone this before."

I feel pride and affection glitter in my chest. She showed me. She showed me on purpose. "No one sheen my teef."

"Can I see them again?" she asks, her voice careful. "I didn't really get a good look last night."

I open my mouth wide, and after a moment's pause for permission, Alphabet runs her finger along my teeth. I watch her eyes scan the many rows, and am surprised that, when her eyes meet mine, they are not full of horror, or voyeuristic curiosity, but something else, something hungry and needing and good.

She tilts my chin with her finger so that our eyes meet.

Then she leans in and kisses me.

Maybe I should think about how my parents could come home at any moment. Maybe I should worry that her lip will catch on my teeth again. Maybe I should be worried that she'll try and eat my blood.

But I don't.

For the first time in my short life, I let myself disappear into a kiss, a full one, my mind clear except for the feeling of Alphabet's mouth on mine, our lips careless. We are monsters, warm and tender and trusting.

And for once, I understand why Mother made her choice.

For once, I let myself love recklessly.

JINJU'S PEARLS

June Hur

I did not choose the sea. The sea chose me, holding me in her desperate embrace.

For five years, I descended into the freezing dark with other haenyeo fish-divers, from dawn until late afternoon, holding our breaths as we harvested abalone, oysters, seaweed, and shellfish. The work was hard, but necessary if I did not wish to starve on this poverty-stricken island of Jeju.

I did often dream, though, of one day choosing my own fate.

A fate that would take me away from the sea.

It was this thought I woke to at first light, and the thought clung to me like the smell of brine as I carried my net and small hand-held tools. Grandmother and I joined the crowd of haenyeos—

mothers, sisters, daughters, aunts—all making their way to the sea while singing a song in unison.

But there was no song in me.

I was tired; rather than sleeping, I had spent hours imagining the scene from weeks ago while visiting the capital of Jeju Island. I remembered the fortressed town, with its neat roads and flared-roofed government offices, scrubbed clean from the hunger and grime that plagued our lives. I had wandered into a bookshop stacked with books that teased me with all the knowledge I did not have. I'd dared not touch the pages with my oyster-stained fingers. And from the shop door, I would catch glimpses of genteel ladies strolling by with their maids, their skin pale and smooth, untouched by the wrathful sun or the salty sting of the sea. I had stared at their silk dresses, at their butterfly pins adorning their perfect hair, and at their embroidered flower shoes that curved up at the tips. I wanted their life—clean, educated, and respectable.

"Daydreaming again?"

I glanced at my grandmother, who walked with a limp; the pressure of the sea wreaked havoc on her body when on land, though when under water, she swam quicker than even me.

"Halmang, you are nearly sixty," I said. "I wish you could live a different life."

"And why would I ever wish that? The sea is our home," Grandmother said. "She is our mother, ever providing for us and never asking for anything in return."

I huffed out a breath and swiped aside a loose strand of my hair, which only slipped free again in the wind. "The sea is like our graveyard. It has taken so many of us already. I would not miss it if I were to never see the sea again."

Grandmother clucked her tongue, hoisting the net higher

under her arm. "Your father would not be pleased to hear you say that."

"The sea took him, too," I mumbled. Father had gone off to fish at sea and had not returned, like many of the men on Jeju Island. I imagined Mother had faced a similar fate; she had to be dead, else why would she have left me when I was only a few days old? How could a mother abandon her infant, unless she had died? "The sea has taken everything from me, and now it's taking my dream."

"What is your dream?"

"My dream . . ."

I stared down at my hand. It looked rough, dry, and almost scaly compared with the hands of respectable women. A memory surfaced, of a fisherman hauling out his catch—an ineo, a creature with the torso of a human yet with a fish tail instead of legs. Crowds had formed around the creature and had stared with repulsion and fear. It was the same look the upper-class cast my way whenever they saw me stepping out of the sea. *It still startles me to see these indecent haenyeo divers*, they would say. *They are half naked! So uncivilized! So unlike us.*

"All I desire," I said, "is to feel less like a fish and more like a human. You know, Halmang, people look at us the same way as those ineo creatures being hauled out of the sea."

Grandmother scoffed. "An ineo is sometimes more human than humans themselves. You should know." She eyed me. "You have an ineo friend."

"Jinju?" I had named the fish-woman "Pearl" for she would always bring me pearls, which I was saving until I had a chest full of them. Enough pearls to dress like the genteel ladies, and to also hire a scholar to teach me to read and write like them.

I might even shed my scales one day and win the affection of a gentleman . . . And fix my fate, finally.

"Jinju is hardly a friend," I explained. "She is just a fish that follows me wherever I go."

"Keeping an eye out for you. Always."

"*Haunting* me. Always."

Jinju had appeared when I had begun my haenyeo training at the age of eleven. I had plunged into the shallow water, looking for sea urchins among the rocks, when I had noticed her quietly observing me, her black hair moving like a cloud of seaweed in the waves. Her skin had looked so pale, almost blue. Or perhaps it was the skylight filtering in through the waves. Her eyes, the entirety of each, were drowned in liquid black. She could be twenty or two hundred years of age—who could say? I had stared back for as long as I could hold my breath, then I had gone back up for air. When I had returned below, she was there still, watching me.

I was eighteen now, a full-fledged haenyeo permitted to dive into the deep sea, and Jinju would always find me, somehow. She would stare at me, never speaking a word, but her gaze always held mine as though wishing to tell me something. Not that I cared to know it. *Ineos are not human*, the villagers often declared, while hauling out their fish-human catch. *They may look like a woman, but they are not a woman.*

Of course, the sight of ineos had grown scarce these recent years. Too many hunted down.

"If you see her," Grandmother called out as I treaded into the water, "tell her Halmang says hello!"

I dived into the sea and clenched my teeth against the freezing water, or perhaps it was trepidation I felt. Jinju always showed up, and sometimes I felt her before I saw her, strands of her mucky hair crawling against my skin.

"Damn ineos," I whispered.

I treaded deeper into the waters, and my attention strayed away from what lurked beneath the sea to a vessel floating in the distance. A person was peering over the boat's ledge, looking confused, and I heard her voice echo, "I heard a splash. Did I imagine it?"

I went underwater and saw a young man dropping into the depth—silk robe billowing as he fell, slowly, slowly, into the darkness below. His eyes were closed; bubbles embraced him. I swam toward him, my heart quickening, and my hands reached out for him when something grabbed my wrist. A touch slippery like algae.

Startled, I shot a look to my side and saw Jinju, the fish-woman. She slipped three pearls into the pouch I always carried, while still gripping me with her free hand, her shell-like nails digging into my skin. Her eyes widened and they appeared all black as she shook her head slowly as though to say, *Do not save him.*

Leave me alone, I mouthed. I wrenched my hand away.

I swam over to the unconscious man. Jinju joined me with concern clouding her brows. Together we brought him to the surface. The vessel was too far away, carried off by a strong gust of wind; the shore was nearer. We hauled the young man's motionless body onto the beach.

After compressing his chest and breathing into him, I watched as his dark lashes fluttered open. He coughed, the look of pain tearing across his features. Then he remained still for the longest time in a sitting position, head bowed, arms draped across his knees as his chest heaved for air. He was a young man, perhaps a year or two older than I, and he had a small mole under the corner of his left eye. He was the most handsome man I had ever set my gaze on.

Nervous, I flicked a glance to my side. Jinju was already gone. It was just the young man and I, and I could tell he was a highborn by his fine silk robe.

"What happened?" he finally asked, his voice hoarse.

"You nearly drowned, and we saved you. I mean, *I* saved you." I told myself that I had changed the "we" to "I" to protect Jinju. "I was out at sea when I saw you drowning, so I brought you back to shore."

He shook his head, hand on his brows. "While standing on the vessel, heading to port, I thought I saw something below. I peered over the boat's ledge, then someone bumped me and I fell in. I swam for as long as I could, but . . ." He looked me over and I wanted to cover myself. "You are a haenyeo."

"Yeah," I replied in the positive.

He asked for my name.

I told it to him.

He repeated my name, and a tremor jolted through me—to hear my name embraced in his mouth. He repeated my name again, then there was a shift in his eyes. Like he found my name familiar. He examined me closer, then blinked, and he suddenly asked, "You are not afraid of the sea?"

"I have grown accustomed to it. It is part of life for me."

"What . . . what does it look like, down there in the waters?"

"Dark."

"You cannot have wished to be a haenyeo."

"No."

The young nobleman and I spent some time together, walking along the shore. I could swear his eyes turned to me on several occasions, gazing at the fullness of my lips, the curve of my jaw, the bareness of my throat. Or perhaps I was imagining this. Perhaps what other girls told me was true—that I was vulnerable, that I yearned too much for the attention of others. But he felt different. I felt as though I had known him for a hundred years. There was a comfort to his presence. And when we parted later in the afternoon, the thought of him filled my skull like the sea.

❀

I did not think I would see him again.

The following week, I perched myself on a rock near the shore, staring at the spot where the young nobleman and I had walked.

After expelling a hundred wistful sighs, I slipped back into the water, and not too much later, I found Jinju peering at me from behind a kelp forest. She swam over, her great tail flickering, and she gave me more pearls.

I wanted to pull away from her touch, but I needed the pearls. As soon as they were secure in my pouch, I kicked off a rock, to get away from Jinju as fast as possible. I swam upward too fast, nearly forgetting the age-old technique of expelling the last reserve of air from my lungs. My head spun. I took in several calming breaths, then peered under the waves again, and there she was—the creepy fish-woman staring up at me.

"Good morning!" a deep male voice called out from the distance.

I looked ahead and saw a figure standing on the shore, waving at me. I swam toward the silhouette and realized it was the young nobleman standing by his horse. My chest tightened as I swam faster, and as I rose from the waters, I smoothed away strands of my drenched hair and wished I could cover myself. I felt like a naked fish, until his eyes took me in, running along the length of my figure. My toes curled in. I felt like a woman for the first time. And he—he was everything I wanted. His silk robe billowed in the fierce island wind, molding to his tall and well-built figure, and his eyes twinkled with mischief. He was handsome and wealthy, and I knew whoever should become his wife would be admired by all.

Imagine, a whisper echoed in my mind, *being embraced by all.*

My heart thrummed to life, unfurling with a yearning that seemed to reach out for him as tentacles. A desperation to possess. To be possessed by one such as he. To become someone else, anyone else, but myself. I tried to tame my heart, not wanting to frighten him away.

But he did not recoil from me. Instead, he tethered his horse to a crooked tree and proffered a hand. I reached out and his long fingers wrapped around mine, and our palms pressed together. It felt so natural, as though we had held hands before in another lifetime.

"Walk with me," he said.

We walked along the coast, and I felt the eyes of the other haenyeos following me, including Grandmother's.

"Have you ever seen an ineo?" he asked.

Without hesitation, I whispered, "I have, sir."

"That is why your name was so familiar to me. You're the girl who has a mermaid following you. I asked about you out of curiosity."

Everyone in my village knew of my "friend" and would stare at me like I was strange. "The villagers must have shared that something must be wrong with me. I do not wish to be followed," I said. "But she will not leave me be . . ."

He squeezed my hand. "You must be special. That is why she follows you."

I blushed.

"Sometimes," he murmured, "I wonder why people hunt for ineos . . ."

"For the elixir of life," I replied, feeling intelligent. "I hear you become more beautiful and younger the more you eat of their flesh."

"But could it be true?"

"Long ago, I heard a rumor. Of a gentleman who is over two hundred years of age, yet it is said he looks to be no more than twenty. Have you heard of this, too?"

"I have heard such stories," he murmured. "But they are simply stories, surely."

"I hear his wives are always doomed to a short life. That is the price that comes with eating ineo flesh."

"Hmm," he said thoughtfully. "Is that so?"

"Rumors claim that over three thousand women had dealings with the ageless man." I paused, afraid that I sounded too vulgar, but he seemed intrigued. "And the women all withered physically and died in the end."

"This is all likely a story with no truth to it, but if it were true, it would seem to me this ineo-eating man wishes to live a long life."

"So much so that he would live with the curse? Of all the women he loves living a short life?"

He chuckled. "Perhaps he does not love the women he has dealings with. Perhaps he is simply—hungry."

I could not understand his meaning, but I sensed that this age-less man was awful. "But why? Why would anyone wish to live forever?" The thought of living forever, diving, toiling through life to barely survive, was an exhausting thought.

"I suppose . . . some never wish to outlive their body," he replied, "because life is better than death. I often think about how much I have seen and how little; about how much the kingdom of Joseon has changed before my very eyes and how much more it will change still . . . I imagine people would want to live forever to see it all. To learn about everything. To live a story with no end. To have wisdom of a thousand years—for one's mind to become the universe itself, rich with everything existence has to offer."

The young nobleman then looked at me and smiled. "To be immortal is to be infinite. Would you not wish that?" He glanced at my haenyeo garb, still dripping wet. Then he examined my expression. "You might not wish it, because you are poor. But a girl like you is worthy of far more than this."

"Am I?" I whispered.

"Did your mother never tell you so? Mine would remind me, every day, that I was precious. That this kingdom could be mine."

"My mother never told me anything. She passed away early, you see . . ."

"Well, I can see it." He reached out and brushed aside a strand of my hair, sending a tremor of confusion down my spine. Did he like me? But why? "You were not meant for this life. If you were to permit me, I would show you how much more to life there is, and you would wish it too—to live forever."

Days like today, I wished Mother were here with me. I could rush over to her, calling out, "Eomang!" and tell her about the young nobleman I had met, and my feelings for him. I wondered what she would say. What kind of advice did mothers give? Wise ones, perhaps. Loving ones.

But I would never know.

She had left me too soon, and even if I could live forever, I knew her absence would still haunt me. Mother had disappeared when I was a few days old. There were no memories of her, except for one: her face a shadow in the sunlight behind; she was cradling me, and I was holding on to her finger. I wish I had never let go.

"Did you see her again?" Grandmother asked.

I looked up from my abalone porridge. For a moment I thought Grandmother was speaking of Mother. Then I saw her examining the pearls I had left out on the table.

"I did." I rubbed my hand against my skirt, to rid the sensation of Jinju's algae-slippery touch, then I picked up my wooden spoon once more. "As usual."

"You know, whenever ineos are caught, they are sometimes kept in ponds like livestock. It is a cruel, cruel thing these villagers do. We must respect the sea and all living within."

I continued to eat. Trying not to stare at the pearls.

"Just this week," Grandmother went on, "an ineo was caught."

"I know, I saw, too." I filled my mouth with a spoonful of porridge, chewing quietly.

"The villagers were discussing whether to sell her or eat her."

"Ineo, ineo, ineo," I said after swallowing. "It is all you ever talk about."

"Then what else shall we talk about?"

"How about the many questions I ask, which you never answer?"

"Such as?"

"Why did my mother leave me, Halmang?"

Grandmother stirred her porridge, her eyes filling up with a faraway look. "A long, long time ago, a childless widower caught an ineo."

I held in a sigh. She always did this. I would ask a question, and she would spin up an elaborate story that had nothing to do with what I wanted to know.

"He had been tempted to keep her for profit, for ineo flesh brings in much wealth. But also, whenever an ineo cries, her tears turn into pearls. In the end, he decided to release her. The villagers asked why he had done so, and he said it was her eyes. Her gaze implored him to let her go. He felt, deep in his heart, that what might give him life and wealth could kill his soul."

I scraped the bowl clean, eating the last abalone.

"Then the ineo swam up to the shore near his home and gave him a gift for his good deed. It was a gift he desired more than anything—a child." Grandmother cast a glance my way, perhaps sensing my frustration as I pushed my bowl aside and grabbed the pearls off the table. "The answer is right before your eyes. Yet you do not see it, because you are distracted by your thoughts of what you do not have."

I was about to stalk off to my quarter when Grandmother called out, "Look at the sea. Look at what you do have. Keep looking until you find it."

"Find what?" I snapped.

"Ask yourself, why does the ineo cry for you?"

"What do you mean?"

"Until you wish to know the truth, you will not hear it, even if I told you."

She said no more, gave me no answers, nor did the sea. The

waters—visible from outside my window—remained as silent and dark as ever.

Two weeks later, the young nobleman sent me an elegant box. Within was a short jacket and skirt made of silk, so smooth and expensive my fingers trembled as I touched the embroidered flowers blossoming along the collar and the hem. The servant who had delivered this gift told me she would escort me to the young noble's mansion.

When people bumped into me in town, they bowed, thinking I was a respectable young lady. And, indeed, I felt that I was one of them. I stuck up my chin, imagining that I was a woman with a hundred servants awaiting me and that I was someone of importance. My steps grew more confident. I was on my way to fix my fate. Soon I would shed myself of my slimy scales and rise from my simple life into a life worth living, a life that gleamed like the brightest of stars.

When I arrived at the mansion, the stately sight swelled in my chest.

"This could all be yours," the young noble said, greeting me and showing me around his estate.

"All mine?" I could barely speak.

"Yes." His smile was intimate. "All of it. I would keep nothing from you."

"But . . . why me?" Had he fallen in love with me so soon? Did he see something in me that I had never noticed before? That even my own mother had not noticed, to have abandoned me on the shore? "I am but a haenyeo . . ."

Without answering my question, he simply whispered, "Come, follow me."

In silence we walked, his knuckles brushing against mine, and with each touch, my heart jolted against my chest.

"I will teach you to be who you wish to be—a young lady. I will bring in the best scholars to teach you how to read and write, and teach you etiquette, and make your life worthy of being lived. And when I receive my government position back on the mainland, you can come live there with me, far away from this gods-forsaken island."

Escape the sea—could I escape the sea?

Thrill fluttered in my chest, yet I could not ignore the tug. The fierce tug of the sea, the waves still pulsing through my veins. The echo of the deep, calling out to me, to stay, to stay. The song of haenyeos surfacing from the freezing dark, hoowi, hoowi, and Grandmother's special dishes—

"You could read all these books and live a thousand lives," he said.

We had walked into a library, with tall bookcases stacked with five-stitched books. On the walls were paintings of young noblemen, but in different robes, different styles of caps, and some paintings looked hundreds of years old. Worn out and the paint faded. Were these paintings of his ancestors? Yet on all the faces of the young men was a small mole under the left eye.

"Come closer," he urged.

I did so, and he offered a book to me. I could not read the title and wondered whether it was a story I already knew, told to me by Grandmother. For she had told me thousands. Or perhaps, within this book, was a *real* story. The ones young ladies grew up reading. The stories that made one respectable and educated.

"This book is a gift for you, but this entire library could all be yours as well, once I teach you to read," the young noble explained. "But first, you must prove something to me."

"Yeah?" I whispered.

"If you wish to be mine, you must catch for me an ineo."

My blood went cold, colder than the depths of the sea.

"Catch a fish, and it will feed you for the night," he whispered. "But catch an ineo, and your life will change—forever."

"I could do that," I said after a pause.

Guilt pinched at me, but I reminded myself of what I had learned on land. Ineos were not human. They were different from us. That was why villagers were permitted to treat them as such—as live-stock.

"I am told the ineo who haunts you is among the last," the young noble interrupted my thoughts, and in his voice was a strain. Panic? Fear? Goose bumps crept along my skin as he leaned in to whisper, his ancient breath stirring the tendrils of my hair. "I have scoured the entire kingdom of Joseon—and only a few remain now, here in Jeju. I want them all."

※

Together we made our way to the port, where we were met by a hired musketeer. The three of us stepped into a boat, and my stomach churned with nervousness as a fisherman led us off to sea. For the whole time I stared at the long musket propped against the edge of the vessel.

"This should be far enough into the sea," the fisherman said.

The young noble bowed his head, then he gave me a dagger and a long rope that was tied to the boat. He then took my chin and drew me near, then nearer, until our lips were touching. "Bring the creature to me, and you will never want for anything again." Then he kissed me lightly.

His lips felt withered.

And guilt beat stronger in my chest.

It was wrong, what he was asking me to do.

I did not need to have read a thousand books to know this truth; I sensed it, as I might sense the current of the sea. I simply knew.

I nevertheless tucked the dagger behind me and dived into the dark sea, carrying down the rope. I later returned to the surface, sucked in more air, then dived and searched again. The water was still frigid. Icier than usual.

Then I saw her.

Jinju was watching me, always watching me.

Gripping the rope tighter, I found myself thinking back on the first time I'd seen her at the age of eleven. I had always assumed she had come to haunt me, yet this time I remembered the way she had untangled seaweed from my ankle, keeping me from drowning. The time she had fought off an octopus, keeping it from wrapping its tentacle around my face. The time she had ushered me away from a shark. Had she been haunting me—or simply watching over me?

I stared at her and no longer saw a thing of monstrosity. She surged toward me like a school of fish, her hair billowing as plants under the sea. She looked wonderful, fragile, and glorious. And I think she knew what I was up to, gripping the rope as I was. Perhaps she could sense the dagger tucked behind me as well. She glanced up, and we both stared at the boat's shadow looming above our heads.

What to do now?

I was running out of breath. I had to decide. If I swam to the surface, she would follow and I would not even need to use my dagger, as the young noble assumed I would. He thought she would fight and struggle to escape, but I sensed she would not. She would follow me to the surface, right into the boat, and the musketeer would pick up his weapon and shoot.

Why does the ineo cry for you?

Grandmother's words rippled through my mind, and suddenly, I wanted to cry. A sob gathered hot in my throat as I swam farther away from the boat, and Jinju stayed close to me. When I was down to my last breath, I quickly made my way upward, the shimmering surface drawing closer and closer.

When I reach the surface, a realization expanded in my chest, *I no longer want a life away from the sea.*

What I wanted, now, was to see the things Grandmother had tried to help me see. I wanted to listen more closely to her tales and all the truths folded within her words. I wanted to know who I was, the side of me hidden in the depth of the sea, always waiting for me behind the kelp forest.

Too afraid to draw attention, I did not expel the poison from my chest in a loud hoowi. Blackness encroached my vision. Darker, darker, until all I saw was a fragment of Jinju, holding me against her cold skin. An explosion filled my ears; her body jolted as the acrid smell of gunpowder pierced my senses.

"Ddal." Blood dribbled out from her mouth. "Neh ddal-ah."

Daughter. My daughter.

Perhaps I had imagined it. I must have. I remembered nothing more after that as my mind plunged into darkness.

When I finally woke up, I was on the shore choking and heaving for air. My hand was full of pearls; they dribbled out onto the sand like drops of tears. And when I rose to my feet, I stared after the trail of blood that disappeared into the water.

"Eomang!" I called out, the waves crashing against my bare feet. "Eomang!"

❦

She has to be alive. I gazed off at the sea from the window of my room. *She has to be.*

I watched the evening waves froth against the shore, the blood-stain washed away. I watched until it was too dark to see anything at all. Then, with a candle lit, I opened the large chest in which I had collected all of Jinju's pearls. A collection started when I was eleven, and now the pearls brimmed to the top.

I could buy anything I wanted with this collection—

But how little I desired now.

At first light, even before the other haenyeos could pass my home, I was running. Darting up hills, tumbling through fields, until my bare feet sunk into sand. I hurried along the black rocks that stretched into the sea, then slipped into the waves. My feet skidded across rocks, more rocks, then nothing, and I was floating in the depth of Mother's heart.

Deep, endless, and unfathomable.

"Eomang," I whispered as my throat tightened and tears burned my eyes. I had done her wrong, yet the waves were warm today, holding me kindly in her embrace. "Eomang, your daughter is here. She is finally here."

SIX THOUSAND MILES

Julie C. Dao

Once upon a time, the world you know begins to disappear.
Drop by drop, it slips through your fingers, glittering like the sea.
You watch it dissolve: the sun-drenched mornings of walking to
school beneath the banyan trees, the scent of ripe durian rising like
heat, Ba's tired hand on your head as he comes home from work,
Mẹ and your aunties rolling bánh cuốn in the sweltering kitchen.
Even at your age, you understand that these days will soon be
taken from you forever.

And suddenly, the cramped house shared by four generations
of your family feels like a palace; the teasing neighbors now
seem admiring courtiers; and the dirty river into which you
dive with your cousins—grudgingly, as befitting a girl nearing
womanhood—is a kingdom of wonder beneath the unforgiving
sun. You have always been a princess, the youngest and most

cherished of the royal daughters, and you never knew it until your riches were almost gone.

But there is an escape from this loss: a country across the world, handsome and strong, with arms full of promises. If you could be together, you would be safe and loved. Your family would want for nothing, and you would see how simple life really was: leave behind a crumbling world to find a better one. Be humble, and earn yourself respect. Work hard, and win a fortune.

So you fall in love with the horizon. Scrape fragments of the old life from your skin like scales. Shut your eyes to the pain of the unknown, like naked feet on sharp rocks. And plunge into the ocean for the last time, singing a love song at the top of your lungs so you can't hear the waves weeping for your loss. You reach those dreamed-of shores, in that kingdom across the sea where you will love and be loved for all time.

But what you didn't know was that the longing would be yours alone.

You rise from the depths with a melody on your tongue, but no one can hear you. You contort your lips to taste their flat, foreign words, but they dry unheard in your throat and your voice shatters, sharp as sea glass. Eyes avert, mouths twist.

Learn English, for god's sake!

So you try harder. You watch them the way a crab hidden in sand watches bigger fish. You adopt their bright clothing and the way they laugh, pale eyes gleaming in pale faces, but no matter what, you can never copy their walk: thoughtless, as though each step costs nothing, as though the press of their feet on this foreign earth does not hurt like daggers biting. You can barely move without the thousand tiny wounds on your legs and soles screaming from where you ripped out your scales and flushed them away to return to the ocean without you.

Go back to your own country!

You move inland, farther from the call of the sea. Blue-green scales still bloom on your legs every month, but over time, you learn to push them back in, housing the shame of your past with your own body, where it will disturb no one. And when your daughters are born, you teach them to do the same: to bow their heads, to speak in soft voices, to only ever please and obey. No matter that the sweeping romance you envisioned was only a dream. No matter that this country seems even more distant now that you are living in it. You teach your girls that pain is the price of love, and that forcing those glassy scales back into their skin will help them belong.

Where are you even from, anyway?

You teach your daughters never to ask you about the past. But try as you might, in the dark undertow of your dreams, you can still feel the cool, endless blue of the Pacific kiss the seeping wounds on your legs. You dream of your scales emerging, your legs fusing into a long shimmering tail, and your lungs taking in their first true breath since you left home.

But in the morning, you push all of it back under your skin.

And for your daughters' sake, you try to forget that any of it had ever existed.

MAI

I swallow my rage as the white woman stares at us from behind the hotel desk. She looks down the kind of long, high nose my mom has always wanted instead of her own flat, wide one and repeats, loudly and slowly, "I can't find your reservation. Did you book a room?"

Mom speaks in her gentlest voice, her Vietnamese accent further softening it. "I did. We have room. My daughter getting married here. The name is Nguyen."

"Wing. W-I-N-G. There's no reservation under that name."

"No, no, *Nguyen*. Loan Nguyen." My mother spells it for the third time.

The woman emits a sigh loud enough to lift a plane off the runway and clacks away at her computer. "Oh, I see it now. You mean nuh-goo-yen. Lone nuh-goo-yen?" she asks, and my mom smiles with infinite patience. "Double queen room. Three nights?"

"Yes. In a room block. For the Nguyen and Jones wedding."

"Oh, the *Jones* wedding!" The woman laughs, rolling ice chip eyes fringed with clumps of mascara. "Just say that next time. It's a lot easier than nuh-goo-yen."

It's the last straw. I'm about ready to jump this Karen, but Mom senses my murderous intent and lays a hand on my arm. "Thank you for your help," she says, sweet and polite.

"Yeah, thanks for your help," I echo, and the woman looks at me, surprised by my perfect English. I make sure she sees me checking her name tag. "Vanessa. I'll be sure to leave a review about your thoughts on pronouncing our name. Though *pronounce* is a loose term here, isn't it?"

"Mai-ah!" Mom drags me away as Vanessa stares after us.

"She's a racist, Mom!" I say loudly, and people all around the fancy lobby look up.

My mother yanks me into an elevator. "You are always so

angry," she says, switching to Vietnamese. "Not everything has to be a fight. So what if she can't say our name?"

I start to argue but reconsider when she pushes the button and leans tiredly against the mirrored wall. Her shoulders slump, shrinking into the space she is forever apologizing for taking up while I shout for more, more, more. Her face is drawn and pale. Traveling has never agreed with her, but flying to Hawaii has been even more of a trial. I swallow my guilt, because *I'm* the one who talked Kim into getting married on an island.

Mom is terrified of the sea. She wouldn't even let me look out of the plane window. My sisters and I know that pressing for answers would mean getting her famous silent treatment, which can last for a whole week. It's the same reason we never talk about the iridescent scales that have appeared on my legs every month since I turned fifteen. When I first woke up that day last year, screaming at the pain of them bursting through my skin like splinter-sharp sequins, it was my sister Thao who ran in to comfort me and gather my bloodied sheets.

"This is natural," she explained. "Kim and I first got these on our fifteenth birthdays, too. It won't be so bad once you learn how to push them back in. Just don't mention them to Mom."

"Why not? Doesn't she know about them?"

"Of course. She has them, too. She taught Kim what to do, and Kim taught me." Thao showed me how to pinch each scale with my fingertips and shove it back under my skin. I threw up twice from the unbearable pain, but Thao was unfazed. "One day you won't even need your fingers. You'll be able to will them right back in as soon as you feel them sprouting."

"What are these? Why do we have them?" I gasped, tears burning my face.

Thao hesitated. "I'm not sure. It's Mom's secret."

What they don't know is *I* have a secret, too. I've been studying the scales and letting them stay longer than a day, which Thao warned me not to do, in case I can't push them back in after. I've even ripped some out, biting down on a mouth guard to keep from screaming. They're beautiful once I rinse the blood off, and I know they have something to do with Mom's fear of the ocean. But where she keeps silent about what scares her, I get angry—angry that my feet and legs hurt with every step, angry that we never talk about the past or the sea, angry that we have to hide it all inside. Angry that no matter what, this country will only ever love people like Vanessa, too distracted by her false charms to hear the beauty of our voices.

On the twelfth floor, Thao pokes her head into the hall. "Kim, they're here!" she yells, then hugs us and whispers, "Thank god. I'm about ready to kick Kim's bridezilla ass." Ignoring Mom's disapproving cluck, she wheels our suitcases into a magnificent bridal suite.

The coral wallpaper is dotted with mother-of-pearl sconces, illuminating a plush salmon rug. The furniture is the bright cream of a shell washed onto shore, and vases spill fragrant white jasmine and beach roses. But all of it is a mere backdrop to the enormous windows through which I see, at last, the ocean: blinding, miraculous. Through the sway of heavy-headed palm trees, it undulates like some creature holding the beach in its glittering arms, shining every shade of blue from indigo to aquamarine. A breeze slips in, bringing with it the breath of salt and the whisper of the sea: *Hush, hush, hush.*

My anger dissolves, obedient for once. I am transfixed, enraptured.

Kim waves her hand in my face. "He*llo*? Is anyone home?" she asks, but jerks backward when I try to hug her. "Just air kisses for now. Don't crease the dress."

She is trying on her gown, a diaphanous chiffon concoction that froths from her body with the palest hint of sea-foam green. Her black silk hair is swept up with pearl pins. She looks like a siren queen surrounded by blond, white attendants all wearing the same long dress of aqua satin. Thao is the only one in deep turquoise, her skirt flaring out like a tail at her knees.

"Hurry up," Kim says. "I want to see both you and Thao in your maid of honor dresses."

"Mom and Mai *literally* just got here," Thao points out. "Give them a minute, will you?"

Kim doesn't like her little sisters telling her what to do at the best of times, so on her wedding weekend, these are fighting words. A screaming match immediately ensues, with the bridesmaids and an older blond woman—the groom's mother, maybe—trying to prevent murder.

"Let's come back later," I tell Mom, but she doesn't hear me. Her eyes are on the ocean outside the windows, a compass lured north. Her face is paler than ever. "You okay?"

She takes a shaky breath. "Let's go."

In our own room down the hall, she crumples onto a bed and lays an arm over her eyes. Our windows only look out onto a courtyard, and I close the curtains so she can nap. Then I slip out, sneaking past the bridal suite. In the lobby, I don't even bother passing racist Vanessa to flip her off. I make a beeline for the beach, the hibiscus-scented breeze tangling my hair. It's almost painful, this desperation to go to the sea before anyone can stop me.

The beaches near the resort are narrow and swarming with

tourists, so I remove my flip-flops and walk until our hotel is a speck in the distance, feeling the sand crumble like sugar between my toes. The air smells like roses and salt and soil after the rain, and the cerulean water and sky are so brilliant I have to shield my eyes. On a quieter stretch of beach, I step into the ocean for the first time.

It's warmer than I imagined. My heels sink into the wet sand and I laugh as the gentle ripples tickle my ankles. I go in until my calves are submerged and suddenly realize that the constant pain in my legs and feet is gone. My head feels clearer, too, like I've never truly breathed before. I feel drunk on joy. I jump and shout and dance with my arms outstretched.

A boy watches me from a short distance away, expertly treading water.

"Nice, huh?" he calls, then slips underwater and swims over. When he bursts back up, I almost have to shield my eyes again because he is as blinding as the water. Drops of the sea cascade off broad shoulders and a shock of jet-black hair. His smile is slow and warm and knowing, like he can picture how my white sundress would cling to me if I dived in with him. "First time in the ocean?"

"Yeah," I say, feeling strangely shy. I have no problem sassing the guys at school, but then again, I grew up with them and most were as white and basic as Velveeta mac and cheese. This boy, on the other hand, is a heady combination of attractive, Asian, and confident. "We don't see a lot of water where I live."

He stands up, and I swear the water takes its time tracing his tan neck and chest. Can't say I blame it. "I bet you spend all your time swimming in pools."

"No, actually. I never learned how to swim. My mom wouldn't let me."

"Really?" he asks, surprised. "You look like a swimmer to me."

My stomach swoops, like his smile somehow tied a knot behind my navel. "How so?"

He points to my legs, which are still knee-deep in the water.

I look down and scream. Every inch of my skin that is touching the ocean has erupted in scales. I collapse on the sand, yanking the hem of my dress over my legs. I hadn't even felt them coming with the usual pain and gore. There isn't any blood, just irides-cent slivers catching the sun like gems. My feet are covered, too, the scales almost fusing my toes together. I look up at the boy desperately. "It's . . . it's a skin condition," I babble. "I'm not a monster, I swear!"

"Hey, it's okay. It's your first time in the ocean, so you couldn't have known," he says in a gentle voice, and points to his own legs. My jaw drops. I had been so busy staring at his upper half, I hadn't noticed the blue-green scales jutting out of the skin beneath his swimming trunks.

"You're like me," I choke out. "I-I've never met anyone outside of my family like me."

"I bet you haven't," he says kindly. "Salt water makes the scales come out. Stay in the ocean long enough, and you'll have a tail. Give these influencers something to post about." He nods at three shrieking white girls in bikinis, trying to jump in unison as their friend films them. Even though they're too far away to see, I tug my dress even harder over my feet.

I realize then that this must be Mom's secret. This is what she's afraid of, and why she avoids the ocean and fought so hard for

Kim *not* to get married in Honolulu. But if this boy can be so calm and matter-of-fact about it, could it really be wrong?

"I'll have a tail?" I croak, and his eyes crinkle at the corners as he holds out his hands. I take them, and they feel as sturdy and solid as the rest of him. "I'm Mai," I add shyly.

He pulls me to my feet. "Huy."

"You're Vietnamese, too?" I ask, surprised.

"Of course." He leads me into the water and pulls me in so deep, I have no time to feel self-conscious about my dress fluttering up above my thighs. Panic shoots through my chest as the ocean presses in around us, but he puts my hands on his shoulders. "Don't worry. I got you."

I kick my legs instinctively, and after a minute, I relax into the sway of the sea. "This is kind of fun," I say as the overwhelming sensation of joy and well-being returns.

Huy laughs, deep dimples bracketing his mouth. His hands are secure on my waist, and I feel a shiver of excitement. I've never even slow danced with a boy and here I am, pressed up against one on my first day in Hawaii. He's all business, though, as he shows me how to move. In no time at all, I'm treading water on my own. "See? I was right. You *are* a swimmer," he says.

In the clear water, I see big scales forming along the insides of my thighs, drawing them together like magnets. I pull my knees apart in alarm. "If I form a tail, can I get my legs back?"

"Yeah, if you don't keep your tail for more than three days. Any longer, and it'll be permanent." Huy plunges underwater and executes a perfect flip. I feel a tug of longing for that careless grace, that effortless joy. He resurfaces, panting. "Hurts like hell to transition, though. I just wanted to try it once. After this weekend, I'm swimming home, permanent tail and all."

"Home?"

He fixes his eyes on the horizon. "Six thousand miles that way. I've been dying to cross the Pacific ever since I turned fifteen and got my first scales." His smile is bashful. "I wanted to practice my English in Hawaii, and now I can say I have."

I stare at him, aghast. "You swam six thousand miles to get here?"

He laughs again. "It's easy with a tail. The journey's the best part: sparkling water, coral shining under the waves, fish swimming around sunken ships. There are so many secrets in this ocean that none of these people can even begin to grasp. They think *this* is living." He gestures to the beach. "But life, *real* life, is across the sea where I come from. Where *you* come from, too."

I gaze across the Pacific, filled with a helpless yearning. "My mom left her home years ago. She never talks about it or the scales. If she caught me swimming with you, she'd kill me."

Huy shakes his head. "But why? The ocean is beautiful. Our home is beautiful. It belongs to us, and we to it. Why did she give it all up for *this* place?"

I tread water, considering his question. I think of all the years I've fielded questions like "Where do you come from?" even though I was born here. I think of how white people stare and shake their heads when we speak Vietnamese in public. I think of racist Vanessa and the hundred other instances of bullshit microaggressions I've endured.

"I guess Mom wanted a better life," I say.

Huy raises a brow. "I came here for fun, but it isn't who we are," he says. "We don't belong here and never will. You can't grow roots in rotting soil, and that's what this place is. It doesn't want us, Mai. All its promises are just a dream."

I want to argue, but I can't. Truth is, I haven't wanted to consider too closely the idea that Mom might have given up everything she knew for an empty promise. I ache at the memory of her cleaning toilets and sticky floors at the diner so that Kim and Thao and I could get an education. I don't want to believe all that was for nothing.

Huy turns suddenly. "Mai," he says, low and eager and intense, "come with me. I can teach you how to swim, and how to use your tail."

"That's crazy!" I burst out. "I don't even know you."

"So what?" he persists, his eyes starry with hope. "I can tell you haven't been happy here, and your mom probably hasn't, either. I'll take both of you."

"I have a sister getting married in two days and another one finishing up college."

"That's fine. They can live their lives here. But you and your mom can go with me."

I look at the horizon in disbelief. I'm not sure which is more overwhelming: the idea of swimming six thousand miles with a boy I've only just met, or the fact that a part of me is actually considering it. "You said if I keep my tail for longer than three days, it becomes permanent," I say. "I won't be able to get my legs back. And if that happens, I won't ever see my sisters again, will I?"

His silence is all the confirmation I need.

I turn and kick back to shore. I will my scales back into my legs, and the minute I stand up on solid ground, the old pain stabs into my feet like daggers. For a fleeting moment, I wonder if this boy's determination to go home and leave behind the sharp rejection of the new world doesn't make a strange kind of sense. "I need to think about it," I say.

"Yeah, of course," Huy says, hiding his obvious disappointment with another disarming smile. "I'm here until Sunday. In the meantime, come back and swim again? Maybe tonight, if you can?"

Without waiting for an answer, he disappears underwater, his scales shimmering.

I come back every night that weekend. I can't focus on the wedding, not with the ocean calling and the boy who offered up its secrets waiting.

On Thursday night, I ditch my sister's cocktail hour, refusing the themed drinks under the pretext of being underage when really, I'd rather not sip something called "Oriental Breeze," a name Mrs. Jones clearly thought would best honor her new daughter-in-law's heritage. I tell Thao I'm avoiding a Jones uncle who hit the whiskey too hard and keeps asking me why Asian girls are so beautiful, and within minutes, I'm back in the ocean, my dress flung onto the moonlit sand as scales bloom on my bare legs. I learn to swim with Huy's hands on my waist and his eyes on mine in the shadows. It feels deliciously reckless to be with a strange boy on a dark beach, my unsuspecting family only steps away. I learn to navigate the water in record time, and we swim out farther and farther, mile after mile. I am drunk on the danger of leaving land behind, of surrounding myself with only water and this boy who sees me as I am.

Friday night is Kim's rehearsal dinner in the resort's bougie French restaurant, a separate building on the grounds, which makes it both easier and harder to sneak out: easier, because it's right on the beach, and harder, because so many wedding guests are coming out to smoke or gossip or engage in illicit relations in the palm grove. I almost get caught by the Jones uncle with the Asian fetish, but he's too wasted to really notice as I meet Huy at the water's edge.

It's only the third time we've gone swimming together, but it feels as natural as breathing. The first shiver of delight as I slip into the water, the electric jolt every time his hands find my skin, and the tender, almost embryonic embrace of the ocean cradling my body. And I know a part of me would die if things went back to the way they were—if I left Hawaii with my silent mother and pretended I had never gone into the sea, or met this boy who accepts the *real* me, or seen my legs fuse together into a long, perfect tail.

Idyllic as it is, there's always pressure from Huy. His passive-aggressive remarks dig at my hesitation, Mom's decisions, and the fact that my sister is marrying a rich white guy. "The ultimate American dream, huh?" He speaks in a light tone, so I'll know it's a joke, but with a hint of judgment, so I'll know he thinks Kim's a cop-out like Mom.

"Just because you don't agree with their choices doesn't make them wrong," I point out.

"It's not about right or wrong. It's about being faithful to where you come from."

"Oh, so you're calling them traitors."

He sighs. "Stop putting words in my mouth. I want to help you. We've got a connection. Not just this," he adds, taking my hand. "But something deeper. We come from the same place, and you seem lost. I want to help you find what you're looking for."

Slowly, I pull away. "We're strangers. How the hell do you know what I'm looking for?"

"Why are you so tense tonight?"

"Because you're being judgmental and pushy. You can try to help without offering a commentary on everything you think my family has done wrong."

"I told you, it's not about right or wrong! It's about what's *better*. Do you think walking on two feet, on *this* land . . ." He gestures to the sand like it's poisoned. "All that pain with every step . . . do you think that's what you were meant for? I'm pushy because I care about you."

"You don't even know me!"

"I do. You and I, we're the same."

"Mom wants me to pretend I can't grow a tail. *You* want me to pretend I don't want my legs. Honestly? I'm sick of everyone telling me what to do." I swim back to shore, and on the sand, my tail gleams in the moonlight like sea glass. But before I can will it away, Huy follows and puts a gentle hand on my hip, like he can't bear for my legs to return. Desperation and longing cloud his eyes as his hand strokes the length of my tail, making me shiver.

When his lips find mine, I realize he does care—or at least, he *believes* he does. I put my hand on his to stop him, even though it's torture.

"I have to go," I say, and with all the willpower I have, I push my scales in, split my tail into legs, and walk away, wincing with every step.

🐚

On Saturday evening, Kim marries Ted Jones with all the glitz and glamour her heart could desire. She floats down the beach on a carpet of white rose petals and kisses him at sunset beneath a chiffon tent, but all I can think about is the ocean stretching out behind me. As the maids of honor, Thao and I stand closest to the bride, facing the guests and maintaining perma-smiles so we don't get caught on camera with resting bitch face. Thao seems distracted, too, and as we move back down the aisle, she whispers, "Mom knows where you went last night."

My throat goes dry. "What?"

"You're not as sneaky as you think," Thao says wryly. "I knew it had to be a boy, so I tried to stop her from leaving to look for you. But she insisted on checking the beach."

"What did you see?" I demand.

"Nothing explicit. Just the two of you swimming, but that was enough for Mom." Thao sighs. "You know how she is. What the hell were you thinking, Mai?"

The whole time we pose for photos, I think about Mom. She *has* been quieter, only speaking curtly to me—her usual signal that I have somehow displeased her and that she will punish me with silence instead of telling me what I've done. It's her signature parenting style, but I never thought it would be because of my secret swim lessons.

"Did you use protection, at least?" Thao hisses.

"We didn't have sex!" I snap, and a blond bridesmaid darts a curious glance at us. "All we did was swim, and you and Mom are acting like I murdered someone."

"Don't use that tone with me," Thao says coldly. "I'm just pointing out that you know Mom has a thing about the ocean. Don't go swimming, or at least hide it better."

"Hide it? I'm so fucking sick of having to hide everything!" I explode. Everyone stares as I shove my bouquet at Thao and stride off, mumbling an apology to a pissed-off Kim and her puzzled husband. I rip off my shoes, these strappy torture devices that somehow make walking even *more* painful, and throw them into the darkness as I march down the moonlit beach.

No matter what I choose, I will have to live a lie. To please Mom, I would give up my tail and pretend none of this ever happened. To please Huy, I would abandon my family for him and somehow convince myself it's the "better" choice.

Everyone wants me to be either one thing or the other.

But I'm not.

Sometimes I have legs, but sometimes I have a tail. I have skin, but I also have scales. I carry inside me the home Mom left behind, but also the new home she made for us. How can I choose between two parts of my own self? And why should I have to?

"Mai!" Huy yells. He's in the water not far away, but I ignore him and keep walking.

"Mai!" someone else shouts. It sounds like Kim or Thao, but I ignore them, too.

I reach an empty stretch of beach, where the ocean drowns them all out. There is only me and the moon and the water, and I unzip my dress. I step into the water in just my bra and slip and watch my scales emerge and my feet and legs fuse together. I move my arms with powerful strokes, my tail maneuvering the sea with all the confidence I have gained these past few days. I have never done a flip before, but I've watched Huy, so I imitate his movements and pull off a few imperfect ones. I spring through the surface like a dolphin, my anger abating as bubbles of joy and triumph rise inside me. I laugh, my voice ringing through the air.

Huy is nearby, watching me with a brilliant smile.

"This is not for you!" I yell over the crash of the waves. "I'm not going with you!"

His smile drops.

"This is for me!" I turn away, flipping and splashing and soaring with the deepest peace I have ever felt. For the first time, I have spoken the truth. I have embraced myself as I truly am.

I leave Huy a speck in the distance, watching me with what I'm sure is disappointment and judgment. I couldn't care less. I laugh again, and that's when I see Mom and Kim and Thao on the beach. My sisters stand slightly behind my mother, dresses fluttering in the breeze. It's hard to read their expressions in the darkness, but I don't think they look angry.

I swim toward them and surface, giving them a good look at the long, sparkling blue-green tail below my torso. Kim's hands fly to her mouth, and Thao stares with mingled longing and wonder. It's Mom's face that captures me the most, though. It's pale as the moon, and her lips are parted in an unspoken cry and her eyes shine with tears.

"This is who I am, Mom. Land and water. Girl and fish. I'm not going to choose between them, the old home or the new. I don't need to." I hold out my hands. "*We* don't need to."

"Mai." My mother's whisper is so full of yearning, it makes my heart ache.

I push myself out of the waves, still extending my hands to her. I am half afraid she won't take them, but she does. Her fingers squeeze mine as she kicks off her heels and presses her feet into the sand, taking slow step after slow step to the ocean's edge. Behind her, Kim and Thao take each other's hands and watch with breathless hope. A tear slips down Mom's cheek.

She steps into the sea.

Acknowledgments

We would like to thank our agents, Lara Perkins at Andrea Brown Literary Agency, and Suzie Townsend and Sophia Ramos at New Leaf Literary. This collection wouldn't be possible without your championing our wild ideas. Thank you to the wonderful team at Feiwel & Friends, especially Jean Feiwel, Foyinsi Adegbonmire, Liz Szabla, and everyone who worked on this collection. Last but not least, we are endlessly grateful to the authors of *Mermaids Never Drown* who trusted us with their stories.

Mermaids forever.

Contributors

DARCIE LITTLE BADGER is a Lipan Apache writer with a PhD in oceanography. Her critically acclaimed debut novel, *Elatsoe*, was featured in *Time* magazine as one of the best 100 fantasy books of all time. *Elatsoe* also won the Locus Award for Best First Novel and is a Nebula, Ignyte, and Lodestar finalist. Her second fantasy novel, *A Snake Falls to Earth*, received a Nebula Award and a Newbery Honor and is on the National Book Awards longlist. Darcie is married to a veterinarian named Taran. Darcie is #TeamFins.

KALYNN BAYRON is the *New York Times* and Indie bestselling author of the YA fantasy novels *Cinderella Is Dead* and *This Poison Heart*. Her latest works include the YA fantasy *This Wicked Fate* and the middle grade paranormal adventure *The Vanquishers*. She is a CILIP Carnegie Medal nominee, a two-time CYBILS Award nominee, and the recipient of the 2022 Randall

Kenan Prize for Black LGBTQ fiction. She is a classically trained vocalist and musical theater enthusiast. When she's not writing, you can find her watching scary movies and spending time with her family. Kalynn is #TeamFins.

PREETI CHHIBBER hails from Atlanta, Georgia, and is an author living the dream and writing her favorite characters. The first book in her Peter Parker trilogy, *Spider-Man's Social Dilemma*, came out in 2022. She's also a speaker and freelancer. She's written for SYFY, Polygon, and *Elle*, among others. Find her cohosting the podcasts *Desi Geek Girls* and *Tar Valon or Bust*. You might recognize her from one of several BuzzFeed "look at these tweets" lists. Find out more at PreetiChhibber.com or follow her on social media @runwithskizzers. Preeti is #TeamFeet.

REBECCA COFFINDAFFER (they/ she) grew up on Star Wars, Star Trek, fantastical movies, and even more fantastical books. These days they live in Kansas with their family, writing stories about magic and politics, spaceships, far-off worlds, and people walking away from explosions in slow motion. Rebecca is #TeamFins.

ZORAIDA CÓRDOVA is the acclaimed author of more than two dozen novels and short stories, including the Brooklyn Brujas series, *Star Wars: The High Republic: Convergence,* and *The Inheritance of Orquídea Divina.* In addition to writing novels, she serves on the board of We Need Diverse Books and is the coeditor of the bestselling anthology *Vampires Never Get Old,* as well as the cohost of the writing podcast, *Deadline City.* She writes romance novels as Zoey Castile. Zoraida was born in Guayaquil, Ecuador, and calls New York City home. When she's not working, she's roaming the world in search of magical stories. For more information, visit her at ZoraidaCordova.com. Zoraida is #TeamFins.

JULIE C. DAO is the critically acclaimed author of many books for teens and children. Her novels have earned starred reviews from *Booklist, School Library Journal,* and *Publishers Weekly,* won recognition as Junior Library Guild selections and Kids' Indie Next List picks, and landed on multiple best-of-year lists including YALSA and the American Library Association. A proud Vietnamese American who was born in upstate New York, she now lives in New England. Julie is #TeamFins.

ADRIANA HERRERA was born and raised in the Caribbean, but for the last fifteen years has let her job (and her spouse) take her all over the world. She loves writing stories about people, who look and sound like her people, getting unapologetic happy endings. Her Dreamers series has received starred reviews from *Publishers Weekly* and *Booklist* and has been featured in the *TODAY* show on NBC, *Entertainment Weekly*, *OPRAH Magazine*, NPR, *Library Journal*, the *New York Times*, and the *Washington Post*. She's a trauma therapist in New York City, working with survivors of domestic and sexual violence. Adriana is #TeamHybrid.

JUNE HUR is the bestselling author of YA historical mysteries *The Silence of Bones*, *The Forest of Stolen Girls*, and *The Red Palace*. In addition to being nominated twice for the Edgar Awards, she's been featured on *Forbes*, NPR, the KBS, and the CBC. Her fourth novel, *A Crane Among Wolves*, comes out in 2024. Born in South Korea and raised in Canada, she studied history and literature at the University of Toronto and formerly worked for the Toronto Public Library. She currently lives in Toronto with her husband and daughter. June is #TeamFeet.

KATHERINE LOCKE is the critically acclaimed award-winning author of *This Rebel Heart*, *The Girl with the Red Balloon*, *What Are Your Words?* and other titles. They also coedited and contributed to *This Is Our Rainbow* and *It's a Whole Spiel*. They live and write in Philadelphia with their feline overlords and an endless supply of chai lattes. They can be found online at @bibliogato and KatherineLockeBooks.com. Katherine is #TeamFins.

KERRI MANISCALCO grew up in a semihaunted house outside New York City where her fascination with gothic settings began. She is the #1 *New York Times* bestselling author of the Stalking Jack the Ripper quartet and the Kingdom of the Wicked series. Kerri is #TeamFeet.

JULIE MURPHY lives in North Texas with her husband who loves her and her cats who tolerate her. After several wonderful years in the library world, Julie now writes full-time. When she's not writing or reliving her reference desk glory days, she can be found watching made-for-TV movies, hunting for the perfect slice of cheese pizza, and planning her next great travel adventure. She is also the #1 *New York Times* bestselling author of books for all ages including *Dumplin'* (now a film on Netflix and one of *TIME* magazine's 100 Best YA Books of All Time), *Dear Sweet Pea,* and *If the Shoe Fits.* She is also the coauthor of *A Merry Little Meet Cute.* Julie's work has been featured by *Good Morning America, Teen Vogue,* the *New York Times, Vanity Fair,* and more. Learn more about Julie at JulieMurphyWrites.com. Julie is #TeamFins.

NATALIE C. PARKER is an author, editor, and community organizer. She has written several award-winning books for teens and young readers and has edited multiple anthologies including the Indie Bestselling anthology *Vampires Never Get Old.* Her work has been included on the NPR Best Books list, the Indie Next List, and the TAYSHAS Reading List, and in Junior Library Guild selections. In addition to writing, Natalie also runs Madcap Retreats, which has partnered with We Need Diverse Books and Reese's Book Club to host the writers workshops for their new internship Lit Up. She grew up in a navy family, finding home in coastal cities from Virginia to Japan, and currently lives with her wife on the Kansas prairie. Natalie is #TeamFins.

GRETCHEN SCHREIBER grew up between the hills of Kansas and the hospitals of Minnesota, but now calls the hills of Los Angeles home. After getting her MFA from the University of Southern California film school, she works as a professional bookworm for Hello Sunshine, Reese Witherspoon's media company. She is always down to run away to Disneyland or a bookstore. Gretchen is #TeamFins.

MAGGIE TOKUDA-HALL is the author of *The Mermaid, the Witch, and the Sea*, her debut young adult novel, which was an NPR, *Kirkus*, *School Library Journal*, and BookPage Best Book of 2020, and its sequel, *The Siren, the Song, and the Spy*. Her graphic novel, *Squad*, is an Ignyte and Locus Award–nominated comic book, and her newest picture book, *Love in the Library*, has received starred reviews from *BookPage*, *School Library Journal*, *Booklist*, and *Publishers Weekly*. She lives in Oakland, California, with her husband, two kids, and objectively perfect dog. She is perfectly capable of drowning. Maggie is #TeamFins.

JULIAN WINTERS is the author of the IBPA Benjamin Franklin Gold Award–winning *Running with Lions*; the Junior Library Guild selections *How to Be Remy Cameron* and *The Summer of Everything*; the multi-starred *Right Where I Left You;* and *As You Walk On By*. A self-proclaimed comic book geek, Julian currently lives outside Atlanta. He can usually be found swooning over rom-coms or watching the only two sports he can follow—volleyball and soccer. Julian is #TeamFeet.

Thank you for reading this Feiwel & Friends book.
The friends who made

MERMAIDS
NEVER DROWN

possible are:

Jean Feiwel, Publisher
Liz Szabla, VP, Associate Publisher
Rich Deas, Senior Creative Director
Anna Roberto, Executive Editor
Holly West, Senior Editor
Kat Brzozowski, Senior Editor
Dawn Ryan, Executive Managing Editor
Jie Yang, Senior Production Manager
Emily Settle, Editor
Rachel Diebel, Editor
Foyinsi Adegbonmire, Editor
Brittany Groves, Assistant Editor
Julia Bianchi, Junior Designer
Ilana Worrell, Senior Production Editor

Follow us on Facebook or visit us online at mackids.com.
Our books are friends for life.